CW00516049

SIREN STORIES
Presents

Emerald Wren

and the

Coven of Seven

J.J. Barnes

For Bear, Boyo and Boo

Chapter One

"Do you know what this is?" asked Emerald Wren's grandfather, fixing her with a piercing stare, his pale blue eyes unblinking.

Emerald looked at the bronze object in his hands and raised an eyebrow. "A jug?"

"Foolish child!" he said

"I am not a child!" Emerald retorted. She was terrified of her grandfather even though she'd never admit it.

"But you are foolish?" he asked, a slight twinkle of amusement creeping into his expression for just a moment.

"Well, no," she said crossly. "I'm not that either."

"This is a lamp," he said, his face returning to the set of stern authority.

Emerald peered at it, glanced at the Morecroft lamp her mother had on the chest of drawers in the corner, then looked back at the object her grandfather was holding. "A lamp... like Aladdin?"

"Says the girl who proclaims herself not to be a child," he said

"I'm eight. It's a legitimate frame of reference."

The hint of amusement seemed to creep across his face again for just a moment. "Fine. Now, listen to me closely, young lady," he said. "This lamp is yours. It is an object of great power and great significance, and it is to be respected. You must not use it until you are absolutely ready, and absolutely certain it is the right time. Do you understand?"

"How will I know?" asked Emerald, too curious now to smart talk him and not taking her eyes off the lamp.

"You'll know," he said firmly. "Do not take it for granted. And when the right moment presents itself, you will hold in your hands the power to change the world."

"What if the world doesn't need changing?" asked Emerald.

"The world always needs changing," he said. "And this time it is you who is tasked with the job of doing it."

ð

"Abi?" Emerald said into her phone, yawning as she spoke. "Are you alright?"

"I'm sorry I woke you," came Abigail Stone's quiet voice. "I got a vision, I needed to share."

"It's fine," Emerald sat up and looked at the time. It was half past two in the morning. Abigail usually waited until the coven got together before talking about her latest vision for them to work on, she wondered what was so urgent. "What did you see?"

"I've never had anything like this before," said Abi. "It wasn't like normal. It was words, just over and over and over."

"What words?"

Abigail hesitated then said carefully, "She walks amongst us but all alone, her life is real but not her own."

"Weird," said Emerald, rubbing her eyes and trying to stifle a yawn. "Is she the one we're saving, or the one we're saving from?"

"I don't know," said Abigail. Emerald heard a hasty whispered discussion on the other end of the phone then, "And it was hot."

"Hot?" asked Emerald. "Abs... I don't know if that's something I need to know about."

"Be serious, Emerald!" came Carla's voice from the other end of the phone.

"Sorry, go on Abi."

"It was like the words were hot," said Abigail. "Or the person saying them... I'm not sure. It's hard to describe. But I felt really hot."

"Her skin was burning," said Carla. "She was roasting hot and thrashing around before she woke up."

"Is that normal?" Emerald asked.

"No," said Abigail. "Not at all."

Emerald pulled a pen off her bedside table. "Say those words again for me?"

"She walks amongst us but all alone, her life is real but not her own," said Abi again.

Emerald balanced her phone between her shoulder and ear, and scribbled the words on her hand. She rubbed her eyes, her whole body ached. She needed these few hours of sleep badly. "Okay," she said. "I'll have a think. We can talk about it when we're all together later. Try and get some rest now."

"You too," said Abigail.

"Goodnight, Em," said Carla.

"Goodnight," said Emerald.

Setting the phone back on her bedside table Emerald lay down and stared at the ceiling, wondering if she should wake Maram but deciding against it. Her latest bonehead boyfriend was probably in there with her and she wasn't in the mood to face him. It could wait and she had to be up in three hours. Tiredness won out and she closed her eyes.

ð

"FADIUS KALM," boomed a deep and hollow voice, shoving Fadius into consciousness.

Fadius blinked and looked around then gasped in horror at the bloody corpse at his feet, dizzily shoving himself away from it, scraping his elbows across the brick work and putting his hands in the filth of the street below.

"What's going on?" he whispered, staring around the alley he was sitting in. His head hurt, his feet hurt. Blood was congealed on his hands and legs and he had no idea why he was there.

"FADIUS," came the voice again, so loud it felt like his head was collapsing in on itself. "YOU HAVE SINNED."

"What?" he said again, fear making his voice quiver. "Who is this? Where are you?"

"YOU QUESTION WHO I AM, FADIUS KALM?"

Fadius trembled and looked around in the darkness. "God?" he finally whispered, crossing himself for the first time since childhood. For the first time since he had escaped his parents' home. For the first time since he had walked away from his faith, never intending to look back.

"I AM GIVING YOU THE CHANCE TO REDEEM YOURSELF, FADIUS," the voice ricocheted around his brain, and he clutched at his head in agony. "YOU HAVE SHAMED ME. YOU HAVE SHAMED YOURSELF."

"Did I... Did I kill him?" Fadius asked, looking at the body and feeling vomit rising in his gut. He turned and threw up on the ground.

"WEAKLING!" roared the voice.

"Who is he?" asked Fadius, tentatively holding out a hand, wanting to turn his face, but stopping.

"HE IS IRRELEVANT. HE FAILED." Fadius wished the voice would stop, it was agonising. "YOU HAVE A CHANCE TO REDEEM YOURSELF WHERE HE COULD NOT. YOU HAVE THE CHANCE TO WASH AWAY YOUR SIN WHERE HE DIED IN FILTH."

Tears crept from Fadius' eyes. Filth. He remembered his father calling him filth as he beat him with a leather belt or ripped out tufts of Fadius' hair with his huge, red hands. He remembered the venomous look in his eyes, the furious curl to his lip. Filth in the eyes of the Lord. Had his parents been right for all these years?

"YES," said the voice. "YOUR PARENTS WERE RIGHT TO BEAT YOU. AND NOW YOU WILL MAKE AMENDS."

"Yes, Lord," Fadius sobbed, his body shaking and his stomach churning, threatening to explode once more. "Anything you say, Lord."

"HANNAH MONROE," the voice said. "BURN HER."

ð

Emerald slipped on her shoes and examined herself in the mirror. She looked as tired as she felt. She always looked as tired as she felt. The late night phone conversation with Abi and Carla had set her back, for sure, but not so much that you'd notice. She picked up her concealer and covered the shadows under her eyes.

Waitressing all day was her livelihood and working with her coven all night was her life, but it was taking its toll.

She tied her short brown hair back into a ponytail and stepped out of her bedroom, heading for the kitchen and the coffee machine that had been working away on a timer since 6am, just half an hour earlier.

"Good morning, Guinevere," said Emerald, nodding to the large tabby cat sitting on the coffee table. The cat watched her through narrowed eyes, her tail flicking. "What?"

"Something happened," replied the cat. "You're not telling me something."

"I'm not telling you many things," replied Emerald, taking the coffee pot out of the machine and pouring the contents gratefully into a Bugs Bunny mug. "Such as that I'm considering getting a dog. A large one. Or one of those small yappy ones. A Chihuahua maybe. Or a Great Dane."

"Emerald Wren," Guinevere started to say, but she was interrupted.

"We're getting a dog?" asked Maram appearing in the little kitchenette, her thick dark hair swept up elegantly on top of her head with a clip in a way Emerald knew she'd never be able to accomplish, even if she had enough hair with which to do it. "Awesome. That'll put the kibosh up old fuzzy butt here."

"Abi phoned me last night," said Emerald, pouring coffee for Maram and handing it to her.

"I knew it!" declared the cat proudly.

"Well we always did say you are the wisest of us all, Guinevere," said Emerald, toasting the irritated cat with her drink.

"I never had to put up with this nonsense before you two," said the cat crossly. "My last charge is quite the respected educator now thanks to me. Teaches potion making to young witches, and I bet none of them give him the attitude you two show either!"

"A teacher?" asked Emerald, making a face. "Glad you didn't try and do that to me."

"It wouldn't suit you," said Guienvere, sticking her nose in the air and flicking her tail. "Though I admit I had higher aspirations than waitress."

"You sound like my mother," said Emerald, giving her the finger.

"So, Abi called?" asked Maram, pouring herself a cup of coffee then sniffing it as if it were the elixir of life.

"Vision," said Emerald, getting back on track and checking her watch. They had a couple of minutes before they had to leave. "A weird one. Just words."

"What words?" asked Maram between sips of the coffee.

"She walks among us but all alone, her life is real but not her own."

Maram frowned. "Weird."

"Ladies," said Guinevere. "Perhaps..."

"We're going to be late," said Maram, interrupting her and putting her empty mug in the sink. "We can figure it out later."

Emerald nodded and they grabbed their bags and coats from the back of the sofa where they had landed the night before.

"Maram!" called out Guinevere in a sing song voice as they headed for the door. "Have you forgotten something?"

"No?" said Maram, patting the pockets on her uniform and coat then checking she had her bag. "Oh crap! Yes!"

She pushed open her bedroom door and shouted, "Hey! Steve! Get out!"

"Now?" asked the bonehead, appearing in the doorway in nothing but jeans. "It's the middle of the night!"

Maram bustled into her room, knocking him out of the way and hastily picked up his shoes and clothes then shoved them into his arms and pushed him towards the front door. "I'll call you later," she said.

Below his messy brown hair, Steve peered at her out of bleary green eyes. "Yeah?"

"Sure I will. Right after I've seen a man about a dog," insisted Maram, opening the front door and pushing him out as he tried to a stutter a question, then slamming it shut with a sigh of relief.

"Sure you will?" said Emerald, raising her eyebrows.

"We can just hang out here a moment until I'm sure he's gone," said Maram, peering through the peephole for a moment then looking back at Emerald apologetically.

"As you wish," said Emerald with a sigh and glancing at her watch. When she caught Maram's slapped expression she immediately hated herself.

ð

"I still think this is illogical," complained Stuart Wren, as he stared out across Lewisham, the view afforded from the eighth floor of the Whitewing Annex of The Commission building masked by looming clouds and drizzling rain. "Emerald is a child."

"The Vision all saw the same thing," said Nahla.

"My involvement should have ceased once we established that the necromancy was not the work of the Virilicae," said Stuart

turning from the window. "Bringing my granddaughter into this is completely unacceptable."

"And yet you did it," Nahla observed with a smile before sipping at something that smelled of roses from a crystal tumbler. "I hadn't pinned you as one for being overprotective."

"She is eight years old and I wasn't even permitted to give her what little knowledge we have," said Stuart. "It's not overprotective, it's objecting to illogical decision making. I always win. With illogical decision making I will not win."

"Yet, as I said, you did it," said Nahla again, setting the glass down on the coffee table that sat by the fireplace.

"Yes, well," Stuart said, standing up and heading for the door. "As you say, I did it."

"Stuart?" said Nahla, as he turned the handle.

"Yes?"

Her face softened ever so slightly. "She has time. She won't be eight forever."

"No," he said. "You're right. She has twelve years to prepare for a challenge she has no idea is coming against an enemy she has no idea exists."

"Then hope is not lost," said Nahla.

ð

"So, why did Steve get the boot?" asked Emerald as they took off their aprons at the end of their twelve hour shift. "Picks his teeth? Bleaches his butt hole?"

"Bleaches his butt hole?" asked Maram, pulling a face as she stuffed her apron in her bag.

"What? It's a thing!"

"People are so weird," Maram muttered, then said, "He thought Alaska was a continent and only watches anime."

"Damn, so close," said Emerald, pushing the door open and pulling her coat up around her face as they headed out into the drizzle of the miserable October evening. Emerald tried to catch Maram's eye but she was hiding inside her scarf. It was okay. Maram didn't need the burden of Emerald's constant concern. Emerald shoved her hands in her pockets and kept pace at her side.

They walked home in amicable silence. Emerald's feet ached and her body felt sore. She longed for a hot bath and a good book followed by a deep sleep, but instead was bracing herself for the night shift. They got back to their building and climbed the stairs to their flat. Emerald winced with every step, her muscles begging her to stop.

"Drink?" offered Maram as she walked into the kitchen and retrieved a bottle of cheap Tesco own brand merlot from the counter.

"Always," said Emerald, dropping onto the sofa with a sigh.

As Maram poured the wine into plastic goblets a thunderous knocking sound came from the front door.

"Bloody hell Tig," called Emerald as she heaved herself to her feet and walked to the front door.

"What?" asked the girl on the other side as Emerald pulled it open, her dark eyes glinting mischievously beneath her bright purple pixie cut hair.

"You know what," grumbled Emerald, stepping back and allowing her in. "You'll get us reported for noise pollution again."

"In my defence," said Tig as she pulled her Five Finger Death Punch hoody off her painfully thin body. "I'm pretty sure it was Ben last time."

Guinevere slunk out of Emerald's bedroom and nodded. "She's correct. Two months ago Ben was making fireballs for Celeste to move. He went too big and it blew up."

"I remember now!" said Maram, handing Emerald a glass of wine. "I wasn't there, I was out with with Leo... or Teo... or Rob... anyway. That," she pointed at the black circle on the white ceiling above her head, "was Ben. Two months ago. And Mrs Rogers upstairs reported it."

Tig pointed her finger at Guinevere and winked theatrically. "I knew you'd have my back!"

Guinevere examined her paw intensely. "Yes, well. I take my duties seriously. And it doesn't mean I support your frantic banging at our front door when a sensible knock would do."

Tig winked at the cat again then pulled a half empty bottle of Jim Beam out of her ripped up satchel bag. "Be generous," she said, handing it to Maram. "Where's everyone else?"

"Ben's picking them up so they'll be here any minute," said Emerald, sipping on her wine. It was pretty grim, vinegary and pungent, but it did the job and it only cost a few quid. She'd take it.

A gentle knock sounded at the door as Maram returned with a half filled tumbler of whisky. She handed it to a grateful Tig then went to the door. Emerald sipped her wine, forcing her brain to focus on having enough energy to get through the evening's work before she would finally be allowed to sleep.

Carla hurried into the room, supporting a wobbling Abigail in strong her arms, closely followed by Ben and Celeste, their faces plastered with worry. Emerald could tell Carla was afraid. Whilst always incredibly protective of the fragile Abigail, the pain she was in now had sent her into overdrive. The love between them was palpable. Emerald wondered if she would ever find anyone who cared for and loved her like that. If she'd ever be as safe in anybody's arms as Abi was in Carla's.

"Is she okay?" asked Tig, moving off the sofa and onto the floor to allow Abi the space.

"No," said Carla, her jaw set, as she gently lowered Abi onto the vacated sofa. "She had another fucking vision."

"She was shaking," said Ben, his eyes wide. He looked at Emerald, probably for reassurance that everything would be alright as they so often looked to her, but she had nothing to give him.

"What did you see?" asked Maram.

"Give her a bloody minute," said Carla, batting her away.

Emerald beckoned Maram over to her, knowing Maram's desire to get down to business was sometimes at the expense of the comfort of those around her and that Carla was not to be messed with when it came to Abi.

Celeste smiled wanly at Emerald, fingering at the gold cross that hung around her neck. Emerald nodded silently. At least Celeste's comfort primarily came from her God.

"So much fire!" Abigail cried suddenly, sitting bolt upright and staring at Carla. "Oh God, so much fire!"

"Okay baby," whispered Carla, gently stroking Abi's long dark hair. "We're here. You don't have to talk about it."

"I do," said Abi, clutching at Carla's arm with her thin fingers. "I do. He's coming. He's coming."

"Who's coming?" asked Maram from Emerald's side.

"The fire," said Abi, staring at nothing with a ferocious and desperate intensity. "He's coming for her."

"For who?" asked Maram, leaning forwards.

"I... I..." Abi screwed up her face, contorting the delicate features, and balled her hands into tiny fists. "I can't see!"

"It's okay," said Carla gently. "You don't need to worry about it."

"Yeah, *she* doesn't," muttered Maram, folding her arms. Emerald shot her a look.

"My head," Abigail whispered, putting her hands to her face. "I can't think..."

"Close your eyes, darling," said Carla, gently stroking Abi's hair. "Just rest. You'll be fine soon. Just rest."

Celeste caught Emerald's eye. She was twisting at her cross and looked troubled. Emerald understood. Abigail was struggling to cope with the visions that were growing stronger and more agonising each week and they were starting to break her. Celeste worked with some of the most vulnerable and damaged women in society, saw how their experiences and traumas weighed on them and the look it gave them, and how Abi seemed to be morphing into one of them. Her eyes held that haunted look of the souls fractured by trauma. Emerald recognised it too. She had seen it twice before. And now she was working her ass off to try and make sure she never saw it again.

Chapter Two

"Here," said Emerald as she handed Celeste and Ben a mug of coffee each. "I'd join you but I plan on sleeping like the dead as soon as we've wrapped up."

"We just don't have enough here," said Maram, raking her fingers through her hair as she examined the pages of notes that were strewn across the coffee table.

"If we don't move fast that werewolf will get him," said Tig, gesticulating with her nearly empty whisky glass. "I'm sick of losing marks to that dude."

"We don't know it's a werewolf," said Celeste.

"Could be Guinevere," said Ben, winking at the cat who had taken up residence on Abigail's lap as she napped on the sofa.

"You joke," said the cat, examining a paw, "but we Guardians are capable of a lot more than you people give us credit for."

"Like shredding these assholes to oblivion?" asked Maram.

"Well, that would be a challenge," admitted the cat. "And I am retired after all."

"If the werewolf got Barry The Bastard it wouldn't be the worst thing," said Ben with a shrug.

"He's a misogynistic lowlife," said Maram. "But he doesn't deserve to die."

"You're right," said Ben, nodding. "I apologise."

"And we don't know it's a werewolf," said Celeste again. "We don't even know if there *are* werewolves... wait, do we?"

"Hey Celeste," said Tig with a mischievous grin. "You know when people are impaled on the neck by barbeque forks..."

"We do know," said Guinevere, cutting Tig off with a stern look. Emerald smiled to herself, Guinevere's protestations of retirement hadn't yet prevented her from acting like their supervisor. "And there are. Though not in Britain, particularly. They're usually found in Eastern Europe and South America."

"Oh..." said Celeste, awkwardly. "Never mind."

"But you're right, it's not like it only happens on a full moon," said Maram, shuffling the notes around again. "The last guy, the rapist guy Adam, there's no way he was attacked on a full moon. And there's no way whatever got him was human." She held up a photo of a mauled body. "Yuck."

"So what is it then?" asked Tig. "A well trained hound?"

"Whatever it is, let's try and get there first this time, shall we?" suggested Emerald. She hated death. Loathed it. Nobody, not the rapists nor the abusers, deserved to be murdered. Whoever, whatever, was killing them needed to be stopped before it got the chance to kill again.

"So we're still moving ahead on Barry The Bastard?" asked Carla.

"Of course," said Maram, frowning slightly. "Why wouldn't we be?"

"The fire?" said Carla, looking exasperated. "You said yourself, we don't have enough to move on Barry The Bastard now. This should be our priority."

"We've got more on Barry The Bastard than we've got on Fire Guy!" protested Maram, gesticulating at the paper.

"But if we don't move on Fire Guy some girl's going to get burned!" insisted Carla.

"My vote goes for Fire Guy," said Tig, holding up a hand like she was in school. "I know some old ladies getting ripped off is bad and all, but a few of them losing their money seems a better option than one woman getting burned to death."

"But Barry's moving now," said Ben. "He's always moving. We don't know how long until Fire Guy moves. It could be months."

"If it was months do you think Abi would be in this state?" asked Carla, desperation in her voice.

"Abi's getting weaker," said Celeste quietly. "Her visions are affecting her more and more, even when they're not strong."

Carla turned a furious look on Celeste. "Abigail is strong!" she said. "She's stronger than you and she's stronger than me!"

Guinevere rested a paw on Carla's lap. "It's okay," she said softly. "We all love Abi. We all respect her. Nobody doubts her ability."

"What do you think Emerald?" asked Ben, looking up at her from where he sat on the floor, coffee cup in his hands.

Emerald looked around as all eyes fell to her. She shuffled her feet. She hated being the one they relied on to make the decisions. She could barely look after herself let alone take responsibility for an entire coven of seven. Still, a decision needed to be made.

"I think we prioritise Fire Guy," she said after a minute. "Do some research, get what we can from Abi when she wakes up. Barry The Bastard deserves everything he gets, from us anyway, but if we can save this girl's life that has to come first."

"Agreed," said Carla.

"Agreed," said Ben.

ð

Whilst Fadius had learned that if a woman was reading a book in a coffee shop it was generally considered a universal sign for 'don't speak to me' but the voice in his head had been insistent. He wouldn't have dared go against the instructions of God, so for the first time in his life he found himself flirting with a woman. With a wry smile he realised it would also be the first time his father would have been proud of him.

"Hannah," the blonde woman was saying shyly, looking up at him. "You?"

"Tom," said Fadius, holding out his hand and smiling at her. "Tom Bilson."

Hannah took his hand and shook it. She was young, perhaps twenty one, but tiny. Barely five feet tall. She looked innocent. Vulnerable. She would have been too timid to tell him to go away like a more experienced woman would have done.

She took a sip of her coffee, her other hand nervously clutching the edges of the heavy book in her lap, then carefully tucked a strand of hair behind her ear. "Nice to meet you."

"Hannah," he said, feeling his palms sweat. Everything about this felt unnatural to him but he persisted. "I was wondering if..."

He hesitated. He couldn't. She was just a child. He turned away from her.

"FADIUS," the voice roared in his head and he yelped in pain, clutching his head and staggering.

"Are you alright?" asked Hannah, placing the book on the table in front of her and getting up to him, catching his arm.

"YOU DARE DEFY ME?" the voice boomed.

"No!" he insisted desperately, bending over in pain and clawing at his ears.

"What happened?" asked Hannah, her gentle voice slipping through the resonating agony and offering a cooling blanket of calm. "Are you ill? Do you need a doctor?"

"YOU WILL BURN HER. YOU WILL BURN HER NOW BEFORE SHE BRINGS PAIN! BEFORE SHE BRINGS DEATH! SHE IS EVIL AND WANTS TO DESTROY YOUR LORD!"

Fadius looked up at her. She smiled at him gently. Her soft, plump face and kind brown eyes showed not a hint of menace or danger. He stood up and ran a hand through his hair. "Hannah?"

"Yes?" she asked quietly, tipping her head to the side and looking concerned.

"Are you religious?"

She stepped back, surprised. "No, not at all actually," she said, frowning, obviously confused by the non sequitur. "God is too illogical a concept. I'm Epicurean in my philosophy. It's actually something I'm studying at university. Why do you ask?"

"SHE DENIES ME. BURN HER."

The pain in his head was intense. A screaming, agonising pain that ripped through him, bouncing off his temples then clawing across the back of his skull.

"Would you like to go for a walk in the park with me? I'd love to get to know you better."

"Oh... I..." Hannah looked at her book and chewed on her lip. He knew the idea of leaving with a strange man troubled her. If he was going to get her to agree he had to be smart.

"I'm sorry, that was forward of me," he said, standing up and backing away. "I just so rarely meet anyone familiar with the work of Epicurus and the neon lights in here are setting off my epilepsy. I shouldn't have been pushy, it was completely inappropriate."

"DO NOT FAIL ME FADIUS!" roared the voice in his head.

She needed to see his vulnerability. The combination of complimenting her mind and revealing physical vulnerability should give her both confidence and guilt.

"Oh yes, of course," she said quickly, pushing her book into her handbag and standing up. "I should have realised, I'm sorry! Of course, let's go. The park sounds perfect. It's a shame to waste this lovely day with a book."

"Thank you, Hannah." He held out his arm and smiled at her.

ð

"Why does the booze always run out so fast?" asked Tig, pouring a fresh glass of whisky then holding the bottle up miserably.

"You shouldn't drink so much when we're working," said Celeste, raising her eyebrows. "It distracts you."

"It helps me focus," said Tig, toasting Celeste who rolled her eyes.

"Her life is real but not her own?" said Ben. "What does that even mean?"

"I don't know," said Abi, her voice weak as Carla held her hand tightly.

"And you didn't see anything else?" asked Maram as she pulled a fresh sheet of paper out from under the coffee table and wrote FIRE GUY across the top in purple Sharpie.

"You've asked her that a thousand times!" said Carla.

"It's okay," said Abi, taking her hand from Carla and smiling at her reassuringly. "No. Nothing else. Just the words and a lot of fire."

"What do you think, Em?" asked Maram.

"He might have done it before," said Emerald, leaning forwards. "We don't have anything else so we start there. We'll need someone to take point on researching women who have been burned to death. And we'll need weapons to fight fire. Tig, you good for that?"

Tig held up her glass. "On it."

"I'll meet you at yours tomorrow, yeah?" asked Ben.

"Not too early," said Tig, tipping her whisky glass with a meaningful look.

"We've got another long shift at Vinnie's," said Emerald. "Celeste, you're at the shelter tonight, aren't you? As always, keep an eye out. She could be one of yours."

"Yes of course," said Celeste. "And I can research tomorrow afternoon if I can sleep for a bit in the morning."

"I'll join you," said Carla. "I'm on the doors from eleven but I'll be home around five. I'll meet you after lunch."

"I'll come too," said Abigail.

"Let's see how you are, yeah babe?" said Carla. "No need to push it."

"I'm... I'm..." Abi started to say, then her eyes began to roll back in her head.

"Oh no!" cried Carla as Abi began to shake violently, her mouth hanging open as she slumped back hard against the sofa.

"Abi!" cried Tig, reaching out for her, but Carla held her hand out.

"She's having another one," Carla said quietly. "She needs space. It hurts her."

Emerald felt her heart race. She had seen Abi have visions before but never like this, her reaction had never been so violent. Carla tried to support her, stopping her from falling to the floor with a gentle grip. Her eyes, usually so tough and cynical were filled with tears. Ben ran his hands over his short, scruffy hair and stared at the floor. Celeste knotted her fingers in her black braids and whispered prayers under her breath.

Maram appeared at Emerald's side and took her hand. She felt the calming warmth spread through her arm as Maram whispered, "I'm here, breathe slowly. I'm here."

Abi's shaking began to subside, her breathing slowing down. Carla stroked her dark hair away from her sweat coated face and gently kissed her cheek. "Okay babe, you're coming back."

Abi's eyes snapped open and, with effort, pushed herself up to sitting. "I saw the fire," she said. "And a man. A praying man."

"So our Big Bad is going to burn a priest as well now?" asked Ben, scowling. "What a prick."

"No," said Abigail, biting her lip nervously and eyeing Celeste. "The man, the praying man, he's bringing the fire. He's the one we have to stop."

Celeste stood still for a moment, her mouth dropping open, then she turned and stepped past Emerald and Maram and went into the kitchen. She fetched a glass from the cupboard and filled it at the sink, drinking the water in one go and carefully avoiding the eyes of everyone in the room that were all watching her.

Emerald and Maram glanced at each other. Emerald wondered if she ought to say something but didn't know what.

"I know, okay?" Celeste said after a moment, coming back into the room with her arms wrapped around herself. "I know. You lot all think I'm crazy for still believing and now some priest or religious nutter is coming to burn innocent women and you're thinking I believe in the same stuff as him."

"Not all the same stuff, I hope," said Tig, raising a pierced eyebrow.

"Shut up, Tig," whispered Carla.

Celeste sat back down, clutching the water glass in her hands. "We don't even know what religion he is."

"I don't see the difference between one sky wizard and another," muttered Tig.

"Shut up, Tig!" hissed Maram.

Tig flashed her dark eyes at Maram, threatening to protest but begrudgingly slumping herself down to sit on the floor, elbows on her knees and a sour look on her face.

"Come on, Celeste," said Emerald gently. "Tig's personal issues aside, you know none of us think badly of you for having a faith. We're after him, not his religion. You know that right?"

"Yeah, okay," said Celeste, her fingers finding her cross again. "I just wish people would stop thinking God condones the evil shit they want to do to each other. He's used as an excuse by these violent men and people like me and my family get lumped in with them."

"So let's stop him," said Tig, then offered Celeste her glass. "Friends?"

Celeste laughed sadly and accepted the glass. "Friends," she said, and took a swig.

Tig grinned at her wickedly. "Glad to see you're finally focusing."

ð̌

"The Ubel Project is in motion, Mr Wren," said a young man, standing before Stuart Wren's desk and sweating.

"It is, eh?" said the old man, leaning back in his chair thoughtfully. The man's obvious discomfort caused him no concern. "Has Ms Hussain been alerted?"

"She has, Mr Wren," he said, nodding nervously and adjusting his tie.

"The Vision are all in agreement?"

"Yes sir," said the young man again. "Six corroborating reports. The Stone girl has set the course."

"Thank you, Wilfred."

"You're welcome, Mr Wren," said the young man, then hastily stepped out of the office and pulled the door closed.

Stuart Wren stood, blinked, then appeared with a pop in Nahla Hussain's office on the fifth floor of the Whitewing

Building, almost exactly in line with his own three floors above.

Nahla was standing at a bookcase, studying a book that appeared to have pages made of water that swirled and moved under the light. "Stuart Wren," she said, closing the book sharply so droplets of water splashed out onto the carpet. "I have told you repeatedly not to enter my office without waiting for an invitation. Everyone else manages to respect that. I have a door for a reason."

"I apologise," he said, nodding his head respectfully and only partly in jest. "I shall endeavour to knock next time."

"You're an asshole," she said crossly, then sat down on the edge of her desk. "I assume you're here about Emerald?"

"Yes," he said. "On both charges."

"I've kept close tabs on mine, I assume the same is true of you?"

"Of course."

"Are you ready to start working together again, old friend?" she asked, breaking the frosty demeanour with a genuinely warm smile.

"It's been a long time coming," he said, then went to the door and pulled it open. Looking at her with a wry smile he rapped his knuckle on it sharply.

"Oh do fuck off," she said.

He roared with laughter then closed the door behind him.

Chapter Three

"It is your fault Olivia!" shouted Emerald's father, slamming his hand down hard on the kitchen counter. "Yours!"

"Eric! Please!" Emerald's mother was sobbing, a fear in her voice that Emerald had come to recognise only too well.

"It's your genes that made her turn out this way!" he roared. "My family is strong! Powerful! She has nothing! She is nothing!"

Emerald felt a tear slide down her cheeks. She was sitting at the top of the stairs, out of sight of parents, listening to the latest of their fights over her lack of power. Her father's disappointment and resentment seemed to be growing every day. Whereas once she'd be told to keep trying and it would reveal itself in time, she was now ignored for the most part. He had given up on her.

"I didn't choose this!" wept Emerald's mother. "It's not my fault! I can't change who she is!"

"I should never have married you," he snarled. Something crashed onto the floor and her mother cried out in shock.

"I didn't ask you to!" her mother was starting to get an edge of defiance to her voice. It surprised Emerald. "If you didn't want a mortal baby you shouldn't have made a baby with a mortal!"

There was a sharp sound of skin on skin and her mother howled in pain. "You slut, she's not even mine, is she?"

"What?" her mother's voice was shaking, weak. "Of course she is!"

"Do you know who my father is?"

"I... of course... of course I do!"

"No," he said darkly. "Of course you don't. If you could even slightly comprehend then you'd know that no descendent of Stuart Wren could ever be a powerless mortal."

"You know what?" her mother's voice cried out, agony and fear breaking through every breath. "I am pleased she is powerless. If power makes her like you then she is better off without it."

"This is over, Olivia," her father growled. "I will not waste my life, my power, on a family of worthless mortals. I never signed up to raise a child like that. This is your doing."

"You signed up to raise a child!" protested her mother, her voice strained and broken. "A child not a power! She's your daughter! She was your baby! You can't just leave her! She needs you! We both need you! Please!"

"No," he said. "The world needs me. I'm wasted here."

"Eric! Please!" her mother cried out. "Please!"

Hearing her father's footsteps pounding across the floor, Emerald scrambled up the stairs and, dodging every squeaky floorboard and creaky patch, scurried ninja like to her bedroom at the end of the corridor. Carefully she closed the door as slowly as possible, avoiding any bump of the frame connecting and any scratch of the latch sliding into place, then tiptoed to bed.

Sitting down carefully she felt her heart racing, her hands trembling. She stared straight ahead and let her brain frantically churn, before shooting to her feet and racing to her wardrobe.

"She's wrong. I can change who I am," she whispered to herself as she pulled sweaters and cardigans out from the bottom of the wardrobe, throwing them onto the floor behind her. Buried at the back was a shoe box. Inside the shoe box was the lamp.

Carefully she sat on the edge of the bed and put the lamp in her lap. "I can change the world."

ð

"Jeez, are you okay?" cried Ben, rushing over to Tig who was frantically rolling back and forth over the scrubby grass that constituted a garden behind her ground floor flat, smoke drifting from the charred sleeves of her tatty grey hoody.

Tig stopped rolling and examined her arms, fury in her eyes. "I'm fine," she snarled, pushing herself up.

"Maybe we should take a break?"

"Why? So some evil priest can burn himself some witches because I can't take a little heat?"

"A little heat?" he asked, taking one of her pale arms in his hand. Her skin was red raw. "Tig, we need to get this under some cold water."

"I'm fine," she snatched her arm away. "I'll heal."

"I'm sorry I hurt you," he said, his eyes dropping.

"Well don't be," she said, more anger in her voice than she intended. "We have a job to do. So let's do it."

ð

Celeste's kitchen smelled of baking bread and garlic. She had won a bread maker in the fund raising raffle at work the Christmas before and now took great pleasure in using it any time she had guests. It made her little terraced house feel cosy and welcoming. The whole house was crammed with books, even in the kitchen where she had shelves mounted and laden. Her friends often laughed, or told her to get a kindle, but books were precious and she couldn't bear to part with them. She felt that they added to the homely feel anyway.

"I've found another one," said Carla, grabbing the notebook at her side and scribbling down details. "Belgium. Oven exploded."

"Accidental?" asked Celeste as she poured hot water over some coffee granules. One day she'd have a coffee machine as fancy as her bread maker.

"Allegedly," said Carla with a frown. "Gas leak, they think. Again."

"Name?" Celeste asked, setting the cup of coffee down on a terracotta coaster at Carla's side, sighing at the ring mark on the pine table top. She'd need to sand that out.

"Elisa Denois," said Carla.

"Any history?"

"No... not that I can see."

Celeste went to the white board set up by the table and added the name to the bottom of column B. The columns were about even. "I'm not convinced they're connected, Car," she said, frowning and setting the pen back down. "Are you?"

"No," she admitted. "It's just... it just feels not quite right, you know?"

"If we could stop tracking the ones with no history then it'd cut our workload down by half," said Celeste as she sat down. "Nothing connects the women in column B to either each other or to the women in column A."

"Other than their horrible fiery deaths, you mean?"

Celeste hesitated, her eyes dropping. "Yeah, other than that."

"It has to be too big a coincidence," said Carla.

Celeste shrugged. "I don't know, but I'm willing to go with you on it."

"It's a huge list," said Carla staring at it and shaking her head. "All those women."

"I know," said Celeste, fingering her gold crucifix sadly.

"We'll get him, Cel."

Celeste nodded. "I hope so."

They went back to work in silence for ten minutes or so before Celeste found another.

"Where now?" asked Carla.

"France. We're down to just two weeks ago," said Celeste with a shudder.

"History?"

Celeste scrolled up and down the web pages looking for more about the woman. "Yes," she said after a minute or so. "Car wreck when she was eight. Her father blacked out drunk whilst driving her home from football practice. She was pronounced dead on the scene but revived in the ambulance."

Carla rubbed her eyes. "Jesus Christ," she muttered. "Hang on. Two weeks ago. Do you have a map?"

"Like a road map?"

"No you dick," said Carla. "A world map. What would I want with a bloody road map?"

"I don't know!" said Celeste. "Yeah, hang on."

Celeste got up and went into the living room. She reached behind the bookcase and pulled out a large atlas. She brought it into the kitchen and leaned it against one side of the whiteboard.

"Okay," said Carla turned to the page with an overview of Europe. She picked up the whiteboard pen and put a splodge on Bulgaria. Celeste gasped. "What?"

"Just... pen on my book..."

Carla rolled her eyes then put marks on the white board next to one of the names on Column A and one on Column B. Then two from Column A in Serbia, two from Column B and one from Column A in Croatia. "Do you see?"

"No," said Celeste, looking at the list then the map.

"The dates," she said. "They're moving."

Celeste came over and looked at the map then the names. "Oh my God," she gasped.

"Column A and Column B," said Carla, marking more. "They're connected because they're moving in a line across Europe. The dates all match up. He started in Bulgaria and he's been getting more prolific the closer to Britain he's got."

Celeste gripped her crucifix. "That's the connection. He's coming."

They stared in silence as Carla marked them off one by one, each death by date, moving across Europe. Celeste felt the weight of the deaths weighing down on her. Another woman was going to die in a freak fire and it was up to them to stop it.

A phone began to ring and Celeste gasped, startled. Carla rolled her eyes at her again, then pulled her phone out of her jeans pocket.

"Abi?" Carla said into the phone. "Are you okay?"

Celeste watched nervously. She could hear the mixture of intense love and fear in Carla's voice.

"Okay, I get it. I'll tell her." Carla said, smiling reassuringly at Celeste. "Yes babe go back to bed. Rest. We'll talk later." Carla listened for a moment more then said, "Alright, I love you. Rest, my darling, rest." Then she hung up the phone and set it down gently on the table beside her laptop.

"Is she okay?"

"She had another vision," said Carla, tension in her voice. "In her dream again. I hate that she's getting them in her sleep now, Cel, I hate it so much."

"Why?" asked Celeste.

Carla looked up at her, her eyes full of sorrow. "She has nowhere that's safe anymore. She can't stop them, she can't turn them off or take a break. She can't even sleep through them now. She even tried taking a sedative a couple of weeks ago, a high dose. She was practically comatose."

"What happened?" asked Celeste.

"She got a vision whilst she was out but she couldn't wake up. She got a nose bleed, she was shaking, she started throwing up and I had to get her on her side to stop her drowning in it." Carla started to cry. Celeste leapt out of her seat and flung her arm around her friend. Carla's large frame and solid muscles suddenly felt vulnerable and small as Celeste held her close. Celeste had never seen Carla cry before. It was alarming. "I thought she was going to die. I was going to call an ambulance but it stopped on its own after a minute and she went back to normal."

"Why didn't you tell us?" Celeste asked, pulling back from her and cupping Carla's face in her hands. "We would have been there for you!"

"Abi didn't want me to," said Carla, taking Celeste's hands away and straightening up, her tough façade coming back. "I respect her wishes. She feels like everyone doubts her ability as it is."

Celeste sat back down again. "She's amazing," Carla said gently. "We know that, I promise. We rely on her. Her ability is massive."

"It is," agreed Carla, adjusting her laptop screen and focusing back on her work. "Now I'm going to figure this out so we can catch this asshole and she can get a break from this."

"What was her vision?"

"A shadow," said Carla. "The praying man with the fire is surrounded by a big, dark shadow."

ð

"Oh my God," wept Fadius, as he wretched into the gutter of the alley behind the old shoe factory. "Oh my God. Oh my God."

He couldn't get it out of his head. The way she had screamed as he turned on her, how her body had fallen limply to the ground after he had struck her, the way her skull had cracked on the pavement below. The smell.

"FADIUS," commanded the deafening, torturous voice that split his brain in two. "LEAVE NOW."

Fadius tried to obey but more vomit came erupting from his gut.

"Oh my God," he sobbed.

Had she felt it? She had been alive, he was certain, but unconscious. Had the shy, sweet Hannah Monroe felt the fire as it ate through her flesh? Had she died in excruciating pain or had his fist to her skull saved her from that?

"HER PAIN DOES NOT MATTER!" roared the voice. "SHE WAS NOT THE ONE."

"What?" Fadius stood upright, his head spinning. "She wasn't?"

"NO," came the voice. "YOU WERE WRONG. SHE WAS INNOCENT."

"Me?" howled Fadius, spinning around, his hands to his head as he tore at his hair. "I didn't do that!"

"YES FADIUS," came the voice. "YOU DID. AND YOU WILL DO IT AGAIN."

Sirens screamed louder as the fire engines approached.

"But..." started Fadius.

"LEAVE! NOW!" commanded the voice.

Fadius stumbled away from the alley, away from the skip where the charred remains of Hannah Monroe lay beneath a stolen barbeque and empty can of lighter fluid.

ð

"The bastard got one of mine," snarled Nahla Hussain, throwing open the door to Stuart's office without knocking.

Stuart tried to hide his surprise. "Nahla," he greeted her. "Good afternoon. I must have missed your knock."

"Shut up and listen," she said, slamming the door shut. "He got Monroe's girl."

"Monroe?" asked Stuart, setting his cup down and taking it seriously. "Our Monroe?"

"Yes," Nahla sat heavily in the leather chair on the other side of Stuart's desk.

"Hannah or Georgette?"

"Hannah," she said, rubbing her eyes. "She was just a child."

"How old?" he asked, dreading the answer.

"Seven hundred and four."

"That's no age," he said, looking down respectfully for a moment. "Has Monroe been told?"

"She will be," said Nahla. "She's in The Depths. She has one of Archer's mirrors but leaves it at Base to protect the glass. She'll be unreachable until check in."

"She won't take it well."

"No," Nahla agreed. "Even worse when she finds out we already have people on this."

"She'll understand."

"Stuart," said Nahla sternly. "Tell me the truth. Did The Vision deliver anything of this to you?"

"No," said Stuart. "Nothing."

"Promise me," she said, leaning over his desk towards him. "Stuart Wren. You promise me right now that you were not told."

"Would it have made a difference?" he asked. "Could you have done anything to prevent it? Would you have?"

Nahla sat back. "No," she admitted. "I couldn't."

"Then it doesn't matter whether I knew or not."

"It'll matter to Monroe."

"I'll deal with Monroe, should the time come," said Stuart.

Nahla nodded sadly. "How many more?"

"Mortals or Beings?"

"Either," said Nahla, then shrugged. "Beings. Mortals are of less interest to me."

"If The Vision knew it was coming they're not talking," said Stuart. "And we have to respect their reasoning. Now, if you'll excuse me, I have work to be getting on with."

Nahla stood and went to the door. "Is Emerald ready?" she asked before she left.

"She'll be ready."

Nahla looked down for a moment then closed the door behind her.

Chapter Four

"His eyes are a little further apart," said Abi, watching Maram as she carefully sketched on a pad of A3 paper on the floor in front of where Abi sat on the sofa in Emerald and Maram's flat. "And his hair's a bit longer on top."

"Drink?" offered Emerald from the kitchen.

"Do you have anything that isn't some cuffy, off brand crap?" asked Carla.

Emerald held up a bottle of red wine. "This says it's a... red," she said.

"Where did you buy it?"

"Aldi."

"Yeah, go on," agreed Carla, rolling her eyes.

"Coffee for me please," said Celeste. "I'm doing eleven til nine tonight."

Emerald put the pot on. Ordinarily she'd be on the wine too but with an evening of work ahead of them, a twelve hour shift behind them, and too few hours of sleep to keep her going, there was no way she'd survive without at least one hard hit of caffeine to fuel her.

"How's that?" asked Maram holding up the sketch pad.

"Better," said Abi, stroking Guinevere who was positioned at her side purring. "But he looks too angry."

"He's a woman killer," said Carla. "It makes sense that he'd be angry."

"He's not though," said Abi looking up. "He's not angry, he's scared. And sad."

"He should be scared," muttered Carla. "When I'm through with him."

"He's not scared of us," said Abi, shaking her head. "He's just scared."

"The poor dear," said Emerald as she brought Carla her glass of wine. She sipped it and made a face like she'd been sucking lemons, then sighed and drank more. "Must be such a burden doing all this maiming and murdering. I bet he's thoroughly exhausted by it."

"Yeah I know. I don't feel sorry for him or anything. I just... he's frightened. It's not nice." Abi stroked Guinevere and looked at the sketch thoughtfully. "I dunno. It's still not quite right. Something's not matching up."

A knock came at the door. Emerald handed coffee cups to Maram and Celeste then went to the door and let Tig and Ben in, Tig looking significantly worse for wear and Ben looking miserable.

"What happened?" she asked as Tig stalked past her, dropping her tatty backpack on the floor and hunching up in the corner angrily. She always had an edge to her but she seemed particularly enraged that night.

"We got your protection stuff ready," Tig said as Ben lowered himself to the floor on the other side of the coffee table, rubbing at his hair and chewing his lip. He looked like a chastised puppy, thought Emerald. Forlorn and riddled with guilt. She wondered what had happened that afternoon.

"Are you okay?" Celeste asked Tig.

"What happened?" Emerald asked again, eyeing the red, blistered fingers that were poking out from Tig's sleeves.

Tig being hurt jarred with her. She felt sick. Tig shouldn't be hurt anymore. No wonder Ben looked so sad. He knew what hurting Tig meant. She suspected that had Tig unleashed her anger at him he'd have felt better, instead she was internalising it. Beating herself up for allowing it, for suffering it. Emerald wanted to hold her close like she had when they were young, but Tig would never have allowed herself to display such vulnerability now, so she held back. It didn't sit right with her though.

"The enchantments worked," said Tig, crossly pulling her hands up inside the blackened sleeves and glaring at the floor.

"It was hard," said Ben, looking at the floor sadly. His heart was breaking, she could tell. He couldn't cope with the fact that Tig's pain had come at his male hands.

"We need a Healer," grumbled Carla. "We've always needed a Healer. It's bullshit we don't have a Healer. All covens have a Healer."

"Well we don't have one, okay?" said Tig, slumping back and retrieving a new bottle of Jim Beam from her backpack. She unscrewed the top and took a swig directly from the bottle.

Everyone looked anxiously at Emerald, waiting for her to take charge. Emerald ran her hands through her hair. She hated it. "Okay, so, do we want to see what Tig and Ben came up with first, or what Carla and Celeste learned first?"

"I'll go first," said Tig and tossed some velvet pouches out of her backpack onto the coffee table. "It's sand. I made plenty. My bag's full of them. Throw the sand and it'll absorb the flames before they touch you. But it's not an easy enchantment. Don't waste it. And I've enchanted a good old fashioned blade. It's small but it'll cut through pretty much anything, magic or otherwise. I tried it on something bigger but I couldn't make it hold so for now it's just a little dagger."

"Right, that's really good, well done guys" said Emerald then clapped her hands together and plastered an enthusiastic smile across her face. The mood in the room was cracked, splintered. It was her job to save it. "That sounds perfect! Okay! So, what's next?"

Her cheer was met with a withering glare from Tig and awkward silence around the room.

"Erm, this is the guy," said Maram after a few minutes, turning her sketch pad around. "Well this guy but looking scared."

"What's he got to be scared of?" asked Tig.

"I'm not sure," said Abi quietly. "I can't see. I'm trying, I promise. I'm trying so hard."

"Hey, babe," said Carla gently, taking Abi's hand and squeezing it. "It's okay. You don't need to push yourself anymore. Rest, please rest."

"Carla's right," said Emerald. She understood better than most how hard it is to deal with a power that is bigger than you are and that space from it was essential for survival. "Carla, Celeste, did you manage to find anything we can use?"

Celeste stood up, suddenly looking very business-like. Every time Celeste stepped into a role of authority she seemed to lose the shy timidity that was so much part of her personality. Emerald could see how she did the job she did with such success. Celeste went over to her bag and pulled out some rolled up sheets of A3 paper. "We found out a lot," she said.

"There have been women burned all across Europe for the last few months," said Carla. "Like loads of them. All accidental."

"What do you mean accidental?" asked Tig.

"House fires, gas leaks," said Celeste.

"Accidents with barbeques and bonfires," said Carla. "A car engine exploded, a dress caught a candle."

"I don't follow," said Maram. "We're looking for murders, right?"

"They're in a path across Europe," said Carla. "They started in Bulgaria and we tracked them across Europe. And now it's happening in England."

Celeste rolled out two sheets of paper covered in women's names with descriptions and ages. "Anna Dobrev died in an accidental fire in Kent two weeks ago," she said, pointing to the first list of names. "Misty Rowbottom in a fire in London last week." She pointed to the second list.

"Okay," said Emerald, frowning. "But you said these are all accidental deaths, we're looking for a guy literally 'bringing the fire'. Right, Abi?"

Abi nodded. She looked at Maram's sketch and shuddered. "Yes."

"They were," said Carla. "Or mostly. In a couple there were male suspects seen in the vicinity that were released but they always died shortly after."

"So... accidental deaths and different suspects?" asked Emerald.

"Well, yes," said Celeste "But it's not as simple as that."

"How are the victims connected?" asked Guinevere, sitting up in Abi's lap and craning forwards to see the names.

"But why does it matter?" asked Emerald, frowning. She felt irritated. "What am I missing?"

"Everyone on this first list," said Celeste, holding up the sheet of paper with Nina Dobrev's name on, "has died before."

"What?" asked Maram, cocking her head to the side.

"They've died before," repeated Celeste. "At least for a minute. Nine Dobrev, the woman in Kent, got a heart transplant. She died on the operating table."

"But..." said Emerald.

"But she was revived," said Carla. "When they got the new heart going."

"Sophia Mariani," said Celeste, pointing to another name. "Drowned in a swimming pool as a child. Brought back with mouth to mouth."

"Her life is real but not her own," said Maram, her voice sounded far away. "That makes perfect sense. She's alive, but her life isn't her own anymore, someone saved it. She owes them her life."

"I guess," said Emerald, hesitantly. Maram looked at her pointedly. She coughed. "Yes I see. It makes sense."

"She could easily be one of yours then, Cel," said Tig, her voice a mixture of sadness and rage.

"What about the second list?" asked Guinevere, the cat's eyes were narrow. "How are they connected?"

"I'm not sure," said Carla. "I know they died in fires, and I know they follow the pattern across Europe, but other than that I can't really find much on them at all. Anywhere. It's a bit weird actually."

"So they're probably genuine accidents?" asked Emerald, looking at the list. Twenty or so women, all dead. She felt her spine creeping with ice cold twists.

"I don't think so," said Carla. "There's something not right about that. They are perfectly in line with the pattern as the deaths move towards us. The dates of the fires match up exactly."

"It's too big a coincidence," said Celeste. "They're connected by something."

"What could it be then?" asked Ben. "What makes their lives real but not their own?"

"I'll keep looking," said Carla. "Whatever it is I guess they're just not meant to be here."

Maram was about to speak when behind her on the sofa Abigail suddenly screamed out, her eyes rolling back in her head as she was thrown back against the sofa. Maram shot to her feet and Guinevere leapt from Abi's lap.

"What do we do?" asked Emerald as Carla stroked Abi's hair.

"Nothing," she whispered, sadness in her eyes. "Just keep her safe."

Abi began to shake in increasingly violent spasms.

"Is she okay?" Celeste asked in a frightened whisper, looking at Emerald.

"I don't know," said Emerald, helplessly.

As Abi's shaking got worse she began to foam at the mouth, a horrible choking sound rattling from her throat.

"Help me get her on her side!" said Carla, leaping to her feet. "She might vomit."

Together, Carla and Ben tipped the convulsing Abi onto her side as saliva and froth dripped from her mouth and splashed onto the wooden floor below.

"Oh god," whispered Tig, her face ghostly white.

Carla sat back down at her side, tears slowly crawling down her cheeks as she stroked Abi's arm. Suddenly Abi's body convulsed so violently that she was thrown from the sofa, her head cracking on the coffee table as she fell. As Tig and Celeste screamed, and Carla howled in despair, she landed unconscious on the floor, blood pooling from the wound.

ð

"WE ARE CLOSE, FADIUS." Fadius startled awake as the voice blasted into his brain. Where was he? He was sore and stiff, and very cold. He forced himself to sit up. The park bench was wet and the old coat he was asleep under smelled strongly of cigarette smoke. "I CAN FEEL IT. I KNOW IT. CLOSER THAN WE'VE EVER BEEN!"

"What?" asked Fadius, staring into the darkness, his body aching with tiredness. He didn't understand. His brain felt clouded. "What do you mean, closer than we've ever been?"

"SO MANY TIMES WE'VE BEEN DISAPPOINTED BUT NOW," the voice roared. "NOW I CAN FEEL HER. SHE IS SO CLOSE."

"Please don't make me do it again," Fadius whispered. He just wanted to sleep. His brain hurt, he felt sick. His muscles were cramping, his stomach was churning. He wasn't a saviour or a warrior. He wasn't strong. He didn't want to kill anybody else. He just wanted to go back to his dingy flat and his dingy job at the back of a dingy warehouse and he wanted to be left alone.

"ARE YOU WEAK?" roared the voice. "TOO WEAK TO FIGHT THE BEARER OF THE BEAST?"

"Please," Fadius whispered again. He fell to his knees shaking. He was terrified. Betraying his God felt untenable but killing the girl had been horrific, and now he hurt. He was tired. He wanted to die. "I don't want to do this. Please. I can't."

"FADIUS," the voice boomed. "YOU ARE MY HANDS ON EARTH."

Fadius went to speak when he felt something start to surge through this body. He felt hot, intensely hot, but without any pain. His arms started to burn as his muscles began to twitch and swell, blood pumped through his arteries so fast he could hear it pounding in his ears, feel it surging through his brain. He felt good. He felt strong. He felt taller. He felt invincible. He stood up and felt a smile of jubilation spread across his face.

"What's happening?" he gasped, holding his arms out before him. They were throbbing, his muscles were bigger, his hands larger. He felt powerful. He had never felt powerful in his whole life.

"YOU HAVE DONE GOOD WORK," said the voice. "YOU ARE BEING REWARDED. DO YOU LIKE THIS FEELING, FADIUS?"

"Yes!" Fadius stood tall. "Yes I do!"

"EDNA BROOM," said the voice. "BURN HER!"

ð

Emerald sat uncomfortably with a beige plastic cup half full of bitter, weak hospital coffee in her lap. At her side Maram was gnawing anxiously on her thumb nail. The hospital waiting room was small, and the air was hot and unmoving. It seemed to sit in her lungs like a weight. She had to force it out with every breath.

"I'm so sorry," Celeste was saying to Carla. "I can't not go to work, they have nobody to cover me! I swear I would stay if I could."

"Please don't worry," said Carla. "I understand. They need you more than we do right now. I'll let you know as soon as we know anything. I promise."

"We aren't going to lose her, are we?" asked Celeste, fear on her face.

"No," Carla promised her, though Emerald could tell she wasn't certain. "We are not going to lose her."

Celeste nodded and twisted at her necklace, then gave a half hearted wave to the rest of them and headed for the door.

"Everything okay getting cover for you?" Ben asked Carla.

"It'll have to be," she said, sitting down heavily in one of the blue plastic bucket seats. "I left a message for the boss. He can get Danny or Felix in to cover me."

"How are you holding up?" Emerald asked her.

"You're going to have to kill him, Emerald," said Carla bluntly, turning to her with a serious face.

"What?" Emerald felt her mouth fall open and her face contort in horror.

"He's killing women and visions of him are killing Abi," said Carla in a matter of fact way. "You'll have to kill him and soon."

"I… I can't!" she cried, her heart starting to race.

"You can't ask that of her!" protested Maram at her side, leaning forwards angrily.

"Why not?" asked Tig, quietly, not meeting Emerald's eye. "You did it before. When necessary."

"I know but… but… but that's different," Emerald stuttered. She felt panicked, her heart was starting to race.

She tried to focus. To stay calm. "But that's why I know I can't. Please!"

"What if he kills another woman?" asked Carla. "What if Abi's body gives up because visions of him break her?"

"He's burning women to death Em," said Tig. "Burning them."

"I know!" said Emerald, putting her hands to her head and trying to force her brain to stop spinning.

"Guys!" Maram cried out, slipping her hand into Emerald's. She gripped it tightly, concentrating on breathing as slowly as she could. In through the nose, out through the mouth. In through the nose, out through the mouth. "Leave her alone. You're asking her to murder someone."

"Do you think he deserves to live?" asked Carla, her voice still devoid of emotion. She sounded flat.

"No, of course not. Of course he doesn't," said Emerald, gripping Maram's hand, feeling the calming influence of her friend washing over her, trying to force her heart rate to slow, pressing the fear down as she felt her emotions starting to surge through her uncontrollably. She had to calm down. She had to calm down. "But you can't ask me to kill him."

"I'm not asking," said Carla.

A nurse opened the door to the left of the coffee machine and approached them, a clip board in hand. "Carla Martinez?"

"That's me," said Carla, standing up and looking scared.

"You're Abigail Stone's next of kin?" she asked.

"Yes," said Carla. "Is she okay? Is she awake?"

"Yes," she said, smiling reassuringly. "She's awake. She's not out of the woods but she's getting there."

"Can I see her?" Carla stepped forward, her hands out as in in prayer.

"Yes, but only you," said the nurse, looking apologetically at the rest of the group. "We won't be allowing any visitors until 9AM. I'm very sorry. But come back tomorrow and you can all step in to see her, two a time."

"Em, if Abi has anything that can help find him I'll call you," said Carla. "Find him and kill him, Emerald. I swear if she dies because you refuse to kill him then losing us will be the least of your concerns."

Before Emerald could answer Carla turned from her and followed the nurse, the door swinging shut behind her.

Chapter Five

The morning sun was cool and bright and the autumn air dewy and clean. Fadius felt fresh and excited. He felt strong. Crouched in amongst the cold, wet leaves of a blackberry bush, he could feel brambles trying to penetrate his skin but failing and an insect walking over his fingers, its tiny feet tickling the hairs on his knuckles. He could smell dirt and manure, weed killers and somewhere there was the excrement from a cat. He had never felt so alive. It was overwhelming and incredible and intoxicating.

The house he was watching was a neat bungalow with clean windows and a mossy roof. It had a terracotta coloured patio decorated with lawn chairs and potted vegetables and gave way to a neatly mown lawn with well tended flower beds and a small shed painted a cheerful yellow. A small pond with an ornamental fish spraying water from its mouth gave the sound of rain, though none was falling that morning.

An elderly woman with her grey hair clipped neatly back into a bun stepped out of the French windows and onto the patio. She carried a soft plastic bucket filled with tools and gardening gloves, and set it down on the tiles. She smelled the air and looked around, smiling at the nature that surrounded her. Despite her obvious age, she looked fit and competent.

Fadius watched her, confusion suddenly starting to prick into his brain.

That couldn't be the right woman. She was old. Yes she was fit and well but it was physically impossible that this woman could be the one they were looking for. She was far too old to be bearing anything. He started to back away.

"FADIUS," the voice seemed to resonate even more loudly in his brain. "BURN HER."

"But..."

"BURN HER."

Fadius hesitated then nodded and returned to where he had been.

Now on the grass, Edna Broom was strapping pads to her knees and pulling on green floral gardening gloves. She took a portable radio out of her bucket and set it on a tree stump. Turning it on, the sound of the Beatles singing about Father McKenzie writing a sermon that no one would hear filled the air.

She reached into the bucket and pulled out the gardening gloves just as Fadius stepped out of the bushes.

"Oh!" she startled, then looked apologetically at him. "I'm so sorry, I didn't see you there. Are you looking for someone? Are you old Bill's boy?"

"No," said Fadius approaching her.

The warm smile fell from her face and Edna Broom stepped nervously backwards. "Who are you?" she asked, and glanced anxiously towards the house. Fadius reached into the bucket and pulled out a set of keys, then walked towards the shed. "What are you doing?"

As Fadius walked away, Edna started towards the house, so he turned back to her and swung his fist into her gut, knocking her down onto the ground. She howled and fell backwards into a flower bed where she landed with a loud crack, then turned and began to wretch violently.

Fadius unlocked the door and pulled out the lawnmower as the sounds of all the lonely people began to drift away and a man began speaking instead.

"PHILLIP!" Edna called out, her voice straining and weak. "PHILLIP, HELP ME!"

Fadius dragged the lawn mower towards Edna, who watched him with horror on her face, then he turned and returned to the shed where he fetched a can of petrol.

"What are you doing?" Edna wept, trying to get up but crying in pain, clutching at her side as she fell back down.

"You will not bear the beast," he said.

"Beast?" she asked, looking wild eyed and panicked. "What are you talking about? What beast?"

"You will not defy my Lord," he said.

"Lord?" asked Edna, panic in her voice. "Your Lord God? I'm a Christian! I pray! I'm on the parish council! Please, please don't do this. Please!"

Fadius hesitated. She looked so afraid, so vulnerable. He suddenly felt every bit of his six feet five inches of muscle and he loomed over the terrified and injured elderly woman.

"SHE IS LYING," roared the voice.

Fadius nodded obediently and tipped up the can of petrol. He poured some of it onto the mower at his feet then as Edna tried to stand, fighting the obvious pain, Fadius tipped petrol over her head and body.

She fell back, weeping, spluttering from the smell and the fumes. "Please," she begged again, her voice cracking and tears pouring down her cheeks.

Fadius ran the last of the petrol in a line from Edna to the mower, then dropped the can on the floor.

For a moment, watching the woman weeping, petrified, he felt a sense of shame. Of sadness. Of fear. Then he took out a match, struck it, and threw it onto the mower. As the flames roared into the air and the woman's screams died away, Fadius stepped back through the bushes.

Behind him he heard a door open and a man start to shout hysterically. He kept walking.

"SHE WASN'T THE ONE," said the voice. "WE MUST GO AGAIN."

"Yes, Lord," said Fadius, as he walked away from the garden leaving the smell of burning flesh and the wails of a horrified widow in his wake.

ð

"Have you slept?" Maram asked Emerald as she stepped out of her bedroom and spotted her friend hunched over the table, a mug in her hand, studying the lists of names with Guinevere at her side.

"Some," said Emerald, looking up. Maram looked terrible. Her usually olive skin looked grey, her eyes were red. "Have you?"

"No," Maram admitted. "Is there any coffee left in the pot?"

"A bit. Finish what's there and put more on," said Emerald. "We've got two hours. I can get some serious caffeine into my system in two hours if I apply the right degree of dedication."

"Something you've never struggled with," muttered Guinevere.

"We need to talk about something," said Maram as she poured coffee into a mug, her voice hollow. "And I think you know what."

"Maram," Emerald started.

"She walks amongst us but all alone," said Maram, holding the cup in her hands and looking over the top of it at them, her face grim. "Her life is real but not her own."

"You don't know," Emerald said.

"She does," said Guinevere.

"You can't possibly know!" Emerald protested.

"Of course it's me!" cried Maram. "Of course it is! Who else is it going to be?"

"We don't know that!" Emerald stood up. "Maram, you're not going to die!"

"Emerald," said Guinevere, softly. "You need to calm down."

"I can't!" Emerald cried out, her heart starting to race. "I can't calm down! You both think Maram's going to die!"

"Em," said Maram, setting her mug down on the side and putting a hand on Emerald's shoulder. "Breathe. Slowly."

Emerald's head was starting to hurt. Maram couldn't die. She couldn't let it be true.

"Maram," said Guienevere urgently.

"Em," said Maram, taking Emerald's hands. "Listen to me. Just listen to my voice."

Emerald nodded, looking into Maram's eyes and forcing her breathing to slow down. Her skin was prickling, her hands were trembling. "I'm sorry, I'm sorry," she whispered, shaking her head. She was making everything about herself, she was always making it all about her. This was about Maram. She had to calm down. She had to help Maram.

"Don't be sorry," said Maram gently, her cool hands soft and gentle. "I'm here. You're okay. Just breathe slowly. I'm here."

Emerald focused, slowing her breathing. She gritted her teeth and closed her eyes. She had to get control. Calm down. Calm down.

"I'm okay," she said after a moment. "I'm sorry."

"Don't be sorry," said Maram. "Sit. Drink your coffee. You've probably just got too much blood in your caffeine system."

"You've never died before," said Emerald, sitting down and looking at the lists. "Have you?"

"No," said Maram.

"Then it can't be you, can it?" said Emerald.

"What about the second list?" asked Guinevere. "We don't know what connects these women yet."

"We don't know yet if they're part of this at all," said Emerald.

"I don't want to tell the others yet," said Maram, going back into the kitchen and tipping coffee grounds into the machine.

"Do you think that's wise?" asked Guinevere, her voice suddenly stern. "Don't you think they have a right to know?"

"Maybe," said Maram, looking down. Her long hair falling over her eyes. "But I can't. Not right now."

"Maram," said Guinevere. "I really must insist..."

"You're her Guardian, not mine," said Maram, her voice suddenly sharp. "I'm older than you. And you're retired."

The cat sat back like she'd been slapped, she looked hurt. Emerald felt badly for her, Guinevere had been there for

Maram just as much as she had ever been there for her. But Maram had a point. This wasn't their information to reveal.

"I won't say anything," Emerald promised, then looking apologetically at Guinevere added, "It's not my choice. I have to respect Maram."

"I'm sorry Guin," said Maram, losing her edge and sinking onto the sofa dejectedly. "I just can't face it. Not yet."

"Nobody will think less of you," said Emerald.

"You don't know that," said Maram, clutching her cup tightly in her hands. "I think less of me."

"We won't say a word," promised Emerald. "We need to figure out if these women are connected to the case and what connects them before we can even be sure it's you anyway, right?"

"Yeah," said Maram. "Right."

ð

Trembling, Emerald took off the top off the shoe box and revealed the brass lamp inside. If ever the world needed changing it was now. She could fix things. But she was afraid.

Holding the lamp in front of her and thinking back to the stories she had read and the movies she had seen, she carefully rubbed her hand on the side of the lamp.

The lamp began to vibrate and a pungent turquoise smoke began to drift from the spout. Gasping, Emerald set the lamp down on her fluffy rug and rushed backwards, scrambling up onto her bed and pulling her knees close. She realised that she hadn't fully believed. Part of her thought her peculiar grandfather had been mocking her, setting her up to be laughed at. But it was real. It was happening.

The smoke was getting thicker now and Emerald could barely see through it. She was surrounded. The smell was sweet but tingly. Cloying. Like spiced potpourri. Small golden lights started drifting around, flickering like specks of dust catching the light on a sunny day but much, much brighter.

Emerald coughed heavily, her knees pulled up to her chin and her eyes closed tightly. After a minute she felt herself breathe more easily and when she looked up again the smoke was gone. A girl, young and thin, dressed in a ragged dress tied with a rope at the waist, was curled up in the foetal position on her rug next to the lamp.

"Hello?" she asked, annoyed at how timid her voice sounded.

The girl seemed to sigh a sound of despair then pushed herself up onto her knees. She knelt before Emerald, not looking up, with her thick dark brown hair hanging down across her face. "Yes, master," she said, sadly.

"Who are you?" asked Emerald, slipping off the bed onto her knees to match the forlorn girl.

"I'm your genie," said the girl and looked up then startled. "Oh! You're just a child!"

"Well so are you!" retorted Emerald.

"I am?" asked the girl, holding out her hands and examining them. "I am!"

"You're surprised?" asked Emerald, fascinated and confused.

"I haven't been a child in... I don't know..." said the girl, standing up and looking down at her willowy body. "A very long time. A very, very long time."

"I don't understand," said Emerald. She resented it when things confused her.

"How old are you?" asked the girl, not offering an explanation.

"Eight," said Emerald, pulling herself up proudly and jutting her jaw out. "How old are you?"

"Eight," the girl repeated, a faint smile beginning to tickle over her face. "And you're a girl."

"Yes!" said Emerald, really annoyed now.

"And you rubbed the lamp," said the girl, staring around Emerald's bedroom. "And you're eight. And a girl."

"This is just getting silly now," grumbled Emerald. "I thought I was getting a genie! Who are you?"

"I'm the genie," said the girl, looking at her through brown almond shaped eyes. "Your wish is my command."

"You're a genie?" asked Emerald. "What's your name?"

"Maram, what's yours?"

"Emerald Wren," said Emerald.

"Nice to meet you Emerald Wren," said Maram. "What's your wish?"

"How many do I get?"

"Three," said Maram. "Then I go back into the lamp."

"Then where do you go?"

"I don't know," said Maram, shrugging despondently. "I go back in, then the lamp gets found by someone and I'm called up to serve. I belong to my master until the wishes are granted, then I go back in and it starts again."

"What do you mean you belong to your master?" asked Emerald. She had quite forgotten the urgency of her desire to wish.

"You're my master," said Maram. "You own me."

Emerald shuddered. "That doesn't sound great," she said, wrinkling up her nose. "I don't know if I want to own you. You're a kid like me, not a pet."

"I'm not," said Maram, her face scrunching up like she was holding back tears. "I'm much, much older than you."

"You are not," Emerald protested.

"I suppose not. Not right now," said Maram. "You're eight so I'm eight. I'm usually older. Sometimes a lot older."

"You're being very cryptic," said Emerald, folding her arms. "Is that genie talk or are you just being difficult?"

"Sorry," said Maram. "People aren't usually interested in me. At least not beyond what I can do for them. However old my master is, that's the age I am. It's been that way for hundreds of years now."

"Freaky," said Emerald peering closely at Maram. Nothing about her suggested she was anything except a normal eight year old girl. Except maybe her eyes. "So you've been owned by loads of people?"

Maram closed her eyes and nodded, her head low and her face hanging slack. "Yes."

"And they keep you until they've made their wishes?"

"Yes," said Maram.

"How long does that take?"

"It depends," said Maram. "When women own me they tend to be quick. They decide what they want and they wish for it and then I'm gone. Men are different... When men own me... it's... slow. They make it last."

"Why?" asked Emerald. Something about the way Maram said it made her feel anxious, nauseated. She wasn't sure she wanted the answer but couldn't help but ask.

"They use me for more than their wishes," she said.

Emerald knew she was fairly ignorant about the world. She read a lot and listened a lot, but had the privilege of a mother who protected her from as much unnecessary pain as possible. Still, the look on the little girl's face and the hollow tone to her voice told Emerald that horrible things had happened to her. Terrible things. For hundreds of years. Her head felt foggy. Her heart ached.

"I would never hurt you," said Emerald. "I promise."

Maram smiled at her wanly. "Then I am going to enjoy my time with you. I will treasure every minute of my childhood."

"Can't I just wish you free?" Emerald asked her.

"Wish me free of what?"

"This," said Emerald. "The slave life. Like in Aladdin."

"What's Aladdin?"

"What's Aladdin?" Emerald repeated, her mouth hanging open in shock. "You're an actual real life genie and you've never seen Aladdin?"

"What is an Aladdin?"

"Aladdin," said Emerald. "Is an amazing movie starring Robin Williams as a genie!"

"Okay..." Maram looked confused.

"Look," Emerald got up and went to her bookcase which was filled with illustrated Disney books her mother had been collecting for her since she was little. She pulled her copy of Aladdin down and flipped through the pages, then handed it to Maram.

"He's blue," said Maram, screwing up her nose.

"He's a genie," said Emerald.

"But he's blue!" said Maram, flipping through the pages. "And he can shape shift!"

"So?"

"So this is silly," said Maram. "Robin Williams is not a real genie."

Emerald rolled her eyes. "My point is," she said, taking the book and turning the pages to the end. "Aladdin wishes the genie free. Then he goes on holiday to Hawaii. And I could do that for you."

"Whoever wrote this knows nothing about genies," said Maram. "It's not something I can be freed from. It's just what I am. It's my species. I stay for three wishes, and then I go. It's not an identity I can pick up and put down."

"Oh..." said Emerald.

"It's a nice idea," said Maram with a sad shrug. "But it's in my DNA. I am what I am. Nothing can change that."

"What would happen if I never made a wish?" asked Emerald. "Would you stay eight forever?"

"I'd just grow older as you grow older," said Maram. "I age like a human, I just start from the age of my master and grow from there."

"Then I'll never make a wish," said Emerald firmly, folding her arms and nodding her head. "Ever. And then you never have to go back in the lamp and you never have to be owned by any horrible people ever again."

Maram frowned and cocked her head to the side. She stared intently into Emerald's face. She looked confused. Hopeful. "Really?"

"Of course," said Emerald. "Oh... but I... I do need to make one wish. Just one."

"Of course, master," said Maram, bobbing her head sadly.

"It's Emerald. Or Em. Not master. Never master."

"Of course, Emerald," said Maram, a slight smile playing over her lips.

"And I promise just this one wish. I only need one thing. I need a power," said Emerald, sitting back on the bed and looking up at Maram nervously. "My dad... he left. He's magic and my grandfather's magic and I'm not. He blames my mum and he left us. I need him to come back."

Maram stepped closed to Emerald, her bare feet treading softly over Emerald's green rug. "I'm sorry, I can't grant that wish," she said, tilting her head. "You already have a power."

"What?" asked Emerald. "No I don't."

"Yes, you do," said Maram. "I don't know what it is but you've got it."

"Oh," Emerald said, frowning. Her mind racing about what power she could possibly have. "I guess I have a different wish then."

"What?"

"Make my daddy come home," said Emerald, fighting to keep tears at bay. "Is that something I can wish for?"

"It is," said Maram, then hesitated, chewing her lip. "May I speak out of turn?"

"Don't ask me stuff like that," said Emerald, screwing up her face again. "It gives me the creeps. I'm not your master, remember?"

Maram smiled a little then said, "I don't think you should wish it."

"Why not?"

"You hate the idea of me being owned," said Maram. "Because people force me to do things I don't want to do. To be places I don't want to be. If I made your father come home it wouldn't be because he wants to be here. He'd be trapped. He wouldn't want to be here but he wouldn't have a choice."

"But he'll be home," whispered Emerald, losing the battle as two heavy tears started to slide down her cheeks.

"But he'll be a slave," said Maram. "I can do it, if you wish it, but I don't think it's something you actually want. If you forgive me for being so presumptuous. Your wish will always be my command."

Emerald felt her eyes start to sting as more and more tears rushed to form. She didn't want to cry. She hated crying. But she couldn't help it. Soon they were flooding down her cheeks and as fast as she fisted them away more replaced them. She tried to speak but only a croaking choking sound came out. She gave in and allowed herself the freedom to cry when she felt Maram's soft arms wrap around her shoulders.

"He's gone," Emerald sobbed. "My daddy's gone. And it's all my fault."

"I'm sorry," Maram whispered, hugging her tightly. "I'm so sorry."

The two girls sat side by side on Emerald's bed for a while, Emerald crying heavy tears of despair whilst Maram sat loyally at her side, comforting her.

"Maram?" said Emerald after a while, when her crying had slowed enough that she could speak but still made her voice wobble. "I promise I won't make any wishes," she said. "I promise."

Maram smiled at her. "Thank you," she said. But Emerald could tell she didn't believe her.

Chapter Six

"You girls look tired," observed Vincenzo as Emerald and Maram shrugged off their coats after stepping into Vinnie's, the restaurant where they worked. "You're not eating enough."

"We're eating plenty," Emerald said as she went to the coffee machine and stuck two large cups under the spouts. She pressed buttons that started it whirring and releasing a delicious smell. "It's sleep we're not getting enough of."

"Our friend went to hospital last night," Maram explained, sliding onto a bar stool and resting her head on the bar. "She got sick."

"I'm sorry to hear that," he said. "I'd send you home if I could rely on replacements to show up that work to your standard."

"It's fine, Vinnie," said Emerald, setting one of the now full mugs in front of Maram's resting head before taking a sip of her own. "Keep the caffeine coming and we'll keep the serving going."

The morning was mercifully quiet. For the most part the restaurant was nearly empty with just a man with a laptop eating a panini and a mother with a baby in a pram at her side who seemed to be making a stoic effort to compete with Emerald for caffeine intake that morning. Ordinarily Vinnie would be giving them jobs to do such as stock take or general cleaning, but he backed away into his office and left the girls leaning on the counter, coffee cups in hands.

In her pocket Emerald's phone buzzed. With a quick side eye towards Vinnie's office she pulled it out of the pocket of her red apron and swiped the screen.

"It's Tig. There's been two more women," said Emerald, her hand to her face.

"Burned?" asked Maram leaning in to look at the screen.

"Yeah, a young woman they think was drunk was found in a dumpster, and an old woman whose mower exploded."

"Jesus," muttered Maram, shaking her head. "When and where?"

"Over the last couple of days. Local."

Maram rubbed her eyes. "I can't deal," she said. "This can't be happening."

"We'll keep you safe," Emerald promised.

"Yeah," said Maram, looking up at her with a face full of pain in a way Emerald hadn't seen in many years. "I know."

"I'll ask her to do some research, see if they're columm A or B," said Emerald, starting to tap a reply into the screen.

"Hey," came a male voice from the other side of the counter, startling them both.

Looking up Emerald saw a man in a Kirklands uniform. "Do you have the delivery?" she asked.

"Yeah, in the truck," he said, nodding to Emerald then smiling at Maram. Turning from Emerald he handed a clipboard to Maram. "I need an autograph."

Maram's face lost the haunted look and reconfigured into a shimmery eyed smile. "I'll look after that for you," she said, taking the board and signing her name next to

Vincenzo's address. "You're new. What happened to Margaret?"

"Dunno," he said. "She left. I guess I'm the lucky guy you'll be dealing with now."

"I'll show you round the back," said Maram, smiling at him.

Emerald rolled her eyes. She had been so grateful when the last delivery guy had been replaced with Margaret. Maram's short lived relationship with Bo had combusted fast and Emerald had been on delivery duty consistently until he had left so that Maram could avoid him and she'd had to listen to him opining miserably and endlessly on Maram's perfect cruelty.

ð

Mahalia Odili, a duffle coat pulled over her blue and white nurse's uniform, stepped out of the hospital and trudged slowly towards the bus stop. She looked exhausted. Her face was drawn and steps were dragging. When she finally reached the bus stop, she sank onto the curved yellow plastic bench as if it were a comfortable sofa.

"Long day?" asked Fadius, leaning his elbows on his knees and not looking at her, his large blue duffle bag between his ankles.

"Long day, long night," the nurse said, not looking up. A couple of others waited at the bus stop but nobody paid much attention to the exhausted nurse or the large, muscle bound man.

Fadius remained silent after that, and when the bus pulled up he picked up his bag and followed the nurse and the others in the queue on board. There were several passengers already on board. Fadius moved towards the back and sat six rows behind Mahalia, not taking his eyes from the back of her head.

As the bus moved off he watched her take out her phone and speak to somebody, her head bobbing slowly as she spoke.

The bus stopped, picking up the occasional passenger, ejecting more, as it moved further and further into the more remote areas of the town. After about forty minutes he and Mahalia were the last passengers. When the bus pulled over to a stop, Fadius stood and walked empty handed towards the front.

"Bye," he said as he passed Mahalia.

Looking up she smiled at him kindly, a look of pleasant surprise on her face. "Bye," she replied.

As Fadius stepped off the bus he looked back with momentary regret at the driver, then the doors closed and the bus pulled away.

Fadius started his long walk back into town as behind him the bus erupted with an ear splitting boom and a wing mirror whizzed past him, narrowly missing his head.

"SHE WAS NOT THE ONE," came the voice. "ANOTHER MUST DIE."

"Yes Lord," said Fadius, not looking back.

ð

"What about Steve?" asked Emerald as she pulled out a pint of San Miguel.

Maram shrugged. "What about him?"

"Nothing," said Emerald, setting the pint glass on a round tray next to two glasses of wine and a Pepsi. "Just you know… Matt seems to have replaced him already and…"

"He's nice, okay," said Maram defensively. "I don't owe Steve anything!"

"I didn't say you do!" said Emerald, inwardly kicking herself. "Just wasn't sure you'd broken up with him."

"Well I have, okay," said Maram, slamming a box of straws down and glaring at Emerald.

"Does he know?" asked Emerald, wondering why she was incapable of just biting her tongue.

"Of course he knows!"

"Cool," said Emerald, attempting to sound as chilled out and disinterested as possible. She picked up the tray and headed towards the table where people waited.

"I'm just saying Matt's a nice guy," said Maram as Emerald walked away. "I'm looking forward to our date."

"Good!" said Emerald.

"Yeah," said Maram. "It is!"

Emerald carried the tray to the table and handed out the drinks, smiling as she passed them out, then returned to the bar where a stony faced Maram was waiting.

"Five hours left," said Emerald with a forced cheeriness. "Then back to the relaxing world of after-work work where nothing stressful or tiring ever happens!"

"Maybe you should try going on a date once in a while," said Maram. "Maybe then it wouldn't seem so weird to you."

"It's not weird to me." These conversations were never a good idea. What was she thinking?

"Well obviously it is," said Maram, hands on her hips.

Emerald sighed. With everything so tense already, now was really not the time. "It's fine," she said carefully. "I don't mind who you do or do not date. It's your life."

Maram flinched. "Yeah it isn't though, is it," she spat, and stormed away, the kitchen door slamming behind her.

ð

Tig sipped the coffee and wished there was whisky in it. She eyed her backpack but suspected she might be thrown out of the hospital if she was caught spiking the coffee at 10 in the morning.

"So are we assuming that the old woman, Edna, died in the war?" she asked Carla. She was sitting on the edge of Abi's hospital bed with her phone in her hands, scrolling through various reports.

"We can't know," said Carla. "But 'against the odds, survived' implies it. Not as easy to find info when they're so old."

"She would have been so young," came Abi's faint voice. "I can't imagine going through something like that, you know?"

Tig smiled at Abi, watching Carla squeeze her hand so gently and tenderly. For a moment she wondered if she would ever fall in love, ever feel comfortable with someone running their hands on her skin. She shuddered and instinctively reached for her bag. Catching Carla watching her she pulled her hand back. "But there's practically nothing on Hannah Monroe," she said after a moment, ejecting such thoughts from her mind. "Have you pulled anything up?"

"Other than reports of her death, not much really! Just like the others, it's like she barely existed," said Carla, holding up her phone to demonstrate. "And I could swear that I'm getting fewer results the more I hunt."

Tig frowned and looked at her phone. "I think you're right, you know," she said. "I'm sure her name was included on the voting register before but it's not there now. It's like she's disappearing."

"That's freaky," said Carla, frowning at her phone. "Someone's erasing her, and everyone else on Column B. Pretty sure that's a sign they're connected."

"We've just got to figure the connection out," said Abi.

"And who's erasing them..." said Tig. "Oh fuck it. This is seriously twisted." She reached for the bag, pulled out the bottle of whisky and poured a slug into her coffee.

ð

"Girls!" cried Vinnie as he slammed his office door open. "Have you heard?"

"Heard what?" asked Emerald and Maram at the same time, breaking the awkward silence that had settled over them

"There's been a terrorist attack!"

Customers around the restaurant spun around, mouths gawping, then began rummaging in bags and pockets for phones and tablets.

They followed Vinnie into his office where his television was playing the news, and a reporter was standing on the side of the road with "BUS BOMB" details trailing across the bottom of the screen. "The two victims," the reporter was saying, "are reported to be driver Mason Maddox and his sole passenger, a local nurse; Mahalia Odilli."

"A woman," whispered Maram, leaning close to Emerald. "A bomb means there was fire."

Emerald nodded her head towards the door and the two slipped out. Around the room there was hushed conversation and faces of shock and fear. "I'll phone Carla," said Emerald. She was about to press dial when her phone began to buzz. "Celeste?"

"I've found her," came Celeste's voice. "The one from Abi's vision. She's here."

"Oh my god," Emerald gasped. She looked at Maram and couldn't help but feel joy despite the horror that was surrounding them.

"She's just a kid," said Celeste. "She was moved here at 3AM from the hospital. Her name is Lara O'Neil."

"And you're sure?" asked Emerald, smiling at Maram who looked quizzical, and trying to force her voice to sound sombre and not betray her inner elation.

"Yes," said Celeste. "Her father beat her with a wine bottle because she's in love with a Muslim boy. She's absolutely broken up. Her mother called an ambulance and she's alive, but her heart had stopped so technically before they revived her she had died."

"Jesus," muttered Emerald. "The poor girl, how old is she?"

"Seventeen," said Celeste, sounding absolutely devastated. "We've been working with her all night. Her mum wouldn't come, she stayed with the father. Lara was moved here in secret for her protection because there's quite a few men in the family who are out for her. She's broken. Absolutely broken."

"There's a girl who died at the refuge," Emerald quickly filled in to Maram who looked absolutely stunned. "Celeste thinks she's the girl we're looking for."

"Em," said Celeste. "We need to save her. I mean it."

"We will," said Emerald. "I promise."

"What time can you leave?" Celeste asked.

"Six," said Emerald. "Meet at the hospital?"

"Power up, then back to the refuge," agreed Celeste. "I'm going to stay here for as long as I can to keep watch but hopefully we can get together and back here before anything happens. I can't let him get her. I just can't. This poor girl, Emerald, she needs us."

"We'll be there," Emerald promised, then hung up and filled Maram in on the plan.

"So it's not me," said Maram, her eyes shining. "It's not me!"

"If we can save Lara O'Neil and stop the Fire Guy then it's over," said Emerald, smiling so much her face hurt. "And nobody needs to know. It's over."

The girls hugged tightly, tears of joy and relief starting to pour.

"I know," came Vinnie's voice as his huge, hairy arms wrapped around them both. "Terrorists here. It's just so close to home."

Emerald and Maram glanced at each other. Emerald suddenly felt very guilty. The three stood in silence hugging, with the sound of the news in the background discussing the tragic event.

Chapter Seven

"But if I've got a power," said Emerald, frowning. "Why can't use it?"

They were huddled over mugs of hot chocolate, sitting on a tree stump in the borders of Emerald's front garden at the top of the long, pebbly drive way. It was private and relatively isolated, somewhere Emerald knew they wouldn't be seen by passers-by, affording them the privacy they needed to maintain the secret of Maram's existence.

"I don't know," said Maram. "I don't really know how it works. Maybe it needs triggering?"

"What do you mean?"

"Maybe you need to be in a situation where it's needed before it comes out?"

"So I could throw myself off the roof then I'd be able to fly?"

"Yeah," said Maram. "But don't."

Emerald laughed. "That would trigger it though, right?"

"Unless you can't fly, then you'd just crash," said Maram, kicking her foot in the dirt. "You know your mum is going to notice me eventually."

Maram had been living in Emerald's bedroom for two days so far but they tried to spend as much of the day outside as they could to avoid being noticed. The half term break would be over in three day's time, however, and Emerald hadn't yet figured out how they would deal with the return to school. She tried not to pass on that concern to Maram. She was already dealing with so much.

"One day," said Emerald shrugging. "But she's not really with it right now. We've got time to come up with an excuse."

"I guess," said Maram, nervously, pulling Emerald's old winter coat around herself. "I'm just worried. What if she sends me away? Where will I go?"

Emerald watched her guiltily. She knew Maram should be having a real life but she didn't know how to arrange it. Seeing Maram's joy at being given some of Emerald's clothes to wear, her amazement at experiencing a hot shower, and her wonder at the television really moved Emerald. Things that Emerald considered ordinary seemed to make Maram feel free, yet she was still trapped. Still a prisoner in her master's home and unable to live a real life.

There had to be something she could do. Perhaps her mother would agree to adopt Maram and let her stay if they could find a way to explain the situation. Then Maram could be a daughter, and go to school with Emerald, and stop feeling like she was trapped in a world she didn't belong in. She could have an actual life.

"Hey!" came an aggressive voice from the street, snapping Emerald out of her thought train. "Emerald Wren!"

The two girls looked. A particularly obnoxious boy from Emerald's school, Drew Hartley, was standing on the path with his hands on his hips with his equally unpleasant friends, Max and Al, behind him. Next to her, Maram froze, the presence of aggressive males obviously terrified her.

"What?" Emerald shouted back, trying to sound tough but feeling sick. Drew, Max and Al were of power and had long lorded it over Emerald. She knew being powerless and the child of someone like her father, someone so powerful and so respected by the community, made her a freak. She was excluded from

everything to do with that world and regularly mocked. And she hated it.

"Do you know where your dad is?" he asked, chin jutted out and evil amusement glinting in his eyes.

Emerald felt her chest begin to thud. Her hands trembled. She blinked furiously, she would not show weakness, she would not show him it hurt.

"She doesn't know," laughed Al.

"Tell her," said Max, grinning a nasty grin.

"I know where he is," said Drew, stepping onto the crunchy stones of the long driveway. "Your dad's left you. He's sick of you. He's embarrassed by you."

"I..." started Emerald, feeling the tears burning at her eyes. "I..."

"I, I," laughed Drew, mimicking her pained voice. "Pathetic. Your dad's with my mum! Did you know that? My mum. The great Eric Wren has finally found himself a partner worthy of him!"

"No he isn't!" cried Emerald, standing up and shaking, her tears finally breaking free and burning hot tracks down her cheeks. "You take that back!"

Drew walked towards her with a swagger and a cackle. "You and your mother aren't good enough for him," he spat, then jabbed Emerald hard in the shoulder. "You're powerless and you're pathetic." He jabbed her again, harder.

Emerald yelped and staggered back. She tried to regain her balance but tripped and fell over, landing heavily on her bum. Startled and embarrassed, she cried out in pain. Behind Drew, Max and Al laughed hysterically whilst Drew loomed over her, raising his hands. Emerald cowered back, all pretence at strength gone and fear completely dominating her. She knew what Drew's power was and she didn't want to be on the receiving end of the acid that he had many times threatened her with just for the fun of seeing the fear in her eyes.

"No!" she cried, scrambling backwards. One of the stones below her had a sharp edge and she felt it slice into the palm of her hand.

Drew stood over her with a wicked smile. "Scared are you?" he asked, laughing cruelly. "You should be."

"Stop!" Maram's voice ordered. Emerald looked up at her and saw her standing up and staring at Drew with her face twisted in anger. "You will never put your hands on her again!"

"Who the hell are you?" Drew demanded, looking at her as if he hadn't noticed her presence at all until now.

"Maram," Emerald hissed. "It's okay."

"No it isn't!" snapped Maram, walking towards Drew with a look of absolute fury. "Get away from her! Now!"

Drew looked at Maram, skinny and shaking with rage, and laughed his head off. She looked tiny next to him. Weak. "Get outta here," he spat at her. "This is nothing to do with you." Then he shoved Maram hard in the centre of the chest.

Maram screamed and staggered backwards, a look of absolute horror flashing across her face as she fell to the ground.

Emerald felt her heart race. Her hands shaking. He'd triggered something deep in her heart that she couldn't control. He'd hit her. He'd hit Maram. Maram who had been abused, beaten, hurt constantly her entire life and who Emerald had sworn that she would protect. He'd hurt her.

The air started to feel thin. Emerald's chest felt tight and her eyes couldn't focus. She struggled to breathe. She struggled to process the rage that was surging through her. He'd hit Maram, he'd hit her, he'd stolen her father. No. Her dad hadn't gone to live with that asshole. Not him. He wouldn't have left her mum for another woman. He wouldn't have left Emerald for that awful boy. No. Not someone who hurt Maram. No. She couldn't see. Her brain felt clouded, her heart beat so hard she had stabbing pains in her chest. She couldn't breathe. What was happening?

Somewhere below her she heard screaming. The sound of running feet.

The fog started to clear and there he was. There he was. The boy who had stolen her daddy. The boy who had pushed her down. The boy who had attacked Maram. She saw his friends running away down the driveway but they were irrelevant. She didn't care. The boy who was to blame for everything was standing there. Staring at her. There he was.

There he was.

In her hand.

Screaming.

He did it. He stole him. He stole him and he hurt Maram and he did it.

She flung him across the driveway. He landed heavily on the roof of her mother's car, then dropped limply onto the ground, his body landing with a devastating crunch.

"Emerald," she heard a calm, clear voice breaking through the ocean waves of sound that seemed to be battering her brain. "Emerald."

A soft hand was on her leg.

"Emerald, breathe," said the voice. "Breathe slowly. It's okay. I'm here. Just breathe."

Emerald felt her heart rate begin to slow. The world around her seemed to be coming back into focus.

"I'm here," came the voice. "It's okay. Just breathe."

She opened her eyes and realised she was lying naked on the ground. Embarrassed she pulled her arms around herself. "What happened?" she cried, as Maram quickly draped the borrowed coat over Emerald's shoulders.

"I'm not sure," admitted Maram. "But there's a problem we need to deal with first." She pointed across the driveway where Drew lay bleeding onto the gravel.

"Oh shit!" Emerald gasped, scrambling to her feet.

The two girls hurried over to him, Emerald pulling the coat on properly as they went.

"I don't think he's dead," said Maram, crouching down and putting two fingers to his neck. "At least not yet."

Emerald noticed, not for the first time, how Maram seemed to carry a maturity and knowledge well beyond the eight years of her physical body.

"Did I do that?" Emerald asked.

"Yeah," said Maram, looking up at her. "You did."

"Oh my god!" cried Emerald. "We can't let him die!"

"You're right," agreed Maram, standing up and her face dropping. "We can't."

"Do we call an ambulance?" Emerald asked, looking around frantically. The driveway was long and wide, the road quiet. Nobody would witness this scene unless specifically coming to the house. It was a decision they had to make alone.

"And tell them what?" asked Maram, running her hands through her hair.

"I don't know!" Emerald cried, frantic now. "What do we do?"

"Wish him well."

"Can I do that?"

"Of course," said Maram, bobbing her head in servitude. "It's okay. One wish won't put me back in the lamp."

"One wish," said Emerald, chewing her lip. She looked from Drew to Maram and back again. The blood was flowing and his skin was sallow. His mouth was slack and his arms twisted at funny angles. "Okay. How do I do this?"

"Carefully," Maram advised, then looked down at Drew. "And quickly."

"Okay... I wish," said Emerald, concentrating hard. "I wish that any injuries I caused Drew would be immediately healed."

Maram nodded. "Your wish is my command."

Emerald stared intently at her, waiting for a flash or a puff of smoke but nothing happened. Then below her she heard Drew cough. Looking down she saw the boy sit up and look up at them in horror.

"You're a freak!" he shouted, pushing himself up. He was smeared in blood but there were no wounds, no bruises. He looked completely healthy but very afraid.

"Drew... I'm sorry," said Emerald, nervously. "Please don't tell anyone."

"I'm going to tell everyone! You're a freak!" he shouted at her, then stumbled away from them and ran down the driveway.

"What happened?" asked Emerald, watching Drew run away from her. She had long wished she could scare the horrible bully off but now it had happened she wished it hadn't. Her stomach churned. Nothing good had happened, of that she was sure.

"You... grew," said Maram, fidgeting with her fingers.

"Grew?" asked Emerald, pulling the coat around herself, the chill in the grey air and the cold of the crunchy pebbles under her feet starting to bite into her.

Maram nodded, turning to her with worry in her eyes. "That's why your clothes are gone. They ripped off."

"Jeez," muttered Emerald, staring at her arms and legs, trying to imagine them big, feeling repulsed by her own body. "I mean I know I wanted a power but not Hulking out! I wanted something cool!"

"I guess it's better than crashing to your death though, right?" said Maram.

"I suppose it is," said Emerald, shrugging. "Kinda wish we'd left that triggering little dickhead to die though."

"No you don't," said Maram.

"Nah," agreed Emerald.

"I've never seen anything like it," said Maram.

"And I hope you never see it again!"

ð

When Emerald and Maram stepped out of the restaurant that evening Ben was waiting for them.

"We've got to get up to the hospital," he said as Maram climbed into the front seat and Emerald into the back. "We're meeting everyone there then heading to the refuge."

They rode in tense silence until they got up to the hospital. Ben parked in a side street and they hurried through the falling darkness towards the building then slipped inside.

The corridors were busy with doctors and nurses hurrying about, and admin staff with clipboards discussing things in corners. Visitors carried flowers and balloons, patients whizzed past on beds and in wheelchairs pushed by uniformed porters. Nobody paid any attention to them as they made their way to Abi's room.

They were the last to arrive. Abi was sitting up with Carla at her side. Celeste was standing up, twisting at her necklace and repeatedly checking the time on her watch, her eyes darting about anxiously. Tig was sitting on Abi's bed chewing on her thumb nail.

"Finally," said Celeste as they stepped in. "Let's do this."

The seven of them formed a circle about the bed and took hands. As the unity of the coven formed Emerald felt the familiar rush of power and heat and strength rush through her veins. In that moment she felt she could take on anything. This man, this monster, could never stop them.

"Ready?" she asked as they broke apart, all looking refreshed by the surge.

"Anything to add last minute?" Tig asked, turning to Abi.

"No," she said. "Man, thirties, big. A shadow. Praying."

"We've got this," said Carla, leaning over and kissing Abi's cheek. "Trust us."

Heading back into the corridors of the hospital, the six made their way to the cars, prepared to guard Lara from any potential threat.

ð

Fadius walked quickly through the cool evening air feeling grateful for the early darkness of late autumn.

"Please," he thought to himself. "Please let this be the right one."

ð

Donna Shepherd, the night manager at the Waterside Street Women's Refuge, tapped lightly on the door of Room 17. After a couple of seconds the door opened revealing the pale, frightened face of Lara O'Neil, still swollen and bruised, with stitches carving their way across her forehead.

"Hello Sweetheart," said Donna. "Would you like anything else to eat?"

"N... n... no," stuttered the girl. "Th... thank you."

"Okay pet," said Donna, and held out a piece of paper. "I've got some numbers here for you, and some names. Don't worry about them right now, just keep them safe and focus on getting some sleep. It's been a long day. There's details about counsellors and legal aid on here so if you have any questions tomorrow just come and find me. Just take a look when you get a chance and don't worry, I'll be here."

"Oh... okay," said Lara, her hand stretching out and grasping the paper, pulling it to her chest like it was something fragile and precious.

"It's going to be okay," said Donna, smiling as reassuringly as she could. She had worked at the shelter for years but the harrowed look in the eyes of their new arrivals never failed to make her ache. "If you need us for anything at all we're here."

"Th... th... thank you," said Lara, clearly frustrated by the stammer.

"Good night," said Donna with a small wave.

As she walked back past the rooms, almost all occupied by terrified women, she thought of how afraid Lara was. How really she was just a child. They'd spent all day just helping her adjust to where she now was, promising her she was safe whilst having to tell her that she couldn't see her mother. The evil, bastard who was raising her was already free and resuming his hold of dominance and abuse over the woman who remained in the family home. She couldn't be with her mum when she needed her most but

Donna was certain Lara was in the better place right now. At least here she was safe.

ð

"This traffic!" wailed Maram, slamming her fist on the dashboard.

"I'm going as fast as I can!" insisted Ben.

Emerald looked out the window at the lights of the cars. He was out there, somewhere. And soon he'd be coming for a frightened seventeen year old girl.

Chapter Eight

A curtain twitched on the third floor and the small, frightened face of a child pressed against the glass for a moment before being pulled away and the curtain closed again. Fadius wondered momentarily what had led that child to be living in the women's refuge. What darkness haunted their past.

"NOW, FADIUS," the voice boomed in his head.

"Yes, Lord," he said as he crossed Waterside Street and walked purposefully towards the front door.

ð

Ahead of Ben's car, Celeste turned off Waterside Street down a side road and pulled in at the side. Ben drove in behind her and stopped the car.

"We'll need to go in the back way," said Celeste as they all got out of the cars. "We'll need to be discreet."

"Is there a lot of security?" asked Emerald as they hurried down the street.

"There has to be a certain amount," said Celeste. "But I know a way in. If we can get up to Lara we can explain everything later."

ð

"Hello," said a woman with a long blonde braid and a purple smock uniform behind the desk just inside the brightly lit entrance to the refuge. "Can I help you?"

"Got a delivery," said Fadius, holding up a cardboard box. "From Gibson and Roe."

"The lawyers?" she asked, leaning over to inspect the box.

"That's right, ma'am."

"I can take that for you," she said holding out her hands.

"Sorry, no can do," he said, shaking his head. "This needs to go straight into the hands of the recipient."

"Who is it for?" she asked nervously.

"A... Lara O'Neil," he said, making a show of reading the label.

"Oh right," said the girl, chewing on her lip. "You'll need to wait here. My manager Donna is around here somewhere, I'll find her. She'll need to sign off on this."

"Understood," said Fadius. "I'm okay to just take a seat?"

"Yes, please," said the girl, gesturing to the row of purple flip down seats that lined the wall by the door below a display of women's charities flyers.

The blonde girl tapped a code into a door, opened it, then carefully closed it behind her.

"ONE SEVEN SEVEN ONE THREE."

ð

"This way," said Celeste quietly as they slipped around the back of the building.

When they reached a fire escape door they stopped in a huddle. Tig dropped her backpack into the middle and opened it up. Inside it was full of pouches of sand. "Here," she said. "Take as many as you can fit in your pockets. The moment he tries anything just chuck them and the sand will eat the flames. As long as it's not bigger than anything Ben can make anyway."

"We need to be discreet," said Celeste. "Stick with me and stay quiet."

Celeste tapped in a code on the outside door, pulled it open, and quietly the coven slipped inside.

ð

"RIGHT HERE," announced the voice.

Fadius walked quickly and quietly, turning right where directed and headed town the long, pale grey corridor. The first thing he noticed was how much bigger the building seemed inside than it had from the outside, extending further back in a warren of rooms. If each room housed an abused woman, plus children in some cases, there was more than he had ever imagined. It shocked him.

"KEEP YOUR MIND ON THE JOB, FADIUS," demanded the voice. "HERE."

Fadius stopped and turned to look at the door he was now standing outside. Inside was the girl. The bearer of the Beast. He could stop her before she brought forth destruction.

He held up his hand and knocked brusquely.

ð

"This place is huge," hissed Ben.
"It's smaller than I remember," said Tig, looking around.
"Keep close," said Celeste. "We can't be seen. It's up here."
They followed her closely up a staircase. Emerald could feel her heart racing and her hands trembling. They'd be fine, she said to herself, they'd get there and wait with Lara and they'd protect her. Between the coven and the werewolf they had always got their man before so there was no reason this would be any different.

ð

"Hello?" came a soft voice as a pale skinned girl with strawberry blonde hair and a badly swollen face peered out between the door and frame. "Who are you?"
Fadius smiled at her gently, then with the strength that had been flooded into him, intoxicating him, he kicked the door hard sending the girl flying backwards across the room with a shriek of horror and pain.

ð

"It's the room at the end," said Celeste as they stepped into a corridor. "The last..." BOOM!

The building shook. Thick, black smoke suddenly erupted into the corridor as dust and ceiling tiles cascaded around them and fire alarms began to scream hysterically above them.

Down the corridor doors were flung open as terrified children clung to frightened mothers who coughed and choked on the smoke and dust as they scrambled through the chaos.

"Celeste!" choked out a woman, spotting her and grabbing her hand.

"Run!" Celeste commanded. "Get out!"

Around them they heard screams and cries as terrified and traumatised women fled from the only place they had ever felt safe, babies in their arms and infants at their feet, tripping and stumbling along in panic.

Following Celeste, they pushed through them and raced towards the end of the corridor to where a twisted, blackened door partially blocked the entrance to the source of the smoke and fear, flames licking out from around it.

"Oh god," sobbed Emerald, reaching about frantically for Maram's hand.

"I'm here," Maram's hand found hers and they clung to one another tightly.

Tig reached into her pockets and threw pouches at the flames. They instantly dissolved but were soon replaced.

"We don't have long," said Celeste, looking round at them with eyes wide and full of terror. "We can't be found here."

"She could still be alive," said Maram. "We have to check."

"I'll open it," said Ben, stepping forwards, his hands undisturbed by heat.

Emerald gritted her teeth. She didn't know where to look, what to do. Was Lara in there? Was He in there? She felt herself trembling and gripped hold of Maram's hand more tightly. Keep calm, keep calm.

At her side Tig was shaking violently and looked on the verge of collapsing. She reached out her other hand and took one of Tig's, though she couldn't tell if Tig was even aware, every bit of her seemed so intently focussed on the room.

Ben turned the handle and pushed, but it fell away from the frame as he did and flames immediately burst out at them, the heat was intense and Emerald felt her hair starting to singe as she cried out and staggered backwards.

Together they threw their sand. Credit to Tig it worked amazingly, the heat died down rapidly, the flames dissolving as the sand touched them. Soon they had managed to put the fire out and left behind just a blackened shell of a room, traces of smoke lazily drifting from surfaces.

Tig suddenly let out a howl and spun away, and Emerald saw why. On the floor, twisted up, was the blackened and burned body of a young girl. Celeste began to cry, Carla hit herself repeatedly on the thigh. Emerald clung tightly to Maram's hand and Ben stared at the body with his eyes wide and his face ashen as he ran his hands over his shaved head.

How long they stood like that Emerald didn't know but suddenly she became aware of the fire alarms again. "We have to get out," she said.

"How did he get out?" asked Carla, looking out of the door down the corridor then back into the room. "Look, the oven's open, he must have faked another gas leak. He can't have left long before the explosion but he didn't go past us!"

"The window," said Ben.

Emerald looked and he was right. One of the windows was broken.

"Did he jump?" asked Carla, carefully walking to the window, the floor creaking below her, threatening to cave.

"We're on the third floor," said Celeste as Carla peered out.

"And there's no ledge to balance on," Carla said looking out. "There's blue lights coming though, we've got to go."

They headed for the door quickly, Celeste pausing momentarily at Lara's charred and twisted body to make the sign of the cross. Then they left.

As they raced down the corridor and back down the stairs Emerald became aware of other wailing sirens joining the shriek of the fire alarms. Whatever happened they could not be found there. If they were found they'd have no excuse. They'd be arrested. They couldn't find this monster from prison and what could possibly be done for them? They had to get out. The walls of the stair well started closing in on her. The steps below her seemed to be spongy and moving. She nearly lost her balance, stumbling forwards but behind her Maram pulled her back. Her heart raced and she felt herself start to lose control. Her head was spinning, the smoke, the sirens, the alarms, the fear, the horror, it was overwhelming her and she felt herself start to panic.

Maram put two hands on Emerald's back and violently shoved her through the door and into the cold night air where rain was starting to spit, and Emerald tumbled down with a yelp, her hands scraping over the concrete and her knees striking the ground with a painful crunch. The pain shocked her, spun her back into reality as tears sprung to her eyes and all the energy that had been shooting around inside her was suddenly grounded.

"Not now, Em," Maram whispered at her, helping her to her feet. "We have got to go."

Standing up and blinking tears away furiously, Emerald followed her friends through the darkness and to their cars.

They drove away from the building, past a melee of firefighters, ambulances and police. Groups of women huddled together as they were attended to. The small, pale face of a child stared at them as they passed by, his eyes dark in his white skin. Emerald wondered if this was the worst he had experienced in his few years of life, or if it was just par for the course.

ð

Abi looked up as a nurse named Sarah gently placed a tray of food on the wheeling table in front of her. "Here you go, sweetheart," she said.

Abi start to lift her hand, a weak and slow movement as though she were seventy years older than her twenty years. As Sarah went to help her, Abi sat bolt upright, her eyes wide, and let out a piercing scream of terror.

Sarah stumbled backwards, shocked and afraid, and fell over a blood pressure machine. When she sat up she saw Abi collapsed on the bed and the heart rate monitor dropping rapidly then begin to frantically beep as alarm bells began to ring.

ð

"I flew," said Fadius, his chest heaving with adrenaline.

"YOU FELL," came the voice.

Fadius peered up at the room he had leapt from, blindly obeying without a second thought but certain he was facing imminent death. "I'm invincible."

"AS LONG AS YOU REMAIN LOYAL TO ME, YOUR STRENGTH WILL GROW," came the voice.

Fadius knew he was strong, he felt it. Every time his master was pleased with him he felt a rushing reward of strength and power and heat blasting through his body like an incredible rush of delirious joy. He felt like nothing could stop him. Like nobody could hurt him. And now he could fly. Or fall. He wanted to feel like this forever. He wished he'd had this power as a child. Nobody would ever lay a hand on him again. Nobody would ever stop him again. He was the strength now. He was the power. He was in control.

"Yes, Lord," said Fadius. "Always."

"SHE WAS NOT THE ONE."

"I'll try again," he promised.

Chapter Nine

Emerald and Maram lay side by side on the fluffy green rug in Emerald's bedroom and stared up at the ceiling. Emerald tried to force the image of Drew out of her mind, but could dismiss neither the twisted, broken body nor the near death face of the boy she hated so much.

"I'm a monster," said Emerald, holding up her hands and looking at them.

"You're not," said Maram. "I've known monsters."

"I don't know what I'm supposed to do with it," she said. "It's not good. I can't help people or do anything amazing with it. What's the point? It's horrible. It's evil."

"You're not evil, Em," said Maram, turning to look at her.

"I'm not," she said. "But my power is. I hope nobody ever finds out. I'd rather have no power at all than have this. Do you think I can get rid of it?

"No," said Maram, turning to look back at the ceiling. "I'm sorry. Not without... I mean... if you were to... you know..."

"I won't wish it," said Emerald, shaking her head and screwing up her face miserably. "I won't."

"I'd understand..." said Maram, beginning to tremble.

"I just need to learn how to control it," said Emerald, sighing heavily. "If that's even possible without a teacher."

They stared in silence for a moment when a loud banging came from the front door downstairs.

"Oh my god," whispered Maram. "The boy..."

"My dad..." gasped Emerald, standing up.

The two girls scurried to Emerald's door and raced to the top of the stairs just as Emerald's mother appeared in the hall and reached for the door. Emerald's heart raced, she waited for a shout of abuse, a demand for her to be pulled outside to be thrust into a crowd of pitchfork wielding villagers.

Her mother opened the door and looked around for a moment, then looked down and gasped, "Oh!"

"Are you Olivia Wren?" came a rather haughty voice.

"What? I... uh... what? Yes! What? You're... what?"

"My name is Guinevere. I'm here as your daughter's Guardian."

"My daughter? Emerald? She doesn't need a Guardian... why would she need a Guardian? I'm her mother! What? You're a cat... you're a talking cat."

"I'm a Guardian, Mrs Wren, not a talking cat," said Guinevere as Emerald's mother stepped back, revealing an elegant tabby cat sitting on the doorstep. "And this is precisely why she does need a Guardian."

"But... I..."

Guinevere walked in and sniffed around, then looked up the staircase, spotting Emerald peering through the bannisters. "I'll be upstairs with Emerald," said Guinevere. "Please don't disturb us. We will discuss what is relevant with you when it becomes necessary to do so."

"Wait!" protested Emerald's mother. "I can't just let you... she's my little girl! What are you doing here? Who are you?"

"Mrs Wren, your daughter is in possession of immense power and I am here to teach her how to use it; to guide her through it in a way someone of your... limitations... simply cannot do."

"Power?" asked Emerald's mother, fear in her voice as Emerald turned to Maram who looked as confused as she did.

How did this cat know? What was a Guardian? What was happening? "There must be a mistake. Emerald doesn't have any power... her father..."

"Is a moron," said Guinevere with a sigh. Her voice softened a little. "I can assure you, Mrs Wren, nobody of any real significance has any delusions about your husband."

"Oh, I see," said Emerald's mother, standing a little taller. "Well... carry on."

"Yes," said the cat, all business again. "Now, if you will excuse me."

Emerald watched as the cat approached her, looked past her to where Maram was lurking in the background, then walked passed them and into Emerald's bedroom.

"I guess we follow her?" whispered Emerald.

"That would be wise," came the voice of Guinevere.

Emerald peered over the rail and saw her mother looking up. She had a strange half smile creeping over her lips, and even though her eyes still held the harrowed pain Emerald was accustomed to seeing, it was the most happiness she had seen in a long time.

ð

Emerald flung the car door open, fell onto the pavement and vomited heavily. The speed they had driven mixed with the swamping panic and grief that surged through her body had finally overwhelmed her.

"Come on Em," said Maram, stroking her hair. "We need to get inside."

Emerald choked back a sob and stood up. Carla held Tig close to her and Celeste was clutching her crucifix so tightly it must have been cutting into her fingers. They were covered in dirt and plaster dust. Emerald's eyes burned and her lungs scratched from the smoke. They must have looked like disaster victims.

"Come on," said Ben. "Let's get in before anyone sees us."

Emerald pushed a shaking hand into her coat pocket and handed him the key. Heading into their building and up to their flat, Emerald felt like she was moving through syrup. She couldn't think clearly. All she could see was the charred body of the innocent girl they had been meant to save, all she could smell was the smoke and burned flesh.

Ben opened the door and they staggered into the flat. Guinevere was sitting on the windowsill but hurried over to them, watching with horror on her face as she took in the disarray.

"What happened?" she asked. "Where's Lara?"

"Where's the booze?" asked Carla, ignoring the cat as she helped Tig to the sofa.

"Fridge," said Maram, sinking onto the floor and putting her head in her hands.

"Emerald?" asked Guinevere, jumping onto the table. "What happened?"

Emerald lowered herself down and put her head in her hands. "We failed," she whimpered. "We've never failed before."

"She died?" asked the cat.

"He burned her. In the refuge," Emerald sobbed.

"He's a monster," said Tig. "I need whisky."

Carla went into the kitchen and pulled a box of cheap white wine out of the fridge. "There's some white shit Tig," she said. "And don't worry, Emerald's going to kill him."

"What?" asked Emerald, looking up suddenly. "No!"

Carla turned on her, fury on her face and slammed the wine box onto the counter. "Yes! Emerald you have to! You can! You nearly went didn't you, whilst we were there. I saw you starting to shake and grow. You nearly went. Look at you, your sweater's ripped. It was happening. If he'd been there you could have killed him right there and then. And I'd have cheered you on."

Emerald's heart began to race and she shook her head. "No, no," she stuttered.

"Emerald will not hurt anybody," said Guinevere, suddenly sounding incredibly authoritative. "And it is not your place to make her."

"You are not the boss of this," snarled Carla. "Seriously. This guy is a monster. That girl died! All those women are homeless now! He burned that girl alive, don't you get it? We need to kill him!"

"Then you kill him," said Ben, standing and squaring up to Carla.

"Trust me when I say this," said Carla. "I will try."

Tig went to speak when the sound of a ringing phone cut through the tension. Startled, Carla began patting down her pockets then rummaged in her bag, pulling the ringing phone out.

"I've got five missed calls," she said, the colour draining from her face. She tapped the screen. "Hello?"

Everyone watched and waited as Carla turned away from them, speaking in a whisper.

Carla hung up the phone and turned back to them. Emerald felt like she must look terrible, but was certain that in that moment Carla looked worse. Her mouth hung open, her eyes were wide. She was staring into space. She didn't look like the six foot figure of strength they were used to.

"What?" asked Celeste, approaching her softly and putting a hand gently on Carla's arm.

Registering the touch, Carla's attention snapped back to them. "Abi. She crashed. She's in a coma," she said, her voice quiet. "I have to go... I have to get there... I can't... I have to go to her... She needs me. I need her. I can't, I have to..."

"Come on," said Ben, standing up. "I'll drive you."

"Thank you," said Carla, nodding to him. "Thank you."

ð

"What's the report, Mr Wren?" asked Hubert Greer, as he sat down in one of the leather chairs in front of Stuart and Nahla, cutting Nahla off mid sentence.

Stuart glared at the young man as he sipped his coffee in silence. He was interrupting them in a conversation about the latest Wonder Woman film and he was decidedly unimpressed. Stuart so rarely enjoyed a conversation about anything other than work and for Hubert Greer to be the one ruining it was incredibly annoying.

"We have some movement," he said after a moment.

"Movement?" asked Hubert Greer. "Care to elaborate, Mr Wren?"

"Mr Greer, considering this is really ostensibly my project perhaps I should be the one you are asking to divulge this information?" suggested Nahla, clearly irritated.

"Yes, Ms Hussain," agreed Hubert Greer, raising his head a little to give them a clear line of sight up his rather long nostrils. "Quite right."

"They are crossing paths now," she said, her eyes narrowing. "All appears to be in line to go ahead."

"It's taking longer than we had expected," said Hubert Greer. "And now with the Monroe girl... it's not going well."

"Considering you won't let me take matters into my own hands, are you really surprised?" demanded Stuart, leaning forwards. "It wasn't that long ago that I didn't give you any choice in matters like this, Hubert."

"Yes, well," said Hubert Greer, sitting back in the leather chair, crossing his legs and folding his arms. "My predecessors made a plan and I will be sticking to it. And considering the events of last summer, Mr Wren, I am sure you can understand why I'm likely to trust their instincts over your own."

Stuart glared. "We are missing opportunities. If Emerald were aware of the situation in full..."

"That is not how it is supposed to go," said Hubert Greer, cutting him off. "We will not go against The Vision."

"Guidance!" said Stuart, throwing his hands in the air. "Their word should be taken as guidance only!"

"If your girl pulls this off, we'll speak more," said Hubert, standing and smoothing down his pristine suit.

Watching him walk away, Stuart felt his blood boil. The uppity little jumpstart with his promotion and brand new suit had no clue just how complex it was to deal with so many threads, how much one had to be aware of, how many things had to be considered.

"If your 'girl' pulls this off," sneered Nahla at his side once Hubert had left the lounge. "Your 'girl' could emulsify him."

"I wouldn't begrudge the price of popcorn to watch that either," said Stuart darkly. "Any word from Monroe?"

"She will be sent to us directly," said Nahla.

"This is a godforsaken agency," said Stuart, shaking his head.

"It's the best we've got," said Nahla. "You and I both know that. This isn't the first time we've come into conflict with the greater good."

"Well I'm fed up with it, quite frankly."

"Aren't we all," she said.

ꝺ

"Girls!" cried Vinnie as they stepped into the restaurant the following morning. They had showered off the smoke and debris, but the sick feeling in Emerald's gut couldn't be washed away so easily. "Oh my girls!"

They exchanged a look and then turned with smiles to their boss. "Hi Vinnie," said Emerald.

"Another explosion, another death," he wailed. "This world. This town. Oh girls."

"Going to the dogs," agreed Maram.

"Oh the dogs!" Vinnie flung his hands to his head. "Don't say that! We've not had another dog attack in weeks now! Don't tempt fate, girls, don't tempt fate. I'll get you some coffee, let's just be thankful we're here."

The two headed for the coat rack, shrugging off their jackets and leaving Vinnie to mutter and fret as he made them coffees.

"I don't know about you," whispered Maram. "But I'd go for a dog attack right about now."

"As long as I don't have to do it," said Emerald with a sigh. "He gets in there first often enough. Why not this guy too?"

"I'll keep my fingers crossed," said Maram, putting her arm around Emerald's shoulders and giving her a squeeze.

ð

Celeste peeped round the curtain surrounding Abi's bed. Carla looked dreadful. She hadn't washed since the incident and her hair was lank. She carried a strong smell of smoke about her and her face was gaunt. The bags under her eyes and sallowness of her skin suggested she hadn't slept. Abi, on the other hand, looked almost angelic. Her dark hair was clean and brushed, she lay against clean white pillows, and Carla had placed what Celeste assumed was Abi's childhood bear at her side. She looked small and young. A machine beeped reassuringly at her side.

"Hey," she whispered, realising Carla wasn't aware of her presence and not wanting to startle her.

Carla turned to her, her eyes blinking slowly. "Celeste?" she said.

"Yeah, it's me," she said, and pulled up a chair at her side. "Why don't you go home and get some sleep? I'll stay with Abi."

"No," said Carla, shaking her head. "I'm not leaving her. I'm all she's got. We're all either of us have got."

"She's got me," said Celeste. "And so do you. And everyone else. We all love you and Abi, you know that."

"Nobody loves her like I love her. Nobody else will kill for her," said Carla, stroking Abi's hair. "Even those of us with the strength to do it."

Celeste fingered at her cross. "It's not that simple, Car."

"It is exactly that simple," said Carla, turning to her. "He needs to die. Emerald still refuses despite everything she's seen. Bendek will do whatever Emerald says. I suppose you could if you could move something big enough but I know you won't. And anyway I don't think we could. From everything Abi said it would need something bigger, something stronger, than any of us. Except for Emerald."

"Killing someone is a huge ask," said Celeste.

"She's done it before Cel," said Carla, her eyes hard. "She's done it before. And now Lara's dead. We've failed in the biggest most important job yet and all Abi's pain and fear and suffering has been for nothing. And now she's like this and we've failed her. All she's ever wanted is to stop the pain she feels people suffering, to protect people and now she might die because of it and we didn't even manage the last thing she asked. And that monster, that evil man, who did all of this... he's still out there and he could do it again and again and despite all the strength we have we aren't stopping him."

"I understand," said Celeste. She looked at Abi lying on the bed so still and peaceful. Would the visions be haunting her even in her coma like they did in sleep? "Do you mind if I pray for her?"

"Knock yourself out," Carla grunted, leaning back in her chair and folding her arms.

Celeste knew Carla didn't believe in the power of prayer. And in her most guilty of moments she admitted to herself that she wasn't sure she did either. But it couldn't hurt.

She put her hands together and her elbows on the bed beside Abi's legs, closed her eyes and began to pray. After a few minutes she heard Carla start to snore and smiled quietly to herself. Perhaps her biggest prayer hadn't been answered yet but at least one had.

Chapter Ten

Thanks to spells or magic that Emerald didn't understand, Guinevere had Emerald's school convinced Maram was a foster child and by the first day back after half term she was fully enrolled.

"And the art class!" Maram suddenly gasped, tapping on Emerald's arm repeatedly. "And the French class!"

"Yeah, French sucks," said Emerald feeling annoyed. Maram had been fluent and Emerald was rubbish.

"It's wonderful," she said. "I've spoken so many languages because I just can but I've never actually learned about them."

"Yeah, whatever," grumbled Emerald.

They were walking home in their matching green and grey uniforms with Guinevere chuckling between them. They'd received some funny looks when the cat had silently greeted them at the school gate and escorted them away but she'd been insistent. They were her responsibility and she was going to protect them, especially considering it would be the first time they'd encountered Drew.

"Do you think your dad knows about your power yet?" asked Maram after a minute.

"I dunno," said Emerald. "Drew and his cronies didn't even look at me once."

"He's probably embarrassed," said Maram.

"Masculinity. So fragile," said Emerald, smiling at her with an eye roll as she kicked a stone out of the way and they turned a corner.

"He's probably not getting a lot of attention at home right now anyway," said Guinevere. "The Power movement is on the rise. I've heard chatter. Your father's people are distracted."

"What's that?" asked Emerald. Since Guinevere's arrival and subsequent tutorage she had realised just how little she knew about the world she had been born into. The world she had been excluded from.

"One of the subsects," said Guinevere. "There are different political movements, different power bases. Your father is invested in Power growth. It'll be consuming his attention."

"So he'll be ignoring Drew?" she asked, feeling guilty about the hope in her voice.

"Most likely," she said.

"He always used to ignore me," she said. "And my mum."

"Power is what drives him," said Guinevere. "If you can't be of use you're irrelevant."

"Kind of feel bad for Drew now," said Emerald, wrapping her arms around herself. "I know what it's like to be irrelevant."

They walked on in silence, Maram smiling as the sun shone on her face. Her long, dark hair hung in braids and her face was a little fuller from the meals and snacks Emerald's mother had piled in front of her, grateful to be useful, and Emerald noticed that for the first time Maram actually looked like she belonged in a little girl's body.

"He's still a little shit, you know," said Maram after a minute.

"A little merde, you might say," said Emerald.

"You can't ask where the bathroom is but you can swear," said Maram, grinning.

"Even French has relevant parts," said Emerald.

ð

"We're getting together at the hospital later," said Emerald, reading a text message from Celeste. "Carla's hoping if we come together the boost might pull Abi out of her coma."

"I can't," said Maram as she dried a glass and hung it on the rail over the bar. "I've got a date."

"Yeah but..." said Emerald, setting down the menus she was wiping and turning to Maram aghast. "It's Abi... she's a bit more important than your date, right?"

"She's in a coma, it's not like she's going anywhere," said Maram. "I'll come by after. Steve, erm, Phil is picking me up straight from here. We can do it then."

"We're going straight from here, then back to ours to make plans," said Emerald, her anxiety levels rising. "You need to be there!"

"No I don't," said Maram, tossing her hair over her shoulder. "I will get together with you after."

"Maram, please," said Emerald, staring at her in exasperation. "Priorities!"

Maram turned on her and glared. "Yeah. I have priorities. Abi's fine, she's in a coma, she's not about to die. She'll survive long enough for me to go out with Bill!"

"Phil."

"Whatever!" Maram threw the towel down, picked up a bin bag of rubbish that was waiting to go, and stormed out the back door.

ð

"Hey," said a boy with blonde curls and dimples, leaning over the bus seat in front of them and grinning. He looked late teens and arrogant. Emerald glared at him. "Where are you ladies off to on this fine Saturday afternoon?"

"Fuck off," said Emerald.

"We're just off to the movies," said Maram, smiling at him.

"Oh yeah?" he asked. "What are you going to see?"

"She's thirteen you know," said Emerald, glaring at him. "Thirteen years old."

"Shut up Em," Maram whispered out of the corner of her mouth, before turning her smile back on the boy in front.

"Oh!" he said. "Right. I see."

The boy turned around again and landed heavily on the seat of the bus.

Maram folded her arms and sunk low in her seat, staring away from Emerald in a pout.

"What?" Emerald whispered after a minute.

"Nothing," Maram grunted.

"Fine," muttered Emerald, looking out the window huffily.

"I'm not really thirteen, you know," said Maram in a cross whisper.

"Your body is."

"So?"

"So it matters!"

"It's my body, not yours," said Maram. "I just want to feel alive, Emerald! I want to be alive! And I can do what I want! I belong to me, not you!

"I know that!" said Emerald.

"Do you?" demanded Maram, turning on her. "Do you really?"

"Of course I do!" insisted Emerald.

"Then I don't see why it's any of your business," she said, with a growl of pain. "Assuming I have your permission... master."

"Maram, please," whispered Emerald.

"Whatever," said Maram as the bus pulled into the stop in the town centre. "Let's just go have fun, okay?"

"Yeah," said Emerald, forlornly. "Okay."

They got off the bus and walked side by side in silence until they reached the cinema.

"Two for Angels And Demons, please," said Emerald to the boy on the ticket desk.

He smiled warmly at Emerald and took her money, then handed over the tickets. "Enjoy," he said. "Did you see the first?"

"Yeah," said Emerald. "But the book was better."

"Weird they did it out of order, right?" asked the boy, rubbing his hand over his shaved head and smiling nervously at her.

"There is no accounting for the peculiar choices of film makers," said Emerald. "Nothing passes the Bechdel test."

"The what now?" asked Maram.

"Conversations between female characters not being about male characters," said Emerald.

"Oh," said Maram. "Bloody men."

Emerald nodded and the boy on the desk laughed. "Well I can't promise this passes," he said. "But it's fun."

"Cool," said Emerald, and they headed towards the screen doors.

"He fancied you," said Maram.

"Shut up," said Emerald, rolling her eyes, but grateful that the tension between them seemed to have eased.

"He did," she said.

"No he didn't," said Emerald.

"He definitely did," she said, nodding. "I could tell. You should go get his number."

"I don't want his number."

"I'll get it!" said Maram, turning to go back before Emerald caught her arm. She laughed and they took their seats.

The room was remarkably empty. Just one other couple sat at the back, talking quietly. Emerald checked the time on her phone before turning it off and the film was due to start any moment.

As the light's began to drop she heard the couple behind them begin to get a bit louder.

"Great," Emerald muttered to Maram, nodding her head backwards.

"Idiots," Maram agreed.

The screen lit up and noise started to boom around the room as a dancing frog told everyone to turn off their mobile phones and be quiet. Behind them the couple got louder and suddenly they heard a howl of pain.

"What was that?" asked Maram standing up and turning around.

Emerald stood up too and saw the young man, who looked about eighteen, standing over the girl he was with who had her hand to her cheek where she cowered below him.

"Hey!" Maram shouted.

"Fuck off!" shouted the man.

"We need to get help," said Emerald.

"We need to be help!" insisted Maram.

Emerald pulled anxiously at her sleeve but Maram stormed down the row of seats and marched towards the angry boy who was shouting at his girlfriend now.

"You don't ever give me that shit!" he roared, as below him the girl cowered back in her seat, crying and shaking.

Emerald raced after Maram and pulled at her arm, terrified. What if he turned his anger on Maram? What if he turned it on herself? What if she lost control and did something terrible?

"Leave her alone!" Maram shouted.

"Get outta here, kid!" the boy said, waving an arm at her.

"I'm sorry," pleaded the girl, then the boy smacked her hard across the face again and she yelped, falling off the seat onto the floor between the rows. She curled up in the foetal position below him, sobbing.

Behind them a trailer for Diet Coke was blasting it's cheery music.

"I tell you to give me your phone and you give me your phone, bitch!" he shouted, leaning over her.

He raised his fist and Maram leapt up, grabbing it and pulling his arm back.

"Maram!" screamed Emerald.

The boy turned around and shook his arm, flinging Maram to the ground.

"Who do you think you are?" he demanded, suddenly looking huge as he loomed towards them.

Maram scrambled away, panic suddenly falling across her face. "Em!" she screamed.

"You stupid little bitches!" he followed them.

"No," Emerald whispered, feeling her head start to pulse, blood rushing through her head and her eyes burning. Her hands shaking and her heart racing.

The boy got closer, his face contorted with rage.

"Leave them alone!" shouted the girl behind him, standing up and looking desperate.

She couldn't breathe. She couldn't see. She couldn't focus. She shook her head, screwing up her eyes, trying to steady her breathing but feeling each breath get shorter and harder. The fog swirled in her head and she cried out, putting her hands to her head.

"Woah!" the boy cried out, staggering backwards.

Emerald roared. She knew she was growing. She could feel it. She could feel her body starting to stretch, her clothes starting to rip.

"Emerald!" Maram cried out.

Emerald felt Maram's hand in hers. It was cool and soft. She could feel her calming effect and her heart rate began to slow. She hadn't gone. She hadn't lost it.

"You're a fucking monster!" the boy shouted, and went to swing towards Emerald when he suddenly fell backwards, screaming.

"Get away from them!" came a voice from behind them.

They spun around and saw the boy from the ticket desk marching towards them, a furious look on his face and his hands out stretched.

The man scrambled away, his clothes starting to smoulder, wisps of black smoke rising from him. The girl screamed and ran, pressing herself into the wall of the cinema whilst all the time the sound of an advert for a car ricocheted around the room.

"What's happening?" he howled, smacking at his shirt and jeans, trying to stop the burning.

"Leave!" shouted the boy, dropping his hands. "Now."

Panicked, the man stood up and raced away as fast as he could, stumbling over the seats and bouncing off the door frame as he headed out of the cinema.

Against the wall the girl was sobbing now. Though fascinated by the boy behind them, Emerald approached her cautiously. "Are you okay?"

She shook her head, tears running down her cheeks. "No," she eventually choked out.

"Let's go," said Maram, nodding her head towards the door.

Emerald agreed and led the girl out of the cinema, Maram and the boy following.

By the front door was a small sofa area and Emerald, Maram, the frightened girl and the peculiar boy all sat down.

"He's going to trash my stuff now," sobbed the girl. "I can't go back. He'll kill me if I go back. I can't go home. I've got nothing. He's got everything. I've got nothing left."

"I'm sorry," said Maram, her eyes dropping. "I didn't think..."

"No," she said, shaking her head. "I don't mean you did a bad thing. I just mean... I can't go back. I don't want to go back... but I can't anyway. I don't know what happened... but... I think you freed me."

"Freed you?" asked Maram, staring at her intensely.

"Yeah," she said, with a shrug, tears running down her cheeks as she tried in vain to wipe them away. "It's stupid really I guess. I just... never got away before. I should have left, I couldn't, I couldn't go and now I'm gone and... I don't know how but you scared him. I've never seen him scared."

Emerald noticed that the cinema boy was sitting quietly, listening, but not speaking. She was surprised.

"Do you have somewhere you can go?" asked Maram.

The girl nodded. "I want to go home. To my mum. I... I miss my mum," she looked sad for a moment then looked at them. "How old are you? You're just little kids."

"Thirteen," said Emerald. "We're thirteen."

"Fifteen," said the boy.

"You're brave for kids," she said, smiling. "Adam's a scary guy. What are your names?"

"I'm Emerald and this is Maram," said Emerald.

"I'm Bendek... Ben," said the boy, holding up a hand.

"I'm Sophie." She tucked her hair behind her ear and sniffed heavily. "I'm so glad it's quiet in here right now. There's usually a load of kids around... no offence."

Sophie stood and picked up her bag. She pulled her phone out of her pocket and looked at the cracked screen and tears began to fall again.

"Are you okay?" asked Maram.

"No," she sobbed again. "This bloody phone. I never used it to get help, you know? I never called the police or my mum or anyone and I thought about it a thousand times. I'd have the numbers on the screen and just stare at it and then I'd hear him come home or I'd just chicken out and then I'd delete them again. But I always had it. And I always had that as an option, you know? I knew that as soon as I was brave enough I could phone my mum and even if nobody else believed me and everyone else took his side, I knew my mum would take my side. I knew my mum would come and she'd get me and we could go and she'd believe me. Even if nobody else believed me. This phone kind of... I'm so pathetic," she wept.

"You're not," said Ben quietly.

"This phone was like all I had of my mum," sobbed Sophie. "And now it's broken! All because I smiled at the guy in the restaurant at lunch. I smiled when the waiter brought our food. And it made him lose his mind and now it's broken and this phone was all I had of my mum and now it's broken."

"Do you want to use my phone?" asked Ben, handing it over. "To call your mum now?"

Sophie gingerly took the phone from him and looked at it, then up at him. "Yes," she said after a moment. "Thank you."

Stepping away from the group, Sophie dialled a number and walked to a corner of the room. Emerald watched as she began speaking, then sobbing, nodding and crying, her face a mixture of pure joy and desperate pain. She felt tears pricking her own eyes, then noticed Maram and Ben were similarly emotional.

"My mum's coming," said Sophie when she came back, her face blotchy and pink. She handed the phone back to Ben. "My mum's coming."

The three sat in the entrance hall with Sophie. Nobody spoke much. A couple of people came in to ask what times films were showing and Ben answered, but mostly they just waited. Twenty minutes later a woman with thick brown curls, large glasses and jeans with mud over the knees suddenly rushed in frantically.

"Mum!" said Sophie standing up and suddenly looking so much younger than she had done before.

"Sophie!" the woman cried, raced over and pulled her to her in a huge bear hug, her arms around her and her face buried in Sophie's long dark hair. "Sophie, baby."

"I've missed you mummy," Sophie sobbed into her mother's shoulder.

"Let's go home, baby," said her mum, holding her face in her hands. "I've missed you so much."

"Mum, these are the kids I told you about... the ones who... helped me," said Sophie, turning to them. "That's Emerald, that's Maram and that's Ben."

Sophie's mum looked them up and down seriously then walked towards them and hugged each of them in turn. She smelled of dirt and flowers and moisturiser. She was warm and soft. She was crying.

"Thank you," she said. "You are wonderful and brave and you brought my baby girl home. Thank you."

Sophie waved and allowed her mum to lead her away with her arm around her shoulders and Sophie cuddled in close.

After they had gone, Maram turned to Emerald and said, "Now I feel alive."

"Me too," said Emerald.

"Me three," said Ben.

Chapter Eleven

The delivery boy came ambling through the door and gave an irritatingly cheesy and over confident wink in Maram's direction.

"Maram," said Emerald quietly as Maram picked up her coat. "Please..."

"Drop it, Em," she said, turning away and waving to Phil.

"Please," Emerald said again, hopelessly. She dreaded breaking it to Carla that Maram had chosen a boy over Abi that night. "It might not be safe! He's still out there. Maram... Abi needs you."

"A coma isn't fatal," hissed Maram. "Being me is though, isn't it? I'm going."

Emerald sighed miserably as her friend stormed away, hooked an arm through a somewhat startled Phil's, and stalked out of the restaurant.

ð

"It's not your fault," said Ben as they walked through the hospital corridors.

"Try telling Carla that, will you?" Emerald said with a sigh.

"You're not the boss of Maram," he said. "You tried."

Emerald smiled at him wanly, then turned the corner into Abi's room. The rest of the group were already gathered around Abi's bed, where she lay silently, eyes closed, chest barely moving as she breathed shallow breaths.

"Hey," greeted Carla. "Close the curtains will you?"

Ben obliged as Emerald stood next to Celeste and chewed on her bottom lip. She had to bring it up first, she had to tell Carla before she noticed. She had to do it.

"Where's Maram?" asked Carla, looking around.

"Shit," muttered Emerald under her breath, then looked up apologetically. "She... couldn't make it..."

"What happened?" asked Celeste, looking worried. "Is she alright?"

"She's fine..." said Emerald. "She is... well... you know Maram... she has to..."

"Where is she, Emerald?" demanded Carla.

"Out," Emerald admitted, shuffling her feet. "With a boy."

"Joe?" asked Tig.

"No," said Emerald.

"Mickey?" asked Celeste.

"No," said Emerald.

"Steve?" asked Carla, looking exasperated.

"Bill," said Emerald. "I mean Phil!"

"Seriously?" demanded Carla, standing up. "How could she do this?"

"It's not Emerald's fault," said Ben quietly.

"You think I don't know that?" demanded Carla, turning on him furiously. "Don't be such a lapdog."

"Hey!" protested Emerald, casting an apologetic look at Ben who wouldn't meet her gaze.

"This could have helped her!" raged Carla. "The power boost could have pulled her out! She needs the strength! How could she do that to us? How could she do that to Abi?"

"She... felt like maybe it would be okay..." Emerald muttered. "Maybe we could try anyway?"

"What's the point?" asked Carla, throwing herself back into her seat in exasperation. "We need the whole coven. That's the whole point, right? Without one of us we're roundly screwed, right?"

Everyone sat in silence for a minute then Celeste coughed awkwardly. "So... there are a lot of problems at work. We're struggling to rehome the women, there's no space in any shelters, and the funding is being cut constantly."

"Oh jeez," said Emerald, putting her head in her hands. "I'm so sorry."

"Where will they go?" asked Tig quietly.

"We don't know," said Celeste miserably. "He's destroyed these women. They're terrified."

"Evil," said Ben.

"We need to get structural engineers in and until then we've got women and children we're having to just send back out," Celeste said. "To God knows what."

"I know what," said Tig, shaking her head sadly. "This guy seriously needs to die. He needs to die."

"There's a charity organisation that's in talks though," said Celeste. "It's a long way off being finalised because so many places need support right now and there areb so many people asking for help, you know? But at least there's hope."

"That's something at least," agreed Emerald. She felt sick. What if it didn't come through? What would happen? She had almost let the families in the shelter slip her mind. And so many other people were still needing help. She felt ice creeping down her spine. This world had so much evil in it and now this man had brought even more. Maybe Tig was right. Maybe he did need to die.

"How are we going to find him?" asked Carla. "Is he going to keep going or was Lara the last?"

Emerald picked at her thumbnail. He could still come for Maram. She knew that. Maram knew that. But she couldn't tell them, not without Maram's permission. It would be too big a betrayal. They didn't know what she was and it wasn't Emerald's place to reveal it.

"Without Abi, how can we know?" asked Tig. "If we can't find him we can't stop him. We can't kill him. He's won. He's going to just disappear and do whatever he wants, kill whoever he wants."

"We can look over the lists again," said Emerald. "Work out the connections. We might be able to figure something out. There must be something we can do."

Carla stroked Abi's hair and kissed her cheek tenderly. "Let's go," she said. "If we're going to do this without Abi we're going to have to get our asses into gear right now. And someone's going to have to make Maram realise this matters more than her vagina."

ð

Fadius stood in a doorway, looking out into the evening.

"THERE," came the voice. "ARE YOU READY?"

"Yes," promised Fadius as he watched the dark haired young woman approach. As soon as the man at her side departed, she would be his.

ð

"Maram should be home soon," said Emerald as they pulled up outside the apartment building.

"Good," said Carla through gritted teeth. "I'd like to say a few things to her."

Emerald closed her eyes sadly, the last thing the group needed right now was a fight.

ð

"So," said Maram, gazing wistfully down the street towards her road and away from the young man at her side who was gazing wistfully at her. The evening had been tedious and she was in no mood to drag it out longer than necessary.

"So," said Phil.

"I'll be seeing you around, yeah?"

"Tomorrow?" he suggested.

"Oh, well," said Maram, shifting her feet and tucking her hair behind her ear. "I have an evening job that takes up a lot of time. I am headed there now actually."

"Oh wow," he said, nodding enthusiastically. "Hard worker! I respect that. Not many girls interested in working hard these days."

Maram narrowed her eyes. "I've not found that, actually."

"Oh I," he hesitated. "I just meant you're not like other girls."

"I am exactly like other girls, actually," she said crossly.

"I meant it as a compliment!" Phil said, throwing his hands up.

"Well trying to pit me against other women isn't very complimentary."

"Jesus," he muttered. "Why do I always end up with the crazy ones?"

"Bye Bill," she said, rolling her eyes.

ð

"There she is," said Tig, pointing down the street. Emerald looked and saw Maram in the distance throwing her arms in the air and storming towards them leaving Phil behind her shaking his head.

"Looks like the date was totally worth abandoning Abi for," said Carla.

Emerald nodded sadly. Poor Maram.

She watched her friend walk towards them down the street and gave her a wave. Maram waved a small wave back then slunk towards them, her hair falling over her face. Emerald could feel the guilt coming off her in waves. Next to her Carla practically growled.

Behind her, a man stepped out of a doorway and started to follow.

"Who's that guy?" asked Tig, frowning. "I recognise him."

Emerald's mouth dropped open in horror. "It's him!" she screamed. "It's the guy! MARAM!"

Maram looked up, turned her head, then began to run.

"What do you mean it's the guy?" cried Carla. "What are you talking about!"

"He's coming for Maram!" Emerald screamed. "We have to stop him!"

"What the hell?" cried Tig. "Why?"

"I'll stop him!" Roared Carla, stepping forward.

"EMERALD!" screamed Maram, she raced towards them and fell into Emerald's arms. Behind her the man was approaching at speed.

Carla stepped forward, her hands raised.

ð

Fadius howled in agony as a seering pain ripped into his thigh bone. He stumbled forward, the sound of splintering clawing through him. His leg started to break and he screamed.

"WITCHES!" boomed the voice in his head, and suddenly Fadius felt a surge of power and energy burst through his body. "DO NOT STOP!"

He put his weight on the broken leg, he felt the pain, but it was pain somewhere outside of himself, pain that couldn't stop him, and he smiled. Nothing could stop him.

ð

"He's still coming," cried Emerald.

"Stop him, Em!" begged Tig.

"I can't!"

"Neither can I!" Carla shouted. She looked exhausted. Everything she had was going into breaking the man's bone but, despite a brief stumble, he began to walk forward towards them again. Slower, for sure, but still coming. "I'm giving it everything!"

Celeste waved her arms around and debris from the street began to crash into the man. A bin lid smacked into the side of his face, knocking his head violently to the side. He roared, stumbling again.

"He's stopping!" shouted Carla, holding up her hands again with a look of determination. "We've got him!"

Emerald gripped Maram's hand with relief. They'd stopped him. They always stopped them. Nobody was stronger than her team. Maram was safe.

"NO!" the man raged and stumbled again.

Emerald felt a flood of relief but then the man seemed to regain his balance. He stood up straight with his arms out, his muscles bulging, as his body shook and seemed to swell.

"Keep going!" shouted Celeste as she moved her arms and flung a purple child's scooter across the road and straight at his head.

The scooter pinged away from him, bouncing away without even touching his skin, followed by a broken tree branch, a rock and a dented wheel trim. He laughed a cold laugh. Nothing was touching him. He looked victorious. His eyes were fixed with fierce determination on Maram as she and Emerald shrunk back against the wall.

Ben stepped forward and conjured a fireball in his hands, turning it, growing it, until it was the biggest Emerald had ever seen him produce and the heat that radiated from it was agonising, then he threw it directly at the man who was now just a few metres away from them.

The fireball hit him, burned him, but disappeared without even slowing him down.

They kept trying. Carla hit him so hard her body was trembling, Ben threw fireball after fireball, Celeste hurled everything around that she could lift but nothing worked.

"EMERALD!" Tig wailed. "He's going to kill them! You've got to stop him!"

Emerald shook her head, panic surging in her body. She couldn't. They'd stop him. They always won. They always stopped them. Nobody had beaten them before, nobody. Her heart was pounding, her head was clouding up, she gritted her teeth and closed her eyes, tears pouring down her cheeks as she tried every coping mechanism she knew, everything she had inside her. Don't do it. Don't lose control. Don't.

"Emerald!" Carla cried out.

Emerald opened her eyes and saw the man's fist as it swung into Carla's face. Her head whipped backwards and she crashed into the pavement, her head slamming against the curb and blood spraying. A split second later he hefted a hard kick straight into Celeste's ribcage, she fell backwards, buckled over, winded and shaking, a cracking sound made her scream in pain and she began to vomit across the pavement. Then he rounded on Ben punching him square in the ear, he flew into the wall of the building and fell down unconscious.

He turned on Emerald, Maram and Tig, breathing hard, with a look of venomous joy on his face.

ð

"WITCHES!" the voice boomed again. "NONE OF THEM CAN LIVE."

"Yes, Lord," said Fadius, staring at the three women that cowered before him. They were terrified. They should be terrified. "Witches harbouring the bearer of the beast. Disgusting. I shall not see the seven heads rise!"

He raised his arm.

ð

Next to Emerald, Tig suddenly let out a roar and launched herself at the man, leaping in front of Emerald and Maram and brandishing a tiny dagger in her hands. She landed on his chest, the dagger plunging into his shoulder as he howled in indignation and staggered backwards.

Tig clung on as tightly as she could but the man pulled her from him and threw her like a ragdoll to the pavement in front of him. Swearing with fury, he put his hand to the wound on his shoulder where blood was now oozing out.

Dazed, Tig forced herself to her feet, regained her balance, then flung herself at the man again. As her tiny frame landed on his enormous body, he roared and gripped her around the throat with one hand.

"No!" he shouted at her, holding her away from him by the neck as her feet kicked frantically and her arms thrashed around. Her eyes bulged in panic.

"We have to help her!" wept Maram, gripping Emerald's arm. "You have to stop him!"

Emerald felt tears start to burn her eyes, her body trembling and her breathing started to race. Her friends' bodies were discarded across the ground, blood seemed to be soaking into the pavement, and Tig was foaming at the mouth as her neck was crushed. She could stop it. Her brain was starting to spin, her hands shaking.

Tig squirmed, her legs kicking and her hands clawing at the man's massive arm as she choked and scrabbled with panic. The dagger slashed at his skin but she was losing strength. Her eyes bulged, tears pouring down her cheeks, her face turning purple.

"Emerald!" begged Maram.

Emerald started to let go, the intense sensation flooding her body as she felt herself start to grow, the rage and panic and fear consuming her.

Tig reached up her tiny arm with the dagger held in her hand. Her eyes were barely open anymore.

Emerald felt herself growing more. She hated it. She didn't want it. She had to. She had to give in to it.

With a swift movement, Tig swung her arm and plunged the dagger directly into the man's left eye.

He screamed, gripped Tig's neck so tightly there was a horrendous cracking sound then he turned with a howl of agony and rage, and raced away, flinging her lifeless body against the wall as he went. She landed in a pool of her friend's blood while Emerald and Maram screamed.

Chapter Twelve

Emerald pulled the cotton hood of her top up over her head as an irritating grey drizzle started to run down the back of her neck and cursed herself for not listening to her mother's advice. She was cold and should have taken the raincoat and the scarf.

"I'm telling you," Maram was saying as they walked home from having lunch with Ben. "He likes you."

"Oh get out of it," said Emerald, shaking her head. "We've been friends for years. Not everybody is as driven by their genitalia as you are."

"Then how come you've not paid for a cinema ticket since the day you met him?"

Emerald glared at her friend out of the corner of her eye. "He's a good friend."

Maram scoffed then looked up at the sky crossly. "This isn't cool. I didn't bring my bloody coat."

As if on cue, the rain changed from annoying drizzle to a torrential downpour

Cursing, the two girls ran down the pavement, over the road, and ducked under the awning outside a café on the corner of a small cobbled alleyway.

"It's meant to be May!" grumbled Maram as they stared out.

Emerald chuckled. Hearing Maram complain about the weather was one of her pet joys. It made her seem like she belonged.

A white van whizzed past them driving straight through a large puddle that was forming in the road, spraying rainwater over them.

"Gah!" Emerald shrieked as they jumped back and turned away to shield their faces.

"What's that?" asked Maram, cocking her head to the side and looking down the alley.

Emerald peered in the direction Maram was looking. Through the rain and the shadows of the tall buildings, silhouetted against the grey sky, was a ghostly white shape on the roof of a dark grey building. "It looks like a person," she said.

The two walked down the alleyway, empty other than the large dustbins and trade entrances for the businesses on either side, staring up at the shape on the roof. The rain was thundering, banging off the sides of the bins like rhythmic drumming, and looking up too much was hard as the rain kept getting in their eyes, but Emerald was certain. On the roof, in what looked like just a white cotton nightie, was the figure of a small, pale girl.

"What's she doing?" Maram asked.

"I don't know," said Emerald, wrapping her arms around herself. The combination of the heavy rain and the cold air with the disquieting sight of the girl on the roof was giving her the chills. The girl on the roof, her long dark hair soaking wet and clinging to her clothes, must have been freezing. Her skin, other than the nightie, was bare and the wind was whipping the fabric around her. She was shuffling closer and closer to the edge of the roof.

"What do we do?" Maram asked.

"HEY!" shouted Emerald. "Are you okay?"

The girl didn't hear, or if she did she didn't respond, she just took another step closer to the edge of the roof.

"Is she going to jump?" asked Maram, turning to Emerald in panic.

"I don't know!" said Emerald, feeling sick.

The girl took another step closer. She seemed to be staring out at nothing, not looking down to the street or back to safety, just staring ahead in a daze.

"Oh my God," sobbed Maram, grabbing Emerald's arm. "Emerald what do we do?"

"Should we get someone?" asked Emerald, looking down the alley to the deserted streets either side of the alley.

The girl stepped with bare feet up onto the ledge that ran around the edge of the building.

"I don't think there's time!" said Maram.

They heard someone shout.

"Someone's up there!" cried Emerald, relief flooding through her. "It's okay!"

The girl turned, saying words they couldn't hear, then turned back to the drop below. They heard the voice again and she turned, holding her hands out and shuffled closer to the edge.

"Stop!" Emerald shouted up desperately, then turned to Maram, panic in her chest. They couldn't let that girl die. "We've got to save her!"

"How?" asked Maram, she had a look of tragic acceptance. The wind picked up, whipping against her face until Emerald couldn't tell if it was tears or raindrops making her friend's eyes look so red.

"Maram... I..." Emerald hesitated, then looked back up at the girl on the ledge.

A man was now visible behind her, his hand outstretched. The girl turned away from him, shaking her head, her arms wrapped about herself. She spread her arms out and stared straight ahead.

"Do it!" cried Maram.

The girl lifted her foot and Emerald cried out, "I wish that girl isn't hurt when she lands!"

The girl landed on the ground in front of them as if she had simply jumped from a chair to a carpet. Emerald stared at her for a moment, feeling elation and sickness and and overwhelming sense of guilt, then hurried over and put a hand on her back. She was curled up in a puddle on the cobbled street.

"Are you okay?" she asked.

"I'm not dead," the girl sobbed, looking up. She was the palest person Emerald had ever seen, her eyes looked like dark holes in a sheet and she was impossibly thin. The bones of her spine bulged through the skin on her back, the soaking white cotton nightgown revealing her ribs.

"We... saved you..." said Emerald.

The girl stood and turned a face of absolute fury on them. "Why?" she screamed. "Why would you do that?" Then she looked up at the roof again and Emerald saw the man looking down on them, then he turned and hurried back from the ledge and out of sight.

"To help," said Emerald. "I... we... are you okay?"

"No!" the girl howled. "I'm not! I was free and you fucking ruined it! Now they'll come for me! You should have let me die!"

Behind them a door opened and a group of five men stepped out into the rain. "Agatha," said one of them in a gentle voice. "Why don't you come back inside, darling. You could have hurt yourself falling like that."

The girl looked devastated. She looked broken. She huddled in on herself with her arms wrapped around her frail body.

Agatha went to take a step forward but Emerald stepped in her way. "No," she said. "She's not coming with you."

"Come on now, sweetheart," said the man, his voice dripping with patronising misogyny. "Step out of the way now, she needs to be getting inside and getting dried off."

Maram stepped forward and stood beside Emerald. "I don't think so," she said.

Another man looked angry. "Enough now," he said. "Agatha, get inside."

Agatha stood behind Emerald and Maram trembling, but didn't move towards the men.

The first man stepped towards Emerald, his face arranged in a way that Emerald supposed was meant to look sympathetic, but came across more like a snake attempting to seduce its prey before swallowing it whole. "Come on kids," he said, putting a hand on Maram's shoulder and rubbing it. "Poor Agatha's a confused little girl and she needs to come with us. We're her family. We care for her. Don't go making this unnecessarily hard now."

Emerald looked back at Agatha, who was sobbing, and doubted herself. She was young, much younger than them, and clearly needed help. Was she wrong? Maybe she needed to go with them. She looked at Maram whose jaw was jutted out with determination, her eyes flashing with rage. There was no way Maram was letting anyone get to Agatha, not without a fight.

"Get your hand off me," Maram snarled, pulling the man's hand off her shoulder with disgust. "And never touch me again."

Behind her, Emerald heard Agatha whimper.

"Right," said one of the other men, stomping forwards. "It's raining and we don't have time to piss about like this. Agatha, get your ass inside right now."

He reached out towards Maram and shoved her sideways so she fell onto the cobbled street.

Emerald turned on him with fury as he reached out, clamping an enormous hand round the fragile wrist of Agatha, and yanked her towards him viciously.

"Let go!" Emerald commanded, rage rising inside her, her heart racing, her eyes losing focus. She could hear the blood pounding in her ears.

"Get lost, kid," the man snarled, his hand tight on Agatha's wrist. "This is none of your business."

Maram got to her feet and ran at him, pulling at his arm to free Agatha but two of the men descended on her, dragging her away whilst she kicked and fought at them. Agatha tried to pull her arm free but the man just walked away, dragging her behind him like a dog on a chain, her bare feet scrabbling over the cobbles as she tried to break free.

Emerald roared, and reached out a hand, grabbing the man that was pulling Agatha and lifting him in the air. She threw him hard at the building and he crashed into the bricks with a crunch. Below her, the men who had been holding Maram were panicking, scurrying about whilst Maram scrambled towards Agatha and pulled her into her arms. Emerald smashed into them, sending them flying left and right as screams and howls of pain filled the air, competing with the deafening thunder of rain on bins and cobbles.

A cold hand landed on her leg. Cooling and calming.

"Stop now, Emerald," floated a voice, drifting through her mind and blocking out the wailing, banging, pounding cacophony that overwhelmed her every fibre.

She felt her breathing starting to slow. The fog that was stopping her focusing seemed to clear and she could hear things more clearly again. "Maram?"

"I'm here, Emerald," came the voice. "You're okay, you're okay."

She looked around the alley and saw blood and bodies strewn around. Some of the men were moving a little, coughing and whimpering, others were still.

"We need to go," said Maram, gathering shredded bits of fabric from the ground below them, the rain starting to lighten up and the wind starting to die down. "Now."

Agatha, her eyes wide and her mouth open, turned to Emerald and said, "She's right. We need to go."

The three hurried away through the rain. They ran down the alley and round a corner. Maram pulled them both behind a large dumpster and shrugged out of her coat.

"Put this on," said Maram, handing it to Emerald who looked down at herself and realised she was naked.

"What happened?" asked Agatha. "How did you do that?"

"I have a power," Emerald said, pulling the coat on and doing it up quickly. "It gets a bit out of control sometimes. I'm so sorry."

"Thank you," Agatha said, tears starting to fall down her face. "They'd have taken me back."

"What happened to you?" Emerald asked. "Who are they?"

Agatha opened and closed her mouth for a moment. "I'm... pregnant," she said, her hands on her stomach. She looked sick. "I'm pregnant and... those men... they... this thing in me... they did this to me, they... I was... I can't, I can't, they did this, I can't..."

"It's okay," said Maram, looking at Agatha. "You don't have to talk. I understand."

"You do?" she asked, her voice barely audible and looking into Maram's eyes with such an earnest vulnerability that Emerald felt guilty for even being there. She felt like she was intruding on something incredibly private.

"I believe you," said Maram gently, and wrapped her arms around Agatha who clung onto her, letting out deep and heart wrenching sobs.

Watching them Emerald sensed they were bonding over something of which she had no concept. And she was incredibly grateful for that.

"How old are you?" Emerald asked when the two had separated.

"Fifteen," she said.

Emerald was surprised. She was so small and fragile looking that she had assumed she couldn't be older than eleven or twelve. "And you're pregnant?"

"Yes... it was my pastor... he..." She fell silent. Her eyes dropped as she wrapped her arms around herself.

"Where's your mum?" asked Emerald, completely confused, but then saw Maram shaking her head at her. "I'm sorry..."

"I have nowhere to go," said Agatha. She sounded hopeless. "I have nowhere to go and I've got this thing growing in me and I want it gone and I don't want to be here. I can't go back. I can't go anywhere. They'll make me go back."

"I know!" said Emerald suddenly, an idea coming to her. "I'm sure I know! They've opened a new women's shelter on River Street. One of the feminist pages on Facebook shared it. They'd help!"

"They won't make me go back?" asked Agatha.

"We'll make sure they don't," said Maram. "I promise you, Agatha. We won't let you go back."

Huddled in the alley, they heard sirens starting to sound behind them as the rain overhead stopped.

"Let's go," said Emerald.

"What's your name?" Agatha asked as they hurried out into the street.

"Emerald," said Emerald.

"Maram," said Maram.

"Thank you," she said to them, stopping and looking at them intensely. "I owe you my life."

"You're welcome, Agatha," said Emerald.

"Please," said Agatha. "Call me Tig."

Chapter Thirteen

Emerald stared at the wall of the hospital room she had been in for the last eight hours. A stream of doctors, nurses and porters had been in and out. She had been poked, prodded and examined and found to be fine but shaken and emotionally traumatised. She could have told them that herself, she thought, but would have added burdened by layers of guilt to the list.

The police detective who had been with her for the past thirty minutes was softly spoken with kind brown eyes. He had asked her questions she had pretended not to know the answers to and given her advice she had pretended to listen to. She didn't know where here friends were or what was happening to them. She couldn't get Tig's face out of her mind.

She wanted to go home. Properly home. She felt like she didn't know how to be an adult anymore. She needed to talk to Guinevere, if ever there was a time for the cat to officially come out of retirement it was now, and she desperately wanted a cuddle from her mother.

"Thank you, Ms Wren," said Detective Raza, closing his notebook and nodding in a way that conveyed both sadness and an over familiarity with grief. "I appreciate that this is a very difficult situation, so I am grateful to you for being so helpful."

"Thank you," said Emerald. She felt terrible. She had lied to him when he was simply trying to do the best he could and protect people. Much like she had lied to her friends when they were trying to do the same thing. But what choice did she have?

"Over time you may start getting more memories, things coming back to you," he said and handed her a card. "My name and direct line are on here as well as the number for my main office if for any reason you can't get through. If you remember anything at all, even if you think it's inconsequential, be sure let me know."

"Yes," she lied. "I will."

"I'll be talking to your friends as well, once they're out of surgery," he said as he went to leave. "It's rare nobody knows the assailant personally in cases so brutal as this. This man is a monster. I have faith he will be stopped, Ms Wren."

"Thank you, Detective," she said, trying to force a grateful smile to her face.

He left the room and Emerald sat back on the chair, closing her eyes. She wanted to sleep but hurt in too many ways.

"Emerald?" came a voice, and a young nurse stepped into the room. "The doctors have just brought me your discharge notes, and your friend Maram is out here. You're both free to leave. Am I okay to let her come in?"

"Yes!" said Emerald, standing up.

The nurse beckoned out into the corridor and Maram stepped into the room looking anxious.

"Hey," she said with a half wave.

Emerald fell into her arms and held her close. Maram wrapped her arms around her friend and began to cry into her shoulder.

"I'm so sorry," Emerald sobbed.

"So am I," said Maram.

They sniffed heavily and separated. Maram looked as terrible as Emerald felt. Her face was blotchy and swollen from tears. Dark grey smudges framed her eyes.

Emerald turned to the nurse who was waiting nervously by the door. "Do you know how everyone else is? Our friends who came in with us?"

"I'm not sure," said the nurse. "I'm sorry. I know that our surgical team are doing their absolute best."

"What about..." Emerald hesitated. She didn't want to ask. She had to ask. "What about Tig?"

The nurse's eyes dropped. "Agatha, Tig, is... her body is..." Emerald felt like her guts were being shredded, she wanted to be sick. "She's part of an active murder investigation so she's having a full autopsy."

Maram began to sob uncontrollably. Emerald set her jaw firmly, gritting her teeth.

"She has no family," Emerald said after a moment. She had felt responsible for Tig since the day they had met, and now was no different. "We're her family."

"I know," said the nurse. "We have her history on record. I promise, everyone here is going to do everything we can. We will phone you as soon as your friends are out of surgery and we have it noted down that standard visiting hours are being waved in your case. You can come in as soon as they're out."

"We can't leave," Maram said, wiping at her eyes with her sleeve. "We have to stay here. We can't leave them."

"There's nothing you can do right now," said the nurse. "You should go home and rest. Get some sleep."

"We will," said Emerald. Maram started to protest but Emerald held a hand up. "We need to talk to Guinevere."

"I'm sorry," said the nurse confused. "I don't have a Guinevere on the list. Was she involved?"

"No, no," said Emerald, shaking her head. "She's just our cat."

The nurse opened her mouth then closed it again and smiled kindly. "Okay then," she said. Then patted their arms. "We'll call you as soon as we have any news."

ð

The Bearer Of The Beast and a witch left the hospital as Fadius watched from the bus stop.

The pulpy mess of his eye still caused him pain but he needed the pain to remind him of his weakness. He needed it to remind him of the power of his Lord for letting him survive what should have killed him. He was grateful for the pain. Pain was strength. Pain was power.

"FOLLOW THEM," came the voice.

ð

Walking down the path through the hospital car park, Emerald phoned her mother. The air was cold and she pulled her coat around herself, but it didn't seem to do anything for the icy chill inside her. It was quarter past five in the morning and the sky was still very dark, so she knew that her mother would be panicked by the sound of the phone.

"This is so bad," Maram muttered to herself as they walked, linking her arm through Emerald's and leaning on her shoulder.

"Really bad," agreed Emerald, rubbing her eyes. Tig was dead, her friends were in hospital, the culprit was still out there, they had no idea how to stop him, and he still wanted to murder Maram. They needed help.

"Emerald?" came her mother's voice in the phone. "What's happened? Where are you? Is Maram okay?"

"We're okay mum," she said, giving Maram a smile. There was something comforting about the incredible reliability of her mother's love in the midst of the chaos and disarray of her life. "Something happened. I'll tell you later."

"What happened? Where are you? Are you hurt? Are you sick?"

"We're at the hospital," she said.

"What? I'm on my way!"

"No mum, we're fine, we're walking home now!" she insisted. "We're hoping we could come to yours? Can you come and pick us up at the flat?"

"Oh," said her mum, sounding incredibly relieved. "Of course you can. I'll be at yours in fifteen minutes. Okay?"

"Thanks, mum."

"Is... Guinevere coming?"

"Yes, mum."

"Oh," Emerald heard some shuffling around. "I'll be there in twenty five minutes."

"Thank you," said Emerald, smiling. "Bye mum."

"She freaking out about the moggy?" asked Maram when Emerald had hung up.

"Always," said Emerald. "She's probably plumping cushions or dusting ornaments as we speak."

"And I thought she'd be worried we were hurt," said Maram with a laugh.

"Nothing compares to the fear of Guinevere," said Emerald.

"And we thought we had it bad," said Maram.

ð

Stuart Wren studied the antique text on his desk but his heart wasn't in it. The more he stared at it, the more the mottled pages seemed to absorb the purple ink that spidered across them, until it looked like one giant blur. He pulled off his reading glasses and rubbed his eyes. The Virilicae would insist on having dramatics he was expected to manage, even when he was distracted by far more important things.

A knock came at the door. Grateful for the distraction, he set his glasses down on the desk. "Come in," he said.

The door opened and Masood Raza, one of the undercover agents, stepped into his office.

"Mr Raza," he greeted, standing up. "How did it go?"

"Your granddaughter is a strong woman, Mr Wren," said Masood.

"She is a Wren, Mr Raza," said Stuart Wren, leaning back in his chair and surveying the man before him. "How much did she tell you?"

"Enough to answer my questions," he said, looking over his notes. "Not enough to suggest she has any idea who or why. She's switched on, even in the midst of trauma."

"What did you hear?"

"Not as much as I would have hoped," Mr Raza admitted. "Her thoughts were extremely focussed on the loss of her friend. Very little penetrated that."

"I suppose that is understandable," said Stuart. "But really she should be concentrating on moving forwards."

"As I say, she is a strong woman, Mr Wren. Despite her grief, which was laborious, thoughts were there in the background. I couldn't get much, but enough to know she is already calculating her next move. And that she isn't giving up."

"Well, that is at least something," said Stuart, drumming his fingers on the desk impatiently.

"With all due respect, Mr Wren," said Masood. "I feel she would be more successful with the training and resources we could provide. There's no doubt her team are talented but with the Commission behind her..."

"Thank you, Mr Raza," said Stuart, picking up his reading glasses and pushing them on. "If I need your advice on my grand-daughter I will be sure to ask for it."

"Yes, Mr Wren," said Masood. "Thank you, Mr Wren."

The man stepped out of the room and closed the door. Staring at the pages of the book again, Stuart Wren found it was even more unclear than before. He took his glasses off again and sighed. The Virilicae would have to wait. He stood up then vanished with a pop.

ð

Emerald flung open the door to the flat without any care for the noise she made. Mrs Rogers upstairs would just have to put up with it.

"Guinevere?" she called out. She needed the cat in a way she hadn't needed her since she was a child. She looked up and down the road that she knew so well but felt haunted by memories of the man stalking towards Maram as she ran in fear, and the way Tig's body had fallen to the ground. Nothing was making any sense and the only person who understood the world they lived in better than she did was Guinevere, and right now she needed to understand.

"Where have you been?" asked the cat, hurrying towards them. "Are you alright?"

"No," said Emerald, pulling off her coat and dropping to her knees in front of Guinevere. "I'm really not. Mum will be here in a minute then soon as we get home I need your help."

"Why?" she asked. "What happened? What's going on?"

"You don't know?" asked Maram, sitting down at Emerald's side and frowning.

"Know what?" asked the cat sounding frustrated.

"Tig..." Emerald started. Then rubbed her hands through her hair. "Tig's dead."

"What?" the cat cried. "When? How?"

"This doesn't make any sense," said Maram, standing up. "There was a murder, Em. There was blood everywhere. Ambulances, police. Why didn't Guinevere hear it? Where's the clean up? The guys in the white coveralls and the police tape? It shouldn't be over already. It's not even been a day yet! Where is everyone?"

Emerald frowned. "I don't know," she said, standing up and going to the window. She looked out. The street was clear. It was as if nothing had happened. She hadn't really thought about it as they walked up there, but Maram was right.

"We need to leave," said Guinevere. "Now."

"I know," said Emerald, curiously. "I mean that's why my mum's coming."

"Pack fast," said the cat, looking around the room nervously.

"What's going on?" asked Maram.

"Later," said the cat. "Go and pack."

Emerald stared at the cat for a moment and then obeyed. They had all come to quickly accept that Guinevere knew far more about their world than any of them, and Emerald knew enough to trust her. She wasn't feeling particularly comforted by the cat's reaction, however, and had even more questions than before.

ð

Emerald's mother had taken the news of Tig's death very badly. Whilst all the coven had been lacking in parental figures in some way, Tig had always been Olivia Wren's favourite. Tig's helpless vulnerability as a child, the timid way she accepted hugs as though both petrified of, and desperate for, physical intimacy, had always brought out her most maternal instincts. Emerald often suspected that, had Maram not already claimed it, her mother would have insisted Tig move into their spare room.

Emerald had told her mother as little as possible, but more than she had told the policeman, and together she and Maram had grieved anew as her mother wept between them, her arms holding them close.

Soon her mother sent them upstairs to unpack and settle in with the promise that a home cooked breakfast would await them on their return, and they gratefully hurried away with Guinevere following.

"Right," said Emerald once she, Maram and Guinevere were alone in her childhood bedroom. "Spill."

The cat sat primly with her tail curled around her and a serious look on her face. She slipped back into the Guardian role with ease. It truly suited her.

"The Commission are aware of your activities," she said.

Emerald's spine went cold. She had heard that phrase somewhere before but she couldn't remember when or why. "Who are The Commission?"

"They're the authorities," said Guinevere. "They're the people who sent me. Most Guardians are employees of The Commission in some role or another."

"I didn't know that," said Emerald, remembering the day Guinevere had arrived. How it had coincided perfectly with the activation of her power. "I guess I thought you just... came."

"Yes, well, you were wrong," said Guinevere.

"So The Commission are good people, then?" asked Maram. "Is that why they cleaned up after Tig's death? To help?"

"No," said Guinevere. "They cleaned up to hide the evidence from the mortals. Something about her death would have raised too many questions and drawn too much attention to the wrong things. They have a lot of power, a lot of people, and part of that power is used to maintain the privacy and strength of those with who are part of the magical community. Tig's death would have exposed us. They're erasing it."

"Erasing it..." said Emerald, something sparking another memory in her mind.

Maram sat upright suddenly. "Like on the internet! That woman, Hannah, who was killed! Didn't Carla and Tig say that she was being erased!"

"Yes!" agreed Emerald. "She was being erased off the internet!"

The cat nodded sagely. "That makes sense."

"So if they're the authorities, why aren't they stopping the fire guy?"

"I don't know," said Guinevere. "Maybe they are and it's taking time. Maybe they aren't because he doesn't pose a big enough threat."

"A big enough threat?" asked Maram, angrily. "But he's killing women! Lots of them!"

"Yes," agreed the cat, sadly. "He is."

"Then how is that not a big enough threat?" Emerald demanded.

The cat sighed. "The Commission are not like the mortal police. They don't make decisions on moral judgment. Matters rise and fall constantly, threats come and go. The magical community are constantly involved in petty issues that are resolved without interference. They monitor. Do what is necessary for the greater good. They're don't step into small matters. They're more interested in," she paused and thought for a moment, "the bigger picture."

"Small matters? Petty issues? Women being murdered isn't small or petty. Maram being murdered isn't small or petty! They sound like assholes," said Emerald crossly. "They're authorities and they know about this guy and they let Tig die because it's not important enough to them?"

Maram began to cry. "We're no better. We let Tig die, Emerald," she said. "I could have told them the truth and made sure we were prepared. You could have smashed his head into the ground with a giant fist."

Emerald stared at Maram. She felt numb. "No," she said. "That's not true."

"It is!" insisted Maram. "It is true! We're mad at them for not stepping in when they have the power to because they don't think it's worth it. But literally we did the same thing! It wasn't worth revealing my secret. It wasn't worth you having more blood on your hands! We made that choice just as they have. We're the same!"

"We're better than some bunch of powerful assholes who don't give a shit!" insisted Emerald. "We care!"

Guinevere's tail flicked. "You should respect those powerful assholes, Emerald. They do more than you realise."

"I'll never respect them," she said, feeling fire in her gut. "They don't deserve any respect."

ð

Through a window, Fadius watched the witch's mother crying as she moved around the kitchen, sorting pans of food on the hob and sorting the coffee maker. She looked heartbroken. The sorrow poured from her. She kept stopping for a moment and gripping the counter top with one hand, the other clutched to her chest, as tears ran so freely down her face that she could barely breathe.

"She's sad," he thought to himself as something stirred in him. He had never seen his own mother cry.

Moments later, the witch and the bearer of the beast entered the room and, on seeing the crying mother, hurried to her and held her in their arms. She sobbed as they comforted her, stroking her hair and kissing her, before helping her to a chair. There was such kindness in their movements, such concern. Fadius frowned. They seemed so soft and gentle. So full of love.

"THEY ARE EVIL," came the voice in his head. "DO NOT LET THEIR TEMPTRESS WAYS FOOL YOU, FADIUS. I CAN BRING THE PAIN FROM YOUR MISSING EYE BACK, REMEMBER. YOU DON'T WANT TO FEEL THAT AGAIN, DO YOU?"

"No Lord," he agreed, nodding and stepping back from the window and stepping into the bushy, tree lined border of Emerald's mother's driveway.

He would wait and he would watch. They would not catch him unawares again. He would learn how to destroy them and they would not be able to stop him.

Chapter Fourteen

Celeste blinked, her eyes burning with the brightness of the light overhead. She tried to move, to look around, but a scream of pain bit through her chest and she yelped out as the pain slammed a reminder of what had happened into her.

"Are you okay there, deary?" came a woman's voice. It sounded old and quite rasping.

Celeste looked around, her eyes adjusting to the light and saw she was encased in a hospital bed behind a pale lilac curtain. A machine beeped rhythmically at her side connected to a clip on her middle finger. A drip was hooked to the back of her hand. How long had she been unconscious? Where were her friends?

"Hello?" she asked. Even speaking hurt.

"Now you've woken up I suppose the nurses will be along soon to check on you," came the voice. "They've been in and out a lot."

"How long have I been here?" Celeste asked.

"You arrived a few hours ago," she replied from behind the curtain. "Right before I got my cup of tea."

Celeste frowned, tried to move and cried out again in pain. "Oh god," she whispered, reaching for her crucifix and finding it gone.

A nurse's head poked around the curtain. "Oh, hello! You're awake!"

"Where's my cross?" Celeste asked.

"Everything's safe in your drawer here," said the nurse, pointing to a locked drawer in a cabinet at her side. "We've got the key don't you worry. Not that we don't trust Moira here, of course!"

"They don't think a doddery, little old lady like me could ever do any harm," came the woman's voice with a cackle. "Little do they know."

"How are you doing, sweetie?" the nurse asked Celeste. She looked worried, but as though she was trying not to be.

"The man who..." she stumbled over her words. "Did this. Is he?"

"I'm sorry love, the police haven't found him yet. There's a detective who I'm sure will want to speak to you. He's already spoken to your friends Emerald and Maram earlier."

"Are they okay?" Celeste asked. "Emerald and Maram? Did he hurt them?"

"No, just shaken," said the nurse. "They went home in the early hours of the morning whilst you were still in surgery."

They went home. They walked away. They lied. Celeste felt anger start to boil in her gut.

"And Tig?" she asked through gritted teeth. "Agatha?"

The nurse's eyes dropped and she put a hand on Celeste's shoulder. "I'm so sorry. I'm afraid she didn't make it."

"She's dead?" Celeste asked in horror, the pain in her chest now nothing compared to the screaming agony in her heart. She didn't know what to do. She grabbed at her braids, she clawed at the bedsheets. She couldn't breathe.

Tig was dead. Tig was dead. He'd killed Tig. Emerald and Maram knew he would come for them. They'd left them unprepared and now Tig was dead.

"I'm so sorry, honey," said the nurse. "I'll see if I can get someone to bring you a cup of tea and a biscuit."

"I don't want a fucking cup of tea!" Celeste cried out. She began to cry, each sob tearing at the damage in her chest and making her cry even more. She winced, tried to stop her chest moving and cried out in pain again.

"Of course. I'm so sorry," said the nurse. "I'll go and have a word with one of the doctors and see if we can't bring you some more painkillers. I'll get the key for your drawer as well for you. And whilst I'm at it I'll phone your friends Emerald and Maram. They're allowed access around visiting hours due to your special circumstances and I'm certain they'll want to see you."

"No!" said Celeste, looking up at her. "Don't call them. I don't want to see them."

"Oh," said the nurse, sounding nervous and shifting on the spot. "If you prefer. Of course. Would you like this curtain opened now or would you like a nap?"

"No, you can open it," said Celeste, sniffing and trying to breathe as slowly as possible. "It's claustrophobic."

The nurse pulled the curtain aside and revealed a bed a few feet away where an elderly woman lay in a floral nightgown with green curlers in her hair.

"Hello there," said Moira, a smile on her face and a look in her eye that told Celeste this woman was no doddery, little old lady. Old, for sure, but she looked sharp and fierce. Celeste felt her skin crawl and wished she'd left the curtain closed.

"Hello," said Celeste.

"I'll let you two get acquainted, you'll be roommates for a while I expect," said the nurse, then left the room. It took everything Celeste had not to call out for her to come back. The old woman was still staring at her, she could feel it in the back of her neck as she watched the nurse leave.

"Don't worry, deary," said Moira as Celeste turned back to her. "We'll kill the bastard who did this to you."

Celeste instinctively fingered around for her crucifix again. She didn't doubt for a second Moira meant every word.

ð

"Did you hear what he said?" asked Emerald, sitting on her childhood bed, the morning sun shining cold autumnal light through the window and casting shapes across the carpet. She held a mug in her hands, sipping the coffee like her life depended on it. Her ridiculous lack of work life balance meant she was used to functioning on too few hours of sleep but this was agony.

"Yeah," Maram grunted, rubbing her eyes and slumping low in the beanbag. "Wait, which bit? When?"

"Right before... Tig... He said something."

"I don't remember," said Maram, frowning. "No I do. He called us witches."

"That's not particularly noteworthy," observed Guinevere from the windowsill, her ginger fur glowing in the light. "People born of power have long been referred to as witches."

"No, no," said Emerald. She searched her tired brain, reliving that awful memory, desperately seeking the words that were tickling around the edges, teasing her mind. Something important. Something. "Beast. He said beast."

Maram frowned. "No," she said, scowling as she replayed the memory herself. "He said bearer of the beast."

"Yes!" Emerald cried, sitting up suddenly and slopping coffee over her fluffy dressing gown. "Bearer of the beast! That's exactly it! And something else.... about heads. Seven heads."

"What does that even mean?" asked Maram, slumping back in the beanbag and looking deflated. "That doesn't help us. That's just nonsense."

"No, insisted Emerald. "It must do. It can't just be random crap or he wouldn't be so focussed. And he was talking to someone else too."

"Who?" asked Guinevere. "Someone there or in his head."

"There was nobody else there that I could see," said Maram. "So in his head I guess?"

Emerald sipped her coffee, thinking hard. Lack of sleep and a slight caffeine hangover made it painful. "Are you sure?"

"No... I mean..." Maram rubbed her head. "I think so. I didn't see anyone."

"Someone invisible, maybe?" suggested Guinevere.

"Dammit I'm smarter than this!" Emerald snapped. "I'm too tired. This is ridiculous. I'm missing something! Something we can use to catch this asshole before he comes back for us!"

"I don't think catching him will do any good," said Maram. "It's not like anything slowed him down, is it? You saw how he kept going when Carla hit him with..."

"Oh my God!" Emerald cried, standing up and losing control of her coffee completely. "There was someone giving him power ups!"

"What?" asked Guinevere.

"You're right!" Maram agreed, sitting up excitedly. "When Carla hit him she did slow him down! He stopped and was obviously in pain then something happened to him and then he kept going like it didn't hurt."

"You're sure?" asked Guinevere.

"Yes!" said Emerald. "He didn't drink a potion or cast a spell or anything. He was in pain and he was stopped and then he spoke to someone, then he suddenly got stronger and kept going."

"He did," said Maram, her face falling. "Before he got the power up, he said something to someone he called 'Lord'."

"He's responding to a master," said Guinevere, her tail flicking as she looked thoughtful. "Lord. Could be he believes he's responding to a God. I wonder if that's some kind of biblical thing."

"Does God really want me dead?" asked Maram, her lip quivering.

"Of course not!" said Emerald, waving her now empty coffee cup in exasperation. "For one thing there is no God. Right Guinevere?"

The cat's eyes narrowed. "What makes you think I'd know the answer to that?"

"Because you always know," said Emerald, suddenly feeling a bit confused and not sure why. "And you've never said I'm wrong. You'd have told me."

"I never said you were wrong to *think* that there's no God," she said. "Whether or not there is... that's simply beyond my ken."

Emerald felt like the bottom had dropped out of her world. "Oh."

"Come on, Em," said Maram. "We need to focus. We need to find out what it means!"

"We'll find out," said Emerald, shaking her head and forcing herself to refocus. "We'll go and ask someone who knows about this stuff."

"Celeste's still in hospital," said Maram. "Who else knows?"

"Vinnie?" suggested Emerald.

Maram nodded. "Perfect."

Guinevere stayed silent, her tail flicking as she stared out of the window. She looked deep in thought.

"What's up?" Emerald asked her as she shrugged off her dressing gown and pulled a hoody on over her t-shirt.

"Mm?" asked Guinevere, looking up at her. "Oh, nothing. You go and ask Vinnie. I'll see you later."

The cat stood up and trotted out of the room, sliding round the door and vanishing from sight.

"Is she being weird?" asked Maram.

"Very," said Emerald. "Right, let's get ready. We'll figure this out. And then we'll stop him."

Maram nodded, her jaw set. "Let's go."

Emerald picked up her empty mug and looked at it, then at the stain that was now drying on her carpet. "I need some more coffee first," she said. "And then we can go."

ð

Nahla Hussain heard a knock on her office door and looked up from a Guardian's application she was reading, grateful for the distraction. The application was not good.

"Hello, Ms Monroe," she said with a sinking feeling as she set the paper down. The tiny Fae woman took a step into the room with folded arms. "Thank you for coming."

"Is there a problem, Ms Hussain?" asked Bea Monroe, not coming further than the doorway and looking irritated by the summons. "My work is rather pressing, as you're aware."

"Yes, I am aware, Ms Monroe," said Nahla, gritting her teeth. She found Monroe's abrasive attitude so irritating but was painfully aware of the horrible news she had to deliver. "I'm afraid I have something very unfortunate I have to discuss."

"If my funding is being cut, Nahla, I am going to be taking it up with Baggot," said Monroe, slamming the door and storming towards the desk. "You may not value the Fae as much as others in your department, but I can assure you..."

"Beatrice," said Nahla, standing up and leaning over the desk. "It's about Hannah."

Monroe's face dropped. "Hannah?" she asked, her voice seeming to match the size of her body for the first time. "M... My Hannah?"

"Yes," said Nahla, gesturing to the seat in front of her desk which Monroe lowered herself into. "I'm sorry."

"What happened?" Monroe asked, her hands starting to shake. "Where is she?"

"I'm terribly sorry," said Nahla, hating every second of this conversation and desperately wishing she could be reading the application again. "I'm afraid Hannah was killed two days ago."

"Killed? What do you mean killed? Shes's dead? My Hannah is dead?"

"Yes," said Nahla. "I'm afraid so."

"Who did it?" Monroe demanded, banging her tiny fists on Nahla's desk.

"A demon," said Nahla. "We have people working on it. He will be stopped. I'm so sorry, Ms Monroe."

Monroe stood up, the fury and pride returning to her face, and looked every bit the warrior she was born to be. "He has taken my daughter," she said. "My Hannah. The Fae will not stand for this, Ms Hussain. We maintain our relationship with the Commission for the sake of everyone but this is not something we can leave to you. He took my daughter and I will not sit idly by whilst you *work* on it. Tell me the name of this demon."

"Ms Monroe," said Nahla. "I can assure you, we are on top of this issue."

"The name," she said, leaning forwards. Nahla forced herself not to retreat back into her chair.

Nahla hesitated, then said, "Ubel."

In all honesty she was not certain that she was right to reveal the name, but felt at a loss as to what else to do. Maintaining good relations with the Fae was an essential part of her job, and notoriously challenging. Having Monroe involved in the Resources department was a huge step and she would be an enormous loss to the Commission should she choose to leave. Few were both prepared to, and capable of, mining The Depths.

Monroe turned and walked out of the room, slamming the door behind her without looking back.

Nahla rubbed her eyes and contemplated going to the common room for coffee. Perhaps she could catch Stuart there and find a way to casually reveal that the Fae were now aware of the project, and likely on a vengeance mission.

A knock came at the door and she sighed. "Yes?"

"Ms Hussain," said her assistant Bobby, poking his head around her door. "There's a Guardian here. She doesn't have an appointment but she says you'll want to see her."

Nahla rubbed her eyes then looked at the photograph of the Jack Russell on her desk who purported to be from a long line of Guardians and experienced in work overseas, despite spelling Commission with one M.

"Is her name Cordelia?" she asked him.

"Cor... what?" he asked, looking confused. "No."

"Now is not a good time, Bobby," said Nahla, shaking her head. "Get Dixon or Lewis to cover it. They're well versed in Guardian law."

"Erm," Bobby hesitated.

"Yes?" asked Nahla.

"She says if you don't see her she's going to Mr Wren."

Nahla frowned. Wren had no involvement in Guardians or their work. The Virilicae were not involved with the Guardians in any way, except occasionally in disputes but that wouldn't involve Wren. Unless...

"Is she in the form of a cat, Bobby?"

"Yes, Ms Hussain."

"Send her in."

Guinevere walked into the office, her nose high and Bobby backed out slowly, closing the door behind him.

"Guinevere," said Nahla. "It's good to see you. How have you been?"

"Excuse me if I get right to the point, Ms Hussain," said Guinevere, sitting on the chair Monroe had just vacated and fixing her with a steely gaze. "But I believe you are involved with my former charge and I want to know why."

"I'm sorry, but you're retired," said Nahla, sitting down. She leaned back and folded her arms. "You're no longer authorised. You made that choice and we respected it, but now you must respect us in return."

Guinevere narrowed her eyes and her tail flicked. "I was not informed of any long game when it came to Emerald Wren, Ms Hussain. I do not appreciate being lied to."

"I'm sorry, Guinevere," said Nahla standing and gesturing to the door. "It was a pleasure to see you but you'll need to leave."

Guinevere remained sitting. Nahla held the cat's gaze, a task she was loathe to admit was challenging, the cat's age and pride giving her a certain power in that stare that made Nahla feel oddly ashamed of herself.

"I want to come out of retirement," Guinevere said after holding that stare for an uncomfortably long time.

Nahla sat back down. "Why?"

"Emerald is in danger," she said. "I took responsibility for her guidance and care when I was assigned to her and that is not something I take lightly. I retired as I thought raising her to adulthood was enough, and I wouldn't need access to Commission information any further. Now I believe that was a mistake. Something is going on. My charge is in danger, and I cannot suitably protect her without all the necessary information."

"I won't lie, you were a loss when you made the decision to retire," said Nahla. "But if you come back you'll be put on active duty and all that it entails."

"I understand," said the cat.

"Welcome back to The Commission," said Nahla, dropping Cordelia's application into the bin.

Chapter Fifteen

Emerald and Maram stood outside Vincenzo's in the rain. Emerald sighed. She wasn't looking forward to this. She'd always respectfully avoided the topic with Vinnie before and wasn't looking forward to diving head first in.

"This is not going to be fun," said Maram, mirroring Emerald's thoughts.

"I know," agreed Emerald, shoving her hands in the pockets of her coat.

"I hate talking about religion," said Maram. "It freaks me out."

"Me too," said Emerald. "Especially now Guinevere's confused me so much that I don't even know what I think anymore. I quite liked feeling safe in the knowledge that they were wrong."

"Religious people make me uncomfortable," said Maram. "I'm only just used to Celeste."

"At least it's only one religious person," said Emerald. "And it's someone we know. The only other idea I had was a church full of strangers."

Maram shuddered. "Yeah, true."

"Remember to sneeze a few times," said Emerald.

Maram held up a tissue. "I'm ready."

They walked into the restaurant and waved to the weekend staff who'd been roped into covering their shifts, then knocked on the door to Vinnie's office.

Vinnie opened it and looked surprised to see them.

"What are you doing here?" he asked.

Maram gave an enormous fake sneeze into her tissue.

"Good grief," he exclaimed. "Go home! You'll contaminate my restaurant!"

Maram elbowed Emerald in the ribs. Emerald gave a croaking chesty cough then sniffed dramatically. "We aren't staying long," she promised him, trying to sound bunged up.

"We need some advice," said Maram. "About religious... stuff."

Vinnie backed in and sat down in his desk chair. "I understand, ladies," he said, respectfully. "There's been so much despair since these terrorist attacks struck our city. Take a seat. How can I help?"

"What do you know about The Bearer Of The Beast?" asked Emerald, sitting on one of the chairs against the wall whilst Maram shut the door behind them then sat next to her.

"Beast?" asked Vinnie, in surprise. It clearly wasn't what he was expecting. "Do you mean the Devil?"

"I don't know, do I?" asked Emerald. "I mean, yeah that makes sense I suppose."

"Oh girls," said Vinnie, making the sign of the cross over his chest and looking distinctly uncomfortable. "I understand the need to find a cause. To find someone to blame. To believe there's some monster whispering in these people's ears and making them do evil. I really do." He sighed and leaned on his elbows. "But I'm not the one to be talking to you about such things."

"But you're the only person we have," begged Maram. "Please. It's important."

"I'm sorry." said Vinnie, shaking his head. "And anyway, my Bible knowledge isn't perfect. I'd do anything for you girls, you know that. But this isn't for me."

"Then who?" asked Emerald, looking at Maram in exasperation. Was it really time to go to a church?

"There's a bookshop near here," said Vinnie. "Tabernacle on Heatherton Street. The staff are young and trendy. Enthusiastic. They like to talk about things old fuddy duddies like me prefer to avoid. Ask them."

"Young and trendy?" said Emerald, feeling horribly uncomfortable at just the idea of talking to a bunch of Christian hipsters with fish tattoos and purple hair.

"Enthusiastic?" asked Maram, pulling a face that suggested she felt the same way.

"You want help?" asked Vinnie.

"Yes," admitted Emerald.

"It just sounds like there's going to be a whole lot of Christians there," said Maram.

"And you sound a whole lot healthier," said Vinnie, folding his arms.

Emerald hesitated then forced out a suitably croaky cough. Maram sneezed impressively into a tissue.

"Bye Vinnie," said Emerald, standing up and backing to the door.

The two hurried out of the office and back into the rain.

"Hey, great job making sure it was just one religious person we had to deal with," said Maram, rolling her eyes as they headed for Heatherton Street. "Now we get a whole gaggle of trendy ones."

"Let's just get this over with," said Emerald.

ð

A knock came on the door of Celeste's room. She opened her eyes and looked up to see Ben poking his head around the frame.

"Can I come in?" he asked.

"Hey," said Celeste looking over at her roommate who was sleeping peacefully in the bed to her side. She nodded and attempted to shuffle into a better position but found the pain in her chest too debilitating.

Ben sat down on one of the plastic chairs. There was a large bandage around his head and his face was bruised. He looked sore. "How are you?" he asked her, flinching as he spoke.

She put a hand out and he took it. "Not great," she admitted. "Grateful for the painkillers. How about you?"

"Pretty sure that dude broke my brain," said Ben, putting a scratched hand up to his head. "And the coffee here's crap. Gave me the hit to get my ass up here though so that's something at least. Have you heard from them?"

"Emerald and Maram?" asked Celeste. "No. Have you?"

"No," said Ben. "Do you want to?"

"No," said Celeste. "No I don't."

"The nurse told me [illegible] Tig [illegible]"

Celeste closed her eyes. "It's their fault, Ben. It's their fault. They knew he was coming for Maram and they didn't tell us. Emerald had a chance to stop him and didn't take it. Even for Tig. Even after what they saw he'd done to Lara. They still let him come without warning us, without saving her!"

"I know," he said sadly, tilting his head to the side slightly as he fought through the pain. "But killing... it's such a big ask..."

"Not everyone is up to the task," came Moira's voice, making Ben jump. "Not something I ever struggled with."

"Uh... I... What?" stammered Ben.

They looked over to Moira's bed and saw the old woman sitting up, watching them. Celeste shuddered. She hadn't heard the woman move and had no idea how long she'd been listening to them. The way Moira looked at Celeste always made her feel like spiders were crawling down her neck. There was something intensely unsettling about her.

"You, boy," said Moira, fixing him with a piercing gaze. "You don't look like you have the stomach for the kill either?"

"What? No!" said Ben, looking at Celeste in bewilderment.

"None of us *want* to kill," said Celeste.

"But this man, this one who killed your friend and hurt you," said Moira. "He's still out there."

"Yes," said Celeste, looking at Ben nervously. He looked as freaked out as she felt.

"He deserves to die," said the old woman in a matter of fact voice. "Any man who lays a hand on a woman in anger deserves to die."

"Well no," said Celeste, feeling her palms sweat and her heart flutter. "Not exactly."

"You young things," said Moira irritably. "No wonder this world is going to hell in a handbasket. None of you have any spine. None of you are willing to spill blood for a just cause."

Celeste watched as the old woman settled back against her pillows and closed her eyes.

"Wow," said Ben looking extremely uncomfortable. "So... I guess I'll be going..."

"Stay!" insisted Celeste.

"The caffeine's wearing off..." said Ben, eyeing Moira as he stood up.

"You wimp."

Ben shrugged apologetically and backed out of the room.

After he'd closed the door, Celeste settled back against the cushions, trying to get comfortable and struggling. She wondered how long until her next pain relief. She wondered how much blood Moira had spilled. She shuddered. If Moira put so little value on human life was she really so different from the man who killed Tig and Lara?

"Never rely on a man," said Moira, cutting into her thoughts and making Celeste jump. "None of them are worth the oxygen they waste staying alive."

Celeste looked at her. So peaceful with her eyes closed and a slight smile playing across her lips. Celeste shuddered at what the woman could be picturing in her mind. Her thumb found the nurse button and a light bulb flashed on by the door. She'd need those painkillers sooner rather than later.

ð

"You go first," said Emerald.

"No way!" hissed Maram. "You're the one who thought of this, remember?"

"You're the one bearing the bloody beast!"

"You're the one who... who..."

"Yes?" asked Emerald innocently.

"Dammit. Fine." Maram stomped through the miserable grey rain up to the door of Tabernacle and peered anxiously through the glass door. "It looks... nice."

"Go on," said Emerald poking her in the back.

"What if they try and convert us?"

"I don't think they do that anymore," said Emerald. "You're thinking of the crusades."

Maram pushed the door open and a small jingle bell sounded overhead. The sound of panpipes filled the air and a sweet smelling fragrance infiltrated Emerald's lungs. She coughed.

"Hello there!" chirruped a teenage girl on the checkout. She had blonde dreadlocks, an ornate cross necklace and an organic cotton vest. "Are you looking for anything in particular today?"

"Sort of," said Emerald nervously. "I, well we, we wanted some... advice about... well there's this question..."

"We have a question about Satan and we were told you guys are all enthusiastic about that stuff," said Maram.

The girl opened and closed her mouth for a moment then called out, "Darren!"

"Yes?" replied a young man, poking his head out from a room at the back of the shop.

"Help?" she answered in a high pitch squeak whilst fixing Emerald and Maram with a terrifyingly forced smile and eyes full of fear.

Darren came towards them, laden with heavy books. His grey muscle vest revealed impressive biceps and a tattoo sleeve of religious iconography. "How can I help you?" he asked them.

"They want to know about... Satan," said the girl nervously.

"Okay, any idea what book you're looking for specifically?" he asked, setting the books on the counter next to the girl who looked extremely relieved.

"No," said Maram. "We want to know what someone might mean if they called me the "bearer of the beast with seven heads"."

He frowned and crossed his arms. "Why would someone call you that?"

"I don't know," said Maram. "But I want to."

"I'm sure you do," he said, then turned to the girl on the checkout who was listening in nervously. "Elodie, would you go grab a copy of Revelations on Revelations, and obviously a copy of The Book."

"Oh, yes, okay," said Elodie.

"Take a seat, ladies," said Darren gesturing to some bright green fabric chairs arranged in a crescent around a small table. A picture of a kitten with the words "God hears even the smallest voice" was displayed on the wall above.

Elodie approached and set a copy of the Bible with a jazzy cover, and a serious looking text book on the table, then knelt down on the floor in front of them, gazing up at Darren adoringly.

"So, what's going on then?" asked Darren, apparently oblivious to the young girl's affections. "The bearer of the beast is quite an accusation for someone to lob at a lovely young woman."

Emerald rolled her eyes. Just once she wished they could go somewhere without men flirting with Maram.

"This guy``` wants to hurt me," said Maram. "He hurt my friends last night trying to get to me. They're in hospital. And he's going to try again."

Elodie looked horrified, her hands to her mouth. Darren nodded sadly, a sage frown on his face. "And why do you think that is?"

"Because he's a fucking psycho," said Emerald crossly. "You think it's her fault?"

"Hey hey," Darren said, holding his hands up and nodding again. "I'm just trying to help here. This is some pretty serious stuff."

"I didn't see anything on Facebook," said Elodie, pulling her phone out of her pocket. "Do the police know?"

"Yes," said Maram. "But not about this."

"He said we were 'harbouring the bearer of the beast'," said Emerald. "We think he was talking about Maram. We want to know what it means."

"Well, the beast obviously refers to the Devil," said Darren, pulling the jazzy bible book towards him. On the floor, Elodie gazed at him as though he was spouting wisdom worthy of great poetry. Emerald glared. "But the seven heads changes things. That takes us into Revelation."

"What does it change?" asked Maram.

Darren pointed to the page in the Bible and read aloud. "I saw a woman sit upon a scarlet coloured beast, full of names of blasphemy, having seven heads and ten horns."

"That's it!" said Emerald. "Seven heads and ten horns."

"He thinks I'm going to ride some monster thing?" asked Maram, pulling a face.

"No," said Elodie, from where she sat on the floor. "He thinks you're the monster's mother."

Maram's mouth fell open. "Fuck that!"

"That doesn't make sense!" insisted Emerald. "Why would he think that?"

"You're right," said Darren, frowning and leaning over the books, flipping the pages in each back and forth. "It doesn't make sense."

"So what does that mean?" asked Maram.

"It means he's wrong," said Darren, leaning back and looking thoughtful.

"Well I bloody know that!" said Maram. "I'm not pregnant! And even if I was it wouldn't be with a bloody great dragon monster thing! What the hell?"

"I mean," said Darren. "His motivation is wrong. Whatever he thinks you are, whoever he thinks you are, it's not come from the Bible. He's had the wrong information from somewhere."

"Are you sure?" asked Emerald, leaning forwards.

"Sure," said Darren, tapping on the book. "It's a really poor interpretation. Most people don't read the Bible in full and it's easy to be misled if you're unfamiliar with the text."

"So he's not being told to kill me by God?" asked Maram, a desperation in her voice that surprised Emerald.

"Oh no," said Elodie, gazing at Maram earnestly. "God is love."

"Yes, well," said Maram scowling. "Be that as it may."

"God is love," Elodie repeated.

"Okay then," said Emerald, standing up. "We'll be going now. We've got a lot to figure out."

Maram stood at her side and the two edged out from behind the table.

"Stay," said Darren. "We can make you some tea and phone our pastor. He'll be able to tell you more."

"No no," said Maram, gesticulating. "Thank you. No."

"Do stay," insisted Elodie. "He's wonderful. He'll be able to teach you the truth. God is love."

"I teach the Alpha course," said Darren. "Perhaps you'd be interested in further studying?"

Maram leaned in and hissed, "Crusades!" in Emerald's ear.

The two backed away to the door and Emerald pulled it open, the little bell tinkling overhead, as the two wide eyed Christians approached them.

"Thanks!"

"Bye!"

"See you again soon!" came the voices behind them.

Chapter Sixteen

Celeste stared at the magazine in her hands. A woman with a trolley had been round and left a couple at the bottom of their beds. Celeste was loathe to read about celebrity gossip but, in the absence of anything else, it would have to do.

There was a quiet knock on the door and she looked up.

"How's she doing?" asked a nurse, stepping into the room and peering with concern at the sleeping woman in the bed next to Celeste. She looked concerned, which surprised Celeste. She hadn't been able to discern anything that actually seemed to be wrong with Moira, other than the concerning thirst for blood.

"She's erm..." Celeste searched for words. "Feisty."

"That she is," laughed the young woman. "And how are you doing?"

"Sore," said Celeste. "Is Carla awake yet? Carla Martinez?"

"Yes," she said, looking at the machines next to Celeste. "She's been sitting with her girlfriend since she woke up."

"Can I go?" asked Celeste.

The nurse laughed kindly. "No, honey," she said. "Not yet. You'll need another check over by a doctor before you can go anywhere, and when you do just be aware it won't be far or for long. You need to be careful. But I can let her know you want to see her."

"Thank you," said Celeste, settling back on her cushions and gazing out the window for a moment. "Have you heard from Emerald and Maram at all?" she asked, trying to sound casual whilst her heart raced.

"No, not since first thing," she said, carefully tucking in Celeste's sheets. "I can see if anybody else has taken a message if you like?"

"No," said Celeste. "It's okay. Thank you."

"Okay, honey," she said. "Just beep if you need anything. Another magazine or anything to eat, okay?"

"Thanks," she said, smiling wanly.

Celeste watched the nurse leave then flicked her hand and the door closed shut with a gentle click. She wanted to be alone with her thoughts and the comforting distraction of celebrity scandal.

"Telekinesis," came Moira's voice making Celeste jump in surprise and then wince in pain. "Excellent. I prefer a physical power. The mind powers always seem so self satisfied."

"I... erm... didn't know you were awake," she said, turning nervously to see the old woman watching her with a piercing stare.

"Oh yes, I usually am," said Moira. "I had my suspicions you were of power, of course, but it's nice to see I was right. You and your friends who have been attacked, you're a coven, yes?"

Celeste blinked rapidly. Her heart started to bang and it made her ribs shriek in pain. She hadn't been asked that before. It had always been something they kept secret. She had been raised to keep it a secret, to be ashamed of it, and her parents had refused to engage with her in adulthood since she had refused to stop using her power. Guinevere had, in turn, always insisted on extreme caution and privacy when using or discussing power. To be outright questioned about it was a shock. She wasn't sure what to do. Still, Moira was not surprised and spoke as if it was a world she was already familiar with.

"Yes," she said hesitantly.

"I have a granddaughter," said Moira. "She's about your age."

"Oh," said Celeste, trying to appear interested and keen but wishing she was anywhere else. "That's... nice..."

"I have trained her well and she will need somewhere to go," Moira went on.

Celeste chewed her lip. "Right..."

"A coven cannot function with only five," said Moira, staring her in the eye in the way that made Celeste feel violated.

"There's six of us actually," said Celeste, wishing the conversation would end.

"Six?" said Moira, frowning. "But your friend Tig, she died, no?"

Celeste closed her eyes momentarily, the pain still sharp. "Yes. There's six of us left."

"A coven of seven," said Moira, leaning back and staring up at the ceiling. "How peculiar."

Celeste waited for further comment from the old woman but none came, and moments later she heard light, breathy snores.

"Moira?" she asked. "Are you asleep now?"

There was no answer so she picked up the magazine again and flicked her finger so the curtain around the bed started to trundle round and give her the solitude she craved.

"You could do it without the use of your hands, you know," Moira murmered quietly. "With training."

Celeste startled and the curtain stopped. "Oh," she said, gripping the magazine tightly.

"Just a thought," said Moira, before the snores recommenced.

Celeste tried to go back to reading her magazine but kept the curtain open. She didn't fancy the idea of not being able to see Moira.

ð

Emerald's mother had put the radio on before leaving for work, needing the distraction of the gallery to stop herself dwelling, and Emerald had left it playing. Bruno Mars drifted across the room offering a gentle and comforting sound that seemed quite at odds with how jagged and uncomfortable the world felt around her. Still, it was reassuring.

"We need to go and tell them," she said, pouring boiling water into two mugs in her mother's kitchen. "They need to know what's going on."

"I don't know if they'll want to see us," said Maram, picking idly at a muffin.

"We have to try," said Emerald. "We just have to. The more we all know the better. We need to be ready."

"For next time?" asked Maram.

"Well," said Emerald, setting the cups of coffee on the table then sitting down heavily. "Yeah."

"Because he still thinks I'm going to birth some demon thing and that it's his mission to kill me."

"Yeah."

"Marvellous," said Maram with a sigh, then shoved a handful of muffin into her mouth. "Who knew being human could be so complicated?"

"Hey," said Emerald, her eyes widening. "You're not human!"

"A little louder for the cheap seats in the back."

"The second list!" she said. "All the people on the second list, the ones being erased by those Commission assholes. They're not human!"

"Oh," said Maram, sitting up a little. "Wow. That totally makes sense! Why didn't we see that before?"

"I don't know," said Emerald. "But that's it, right?"

"It must be..." said Maram. "But what else is there?"

"Don't you know?" asked Emerald.

"I lived in a lamp, Em," said Maram. "I hadn't even heard of the Spice Girls til that tequila night with Tig..."

They looked at each other for a moment and Emerald felt sick. They sat in silence for a moment as Bruno changed to Adele.

"I miss her so much," said Emerald.

"Me too," said Maram.

"We need to get this guy," said Emerald. "We just have to."

"Where's Guinevere?" asked Maram. "She'll know how we can check if they're not human, right?"

"No idea actually," said Emerald, looking around momentarily. "But that just proves it, doesn't it? Whoever is looking for you doesn't know who, or what, you are. He's got the prophecy same as us and is just trying to work it out."

"She walks amongst us, but all alone, her life is real, but not her own," said Maram, glaring at her coffee.

"Exactly. The women who were on list two must have been non-humans but living and working amongst humans."

"Do they do that?" asked Maram.

"Well... you do," said Emerald.

"I guess I thought I was the only one."

"Still doesn't explain why he wants to kill you but it's something," said Emerald. "Where *is* Guinevere? Now's the time she'd really be useful."

"We can ask her later," said Maram. "Shall we go to the hospital? Even if they don't want to see us, they'll want this information."

"Okay," agreed Emerald. "Let's go."

ð̌

"We have a problem," said Nahla, opening Stuart Wren's door without waiting for an invitation.

He looked up, and set his pen down. "What now?"

"Monroe," said Nahla. "She's going to war."

Stuart sighed. "Of course she is," he said, rubbing his temples. "I warned her. Letting Hannah be part of a mortal school comes with unnecessary risks."

"It is neither Hannah's fault, nor Monroe's," said Nahla, fixing him with a steely gaze.

"No, I am aware of that," he said, irritated. "But Georgette is not dead. Hannah is."

"So you think these girls should have closeted themselves away, instead of living as freely as others are able, because there are evil men in the world?"

"I think a little precaution is necessary," said Stuart. "The Fae, the Jinn, the Lorelai, they are vulnerable and have an entire network of places they can live. They do not need to put themselves at risk."

"Life is risk, Stuart, and we are all entitled to a life," said Nahla. "And perhaps if anyone is being excluded from public life it should be men! It is men who commit these atrocities, not the Lorelai nor the Fae."

Stuart leaned back in his chair and folded his arms. He bit his tongue, knowing well enough not to transgress by using the words "not all men" in the company of Nahla.

"I see your point," he said.

"I connect with these Beings for a reason," Nahla went on as she sat down opposite him. "I bring them into our world. Enable them to live as freely as they want, without threat of harvesting or death because they should not be excluded from life just for the sin of being born not human. Their presence harms nobody, they deserve the same respect back. That is not their fault, it is the fault of man, and therefore it is not my people who should be punished."

"You're right, Nahla," said Stuart, nodding gravely. "I'll assist in any way I can."

"Thank you," she said. For a moment she sat in the chair, her face awash with emotions, then she stood. "Stuart?"

"Yes?"

"You have faith in The Vision, don't you?"

"They're second only to The Oracles," he said.

"That doesn't answer my question."

"I know," he said.

Nahla paused for a moment then left, shutting the door behind her without a word. Stuart stared momentarily at the door, thoughts racing through his head, then got back to work. There was always more work.

ð

Emerald and Maram walked side by side through the hospital. It was quiet and their feet echoed in the corridors. Emerald felt like they were announcing their arrival with a drum beat.

"Excuse me," said Emerald, leaning on the front desk on the ward they had been released from in the early hours of that morning. "I was wondering if you knew where my friends are? We came in last night..."

"Emerald Wren?" asked the nurse, looking up. "And Maram Jinn?"

"Yes, that's right," said Emerald.

"I'm Becky, I've been briefed," she said with a sympathetic smile. "Everyone's actually in Ms Stone's room."

"Abi?" asked Maram. "Abi's awake?"

"Oh, no," said Becky. "I'm sorry. I didn't mean that. No, she's still unconscious I'm afraid, but her condition is good. She's stable."

"Thank you," said Emerald, and together she and Maram walked through the hospital corridors to Abi's room.

As they came to the door they heard voices inside and Maram put her hand on Emerald's arm, her finger to her lips. They stopped and listened.

"I don't know any other witches," came Ben's voice.

"Me neither," said Carla.

"There are others though," said Celeste. "We're not the only witches in this town, let alone the world."

"Then we can find them," said Carla.

"We've not even agreed to this yet," said Celeste.

"We only found each other by chance," agreed Ben. "And if we hadn't, where would we be now? We're a family."

"We aren't anymore," said Carla. "We don't need them."

Emerald turned to Maram and whispered, "They're replacing us."

"They can't!" said Maram, desperation in her eyes.

"Come on," said Emerald, her stomach knotting up and her hands shaking. She had to stay calm. They were here for a reason.

Emerald knocked on the door and stepped into the room as all the eyes turned to her. Carla's narrowed with rage, Ben and Celeste's widened with shock and worry.

"What are you doing here?" demanded Carla.

"We found some stuff out," said Emerald. "About the guy..."

"The guy you let murder Tig?" asked Carla, standing up.

"Carla... please..." said Maram.

"We don't want you here," said Carla. "We don't need you here."

"Carla," said Ben, putting a hand on her arm which she angrily shook off.

"Please," said Maram. "If we're going to stop him we need to work together."

"Oh so now you want to stop him?" Carla demanded. "Now it's *your* life at risk?"

"Carla," said Celeste gently. "That's not fair."

"No Celeste," Carla snapped. "What's not fair is Abi's in a coma, Tig's dead, Lila's dead, we're all broken and messed up, and a fucking woman killer is on the loose. And it's all their fault."

"I'm sorry," Emerald whispered.

"And you?" Carla asked, turning on Maram with fury on her face. "Are you sorry? It's your life Tig sacrificed herself for. Are you sorry?"

"Yes!" Insisted Maram as tears ran down her cheeks, splashing heavily to the floor as she buckled up in despair.

Emerald wrapped her arms around her friend and glared furiously at Carla. "Do you think we knew this would happen?"

"I don't think you thought at all," said Carla, her eyes losing a fraction of their rage as she took in the sight of Maram crying heart wrenching sobs, but soon focussing again.

"What did you find out?" asked Celeste. Then when Carla turned on her, "We need to know! They're right! He might come back!"

"For Maram," said Carla. "He's not coming for us. He's coming for her. We're safe as long as we're nowhere near her."

"We don't know that," whispered Celeste, gripping her cross. "He's seen us now. We don't know what he's planning. And we can't just abandon her even if he does only want Maram."

"Yes, we can," said Carla. "You can do what you want but I'm staying with Abi. They're on their own. We don't need them."

"Come on Maram," said Emerald. "We'll stop him ourselves."

Maram nodded, snot and tears over her face.

Carla turned her back on them, tenderly stroking Abi's face and gently smoothing out the sheets that covered her.

Celeste and Ben glanced at one another, then at Carla, then at Emerald and Maram, their faces frozen in tension.

"We know it's not your God," Emerald said to Celeste. "Whoever's doing this to him. It's not God."

Celeste stared at her, tears in the corners of her eyes. "You believe me?"

"I do," she said. Then gently led the sobbing Maram from the room.

ð

"She's crying," said Fadius, watching the Witch and the Bearer of the Beast walk away from the hospital. "She looks weak. Frightened."

"DON'T BE FOOLED BY WITCHES, FADIUS," came the voice. "WE MUST BE SURE. WE MAY ONLY GET ONE MORE CHANCE."

Fadius watched as the witch pulled her friend into her arms, letting her sob on her shoulder whilst she stroked her hair, gently whispering in her ear. Such love radiated between them. Such compassion.

"NO FADIUS," the voice boomed in his ear. "WITCHES CANNOT LOVE."

"No Lord," agreed Fadius, bowing his head and backing further into the trees of the wooded area that ran down the side of the hospital grounds.

Chapter Seventeen

"Where have you been?" Emerald asked as they walked into her mum's kitchen to find the cat casually lapping at a mug of tea.

"I had errands," said Guinevere, not meeting her eyes.

Emerald frowned but a heavy sniff from Maram at her side tore her attention away. "Come on, sit," she said. Maram obeyed.

"What happened?" Guinevere asked.

"We tried to tell everyone what we've found out," said Emerald. "But..."

"But they hate us," Maram wept. "Because we killed Tig."

"You did not kill Tig," said Guinevere, flicking her tail. "He did."

"Because of me," said Maram, her large dark eyes full of tears and abject despair.

"Because of him," said Emerald. "And whoever it is who's whispering in his ear."

"Guinevere," said Maram. "Are there others like me?"

"Other Jinn?" asked Guinevere.

"Or other things," said Maram. "People who aren't really humans but living around us?"

"Why?" asked Guinevere, lapping at her tea again.

"Because that's what we think the second list is," said Emerald. "The first list is women who died, we know that. But the second list could be women like Maram. Women who are living fake lives, pretending to be something they're not."

"Ah," said Guinevere, nodding thoughtfully. "I see."

"And when we were trying to look them up they were being erased," said Emerald, peering at the cat suspiciously. "And I think it was the Commission hiding their existence; to protect magic."

"Ah," said Guinevere again.

"So, are there?"

Guinevere hesitated a moment longer than Emerald expected, then carefully said "Yes, there are."

"Like the Power people?"

"Sort of," she said.

"You're being weird," said Emerald. "Why are you being weird?"

"I'm not being weird," the cat retorted.

"You are," agreed Maram. "Very weird."

"You're always weird when you're not telling me something," said Emerald.

"There are people, Beings, who lives amongst humans," said Guinevere, her tail flicking. "Much like some witches live amongst humans, like you do without revealing themselves. Some people of Power remain much more segregated, others partially integrate for things like education or work. It's the same for other Beings."

"Why didn't you tell me?" asked Maram. "I thought I was the only one."

"You didn't ask," said Guinevere. "And anyway, I was sent for Emerald. Not you."

Maram looked like she'd been slapped. The cat sounded so cold. Emerald glared at her.

"You should have told me," said Emerald, quietly seething. "None of us have anyone to teach us. You're all I have, all any of us have. You have a responsibility."

"I do," said Guinevere, looking at her with an oddly calm face. "A big responsibility. Bigger than you can comprehend."

"Alright crypto," said Emerald, turning away from her and feeling increasingly irritated. Time was running out. He could come for Maram at any moment, and everyone was abandoning them. "Come on Maram. We can do this on our own. We don't need them and we don't need her."

Maram stood and looked dejectedly at Guinevere who caught her eye then turned away with a peculiar look on her face.

What did she know? Emerald wondered. She knew something. Why wouldn't she tell them? They really were alone.

ð

The next morning Emerald and Maram went into work and were greeted by a delighted Vinnie.

"Oh you girls," he cried out. "No more days off. The place is in ruins."

He gesticulated wildly. Emerald noticed that the trays were in a slightly different position and there were three dirty glasses left behind the bar. No sign of ruin, but it was nice that someone valued them.

"We'll do our best," she said, patting him on the arm then shrugging off her coat. The normality of the restaurant that ate so many of the hours in their days, normally a chore, now felt like a comfort blanket. She could almost imagine the world was normal again. That life was ordinary.

For much of the shift Emerald was so busy that the trauma of the previous day wasn't able to creep to the front of her mind. She barely spoke to Maram unless it was related to work, and she served customers, cleaned messes, and repositioned the trays with joy. This was easy. This was fine. There was so much comfort to be found in mundanity. The world of magic and violent men was far away. Life was carrying on.

As she was pouring two large glasses of Sauvignon Blanc for a middle aged couple who appeared to be on a first date by the coy glances and pungent cologne, she felt Maram press against her side.

"Look," she hissed, starting to tidy a perfectly neat pile of napkins with urgency, not making eye contact.

"What?" Emerald whispered back.

"By the coat stand," came the reply as Emerald returned the bottle to the under counter fridge.

"What?" Emerald asked, then her mouth fell open. "Holy crap."

There, at a table with a nervous looking elderly woman with neat white curls and sensible shoes, was Barry The Bastard.

"What do we do?" asked Maram.

"I don't know!" said Emerald.

Barry The Bastard handed the elderly woman a menu, then put a black leather briefcase on the table importantly. It was full of paper and files and he shuffled them in his hands for absolutely no reason that Emerald could determine, before closing the briefcase and setting them on top.

"I'll take these then go take their order," said Emerald.

"I'll go clear table 3," said Maram. "Recon."

"On it," agreed Emerald.

Hastily she took the drinks to the couple then took her order pad from her apron pocket and wandered over as casually as she could, catching Maram's eye as she determinedly scrubbed at a non-existent stain on the surface of table 3.

"I understand you're feeling anxious about this, Connie," said Barry The Bastard. "Totally understandable. The world is changing so fast, it must be hard to keep up."

Emerald glared at him.

"Oh, well," said the old woman. "I do try. I like to use the Facebook to keep up with my grandson. He's in Thailand on his gap year."

"Oh Connie," said Barry The Bastard with an obnoxious laugh. "The Facebook. You're so sweet."

Maram's jaw set firmly. Emerald glared more.

"I'm just not sure investing is the right thing for me, right now," said Connie, twiddling her wedding ring. "Greyson has only so recently passed. I'd hate to be hasty."

"Connie, Connie, Connie," said Barry The Bastard, a sickening smile spreading over his lips as he reached out a slimy hand and placed it over Connie's left hand. "Greyson was a smart man. He liked to look after you. He wouldn't have wanted his wife left destitute because she was too afraid to make the smart decisions."

Emerald felt herself make a guttural growl at the back of her throat and Barry The Bastard snapped his face round to stare at her.

"Uh, anything to order?" she asked, plastering a pleasant smile to her mouth whilst aware it wasn't reaching her eyes.

"Coffee. Black." Barry the Bastard said, turning away from her as she scribbled it down. "And for you, dear?"

"Do you have any green tea?" Connie asked, looking up at Emerald and smiling warmly.

"Yes, we do," said Emerald. "I'll sort that out for you right now."

"Thank you so much," said Connie.

Emerald smiled at her properly, then flashed a cold stare at Barry The Bastard who was blanking her. Maram caught her eye and the two retreated to the bar leaving Connie to the mercy of the slimeball.

"What do we do?" asked Maram as Emerald busied herself making Connie's green tea with care.

"I don't know," said Emerald. "We never really got as far as a plan!"

"Any plan we'd made would have involved everyone else anyway," whispered Maram. "We're on our own."

"What if..." Emerald started.

"Excuse me!" cooed a woman's voice.

Emerald looked up and saw the middle aged Sauvignon Blanc drinker leaning over the bar.

"Yes?" Emerald asked, not looking away from Barry The Bastard.

The woman was a bit taken aback but said, "We were trying to catch your eye, we were hoping for another tipple!"

"I'll sort it," said Emerald, still not looking at her.

"Oh, erm," the woman stepped back from the bar and smoothed her dress. "Good. Thank you."

"We can't let him leave," she said once the woman had stepped away.

"Can we do this on our own?" asked Maram.

"We have to," said Emerald. "Don't we?"

"Yeah," agreed Maram. "We have to."

"Get his coffee," said Emerald. "Make it shit."

"On it," said Maram.

Moments later Emerald slowly carried the tray of drinks towards the table whilst Maram dipped away to start scrubbing at the now gleaming table 3 again.

"It's just," Connie was saying, her hands twisting anxiously in her lap. "If I lose it I'll have nothing. I don't think I can give you everything. It's too big of a risk. I'll have nowhere to go, no way of looking after my family."

"Connie, Connie, Connie," said Barry The Bastard, leaning into her. "Think of your grandson. Think of your son. Do you really want to be a burden on them? Or do you want to know you have enough to take care of yourself and leave enough for them to be comfortable as well?"

"Oh I…"

"Do you want them to remember you with resentment? Be grateful when their stress is gone?" Barry went on. "Or to look back with love as they live the lives you've always wanted to give them?"

"Well…"

"Trust me, Connie," he said, his hand crawling over her own once more. "Trust me. Greyson would have wanted your family to have better. Don't let him down."

"I…"

"Just sign here and it's done. Easy. Then I'll be able to triple your investment and all your troubles will be over. I know how hard this is for you. Funerals are so expensive after all."

With tears in her eyes and a quivering hand, Connie tentatively reached out to take the silver fountain pen that was clasped in Barry The Bastard's claw.

Maram stood bolt upright, a frantic look on her face. Emerald looked about wildly, there must be something she could use to distract them. She couldn't let that sweet old woman sign her soul away to the devil.

As Connie's hand went to grip the pen, Emerald let out a cry and tipped the coffee and green tea off the tray. The mug and cup crashed down spraying a scolding hot splash of liquid across the briefcase of paper, the table, and Barry The Bastard's lap.

He howled, leapt to his feet and turned on Emerald with rage.

"You stupid bitch!" he shouted in her face.

Emerald staggered backwards, her heart beginning to pound.

"I'm sorry sir," she lied, panic surging through her as she found herself pressed against a table behind her, noticing how large Barry The Bastard actually was as he loomed towards her.

"You idiot! Look what you did!" he shouted again, smacking at his coffee stained suit. "You absolute..."

From beside him, Maram landed a punch square across his jaw, snapping his head backwards. He fell backwards and landed with a crash across the table, paperwork flying everywhere and Connie crying out in shock as she was left sitting in her chair staring at the debris, mess, and the knocked down man on the floor in front of her.

For a moment the entire restaurant was frozen in time. Nobody moved. Nobody spoke. Nobody even breathed. Then there was a surge of activity. Barry The Bastard staggered to his feet, rage in his face, as Vinnie charged from his office and appeared at their side.

"What happened?" Vinnie demanded.

"You hired incompetent staff is what happened!" declared Barry The Bastard, rounding on Vinnie and pointing an accusatory finger at Emerald. "And a violent psychopath!" The finger moved to Maram.

"I'm so sorry, sir," apologised Vinnie, turning a furious face on Emerald and Maram.

"Sorry?" shouted Barry The Bastard, scooping up his paperwork and briefcase. "Tell it to my lawyers. Come on Mrs Masters, we are clearly not safe in this shoddy establishment."

"Oh, please, sir," said Vinnie, flustered as he tried to coax the pair into staying. "Let's discuss this in my office."

"Not as long as these disgraceful girls are working here!"

Emerald and Maram watched as the man led the anxious Connie away, ranting as he went, whilst Vinnie turned on them with outrage and confusion. "What the hell happened?"

Maram started to speak but he held up a finger.

"I've a good mind to fire you on the spot!" he cried.

"If you could..." started Emerald.

"What?" he demanded. "If I could phone the police? Stop that customer from phoning the police?"

"Just listen for a moment..." insisted Maram. "If we could..."

"Excuse me?" came a voice from behind them.

"What?" Emerald and Maram demanded, turning and seeing the Sauvignon Blanc woman standing behind them giving a little wave.

"I just wondered if you could get our drinks now..."

"No!" they cried out in unison, throwing their hands in the air in utter exasperation.

The woman looked shocked and turned to Vinnie. "The service here is just ghastly!" She stormed back to her table, complaining loudly to the waiting man.

"Girls!" Vinnie looked so angry, so confused. "My girls! What is happening? What are you thinking?"

"It's complicated, Vinnie," said Emerald, then looked over her shoulder towards the door. "And we've really got to go."

"Go?" he cried. "Go? And leave my restaurant in ruins? My customers upset? A potential law suit on my hands?"

"We can't explain right now, Vinnie," said Maram. "I'm sorry."

"You can't just leave!" he said, gesticulating to the mess. "You still work for me! We have a business to run!"

"Fine," said Emerald. "Then we quit. Come on, Maram."

Vinnie looked like he had been slapped and took a step back. Emerald wanted to stay and explain, to apologise and give him promises of returning to sort everything out. She knew in her heart that he would understand. He'd even offer to help in any way he could. But there wasn't time.

Before he had a chance to protest, to plead with them, they grabbed their coats and headed for the door leaving the chaos behind them, the sanctuary of normality destroyed by a man, and stepped into the street.

"He can't have got far," said Emerald. Maram nodded and the two looked around them. Emerald spotted Barry The Bastard leading Connie around a corner at the end of the street and pointed. "Let's go."

They started hurrying after them when from around the corner they heard a piercing scream. Picking up the pace they ran ahead, Emerald nearly colliding with a girl with thick dark curly hair who ricocheted off a wall with a yelp as she flung herself out of the way.

Not pausing to apologise, Emerald and Maram turned the corner and saw Connie cowering against a wall, blood splattered across her face whilst she trembled. In front of her was the blood stained, mauled body of Barry The Bastard, his clothes torn, his skin shredded.

"A dog!" Connie cried out. "A giant dog!"

"That fucking werewolf!" raged Maram.

Chapter Eighteen

"Oh help me, help me!" sobbed Connie, reaching out her hands desperately towards Emerald and Maram.

Behind them they heard someone approach and scream out in horror, then a woman raced past them towards Barry The Bastard, pulling a phone out of her handbag.

A man followed her, and crouched down beside Connie. "Don't worry, my wife's a doctor," he said gently, helping the woman to her feet and letting her lean into his arms, supporting her weight. "Are you okay?" he asked, noticing Emerald and Maram standing there was watching. "Were you hurt?"

"We've got a pulse!" the doctor announced. "He's hurt but he's alive." Then she started speaking instructions into the phone, summonsing an ambulance and giving a detailed description of the condition of the savaged man.

In front of her Barry The Bastard started to groan.

"He's not dead," Emerald whispered to Maram.

"Has the werewolf ever left one alive before?" asked Maram, as they started to back away.

"No," said Emerald. "I don't think so."

"We need to get out of here," said Maram.

The two turned and ran, ducking down an alley and cutting through the streets. Emerald's mind raced and her heart pounded. She had to calm down. She stopped and leant against a wall, putting her head back and closing her eyes. Slow down, slow down. Don't panic.

She felt Maram take her hands, cooling and soothing. "It's okay, Em," she said. "I'm here. We're okay."

"What happened back there?" she asked.

"Erm... well, you burned the bastard, I clocked the bastard, and then some werewolf battered the bastard," said Maram, smiling wryly.

"Good, good," said Emerald with a nod. "Just checking."

ð

Celeste, pain in her head starting to overwhelm her again, lay back against the pillow on her bed. The nurse at her side took her blood pressure and pulse, checking things off on a list, then smiled at her gently.

"You're getting there, honey," she said. "You won't be going home for a while yet but you're definitely on the mend."

Celeste smiled wanly. She wasn't dying to go home. She was dying to leave the hospital, for sure, but home was no lure. Home was empty. She had long envied Emerald the welcoming arms of her mother. Celeste's own parents had equipped her with basic knowledge, understanding of where she came from and why she had this gift, but were themselves disconnected from the magical community, focussing their energy on their religion. Born of power, but not devoted to it. Celeste had left home at eighteen, started working in the refuge and longed to use the power that surged within her. Emerald and Maram had welcomed her into their growing community and finally she had felt like she belonged. Now? Now there was only the feeling of death, loneliness, and an empty flat over a dingy shop and a community that was falling apart, both in her personal life and at work.

If the coven broke what would she have?

The nurse left and Celeste closed her eyes. At least there was darkness.

"Grandma?" came a quiet voice.

Celeste opened her eyes a sliver, peering out quietly. A round faced girl with thick dark curls was standing in the doorway, fidgeting with her hands.

"Lila!" greeted Moira. "My darling. Come here. Tell me everything."

The girl nodded nervously then approached, sitting primly in the blue plastic bucket seat at her side then pulling a spiral bound notebook out of her bag.

"I, erm, I made some notes," she said. "After. So I didn't forget. I wrote it down. Erm. So you could see."

"I don't want your notes," said Moira, waving a hand at her. "I want your feelings. How did it feel?"

"Oh, erm," Lila mumbled, flipping through a few pages of notes. "It felt, erm..." she found a page and tapped on it. "Exhilarating. Yes. Exhilarating and, erm, frightening."

"Exhilarating!" said Moira, clapping her hands together. "Yes. Exhilarating."

Something in Celeste felt cold. She didn't know why, but the whole conversation felt distinctly unpleasant.

"Tell me," said Moira. "Was there blood?"

Celeste turned suddenly and then instantly regretted it. She had planned to stay still and quiet but the question had startled her.

"Oh!" Lila startled, looking at Celeste anxiously, then back to her grandmother.

"Lila, this is my roommate Celeste," said Moira, smiling in a way that made Celeste nervous. "She is a telekinetic."

Celeste opened her mouth to say something then closed it again. Hearing it spoken so casually and to a total stranger without her prior consent felt peculiar.

"Wow," said Lila. "I would love that. I don't have that. That's a great power. I would love that power."

"Lila!" snapped Moira. "Your power is immense. It is noble. We are of great value."

"Oh yes," said Lila, bobbing her head down. "Sorry Grandma. You're right. I know. I love my power. I, erm, I will remember."

"What is your power?" asked Celeste.

"Same as Grandma," said Lila, looking at her through earnest eyes that drooped down at the corners so she looked perpetually sad. "We're shape shifters."

"That sounds great," said Celeste, genuinely impressed and thinking of Professor McGonagall. "What can you change into?"

"I'm, erm, still learning," said Lila. "I can't go too big. Or too small. I can only. I can do animals that are, erm, my size. I am learning though. Grandma is teaching me. I'm learning. I'm studying hard. I'm getting better. Faster. I used to be slow. I'm learning."

"Amazing," said Celeste.

"Grandma though," said Lila. "Grandma is powerful. She can change into anything."

"Anything?" asked Celeste.

"Anything," said Moira, her chin high with pride. "From elephants to mice. But I prefer the form of the noble wolf."

ð

"Okay," said Emerald as they walked home to Emerald's mum's house. "So... we're unemployed..."

"Yep," said Maram.

"We've lost our coven..."

"Yep."

"Our Guardian seems to have cut us off..."

"That she does."

"And the maniac is probably going to come back and try to kill you."

"Pretty much sums it up," said Maram. "Oh, and I broke a nail earlier."

"You did?" cried Emerald. "That's a proper problem."

"I knew you'd understand," said Maram, smiling at her sadly.

"And we thought it was complicated before, eh?" said Emerald.

"We were idiots," said Maram with a sigh.

"I'm glad you're home," said Emerald's mum when they stepped in the front door. "There's... people here to see you."

"Who?" asked Emerald, hope in her heart, the possibility of one of her friends waiting in the kitchen for her bubbling in front of her. They hurried through the door and into the kitchen.

Sitting at the table were two fierce looking, but tiny, women.

They stood. The elder of the two held out a hand. Emerald glanced nervously at Maram who shrugged, then took the hand. It was dry and firm with a strong grip.

"Emerald Wren?" asked the woman.

"Yes," said Emerald, hesitantly.

"Granddaughter of Stuart Wren?"

"Uh, what? I mean, yes. Yes he's my Grandad."

"And Maram, the Jinn?" asked the woman, turning to look at Maram and holding out her hand. Maram nervously shook it.

"The what?" asked Emerald's mother.

"Excuse me, Mrs Wren," said the small woman. "But this is a matter that does not pertain to you. I would insist on privacy at this time."

"Oh," said Emerald's mum. "I see."

"Thank you," said the woman, turning away from her and back to Emerald and Maram.

Emerald's mum looked at Emerald. The small woman was part of the world of magic and clearly had authority. She didn't dare question it.

When Emerald's mother had left and the door was shut, the small woman gestured to the table and offered for Emerald and Maram to sit.

"My name is Beatrice Monroe," said the woman, sitting down. "And this is my eldest daughter Georgette."

"Hello," said Emerald and Maram in unison.

"I am an employee of The Commission," said Monroe.

Emerald sat upright, her eyes narrowed. "Why are you here?"

"You are currently involved in the Ubel Project," she said. "And the man you are hunting, the man who is hunting you, murdered my youngest daughter."

Questions rattled around Emerald's head. What to ask first?

"Hannah Monroe?" asked Maram. "The girl who died last week?"

"Yes," said Monroe. "That was my Hannah."

"My sister chose to live amongst the mortals," said Georgette. Georgette was small in stature like her mother, wiry and strong, but the ferocity in her eyes was very slightly less intimidating. "The man who did this to her deserves to die. You're going to kill him and we are here to help."

"You are?" asked Emerald. She rubbed her head and looked at Maram who looked equally confused.

"Yes," said Monroe. "Where are the rest of your coven? I was led to believe you had a team on this."

"They're..." started Emerald.

"Hurt," finished Maram.

"Witches," muttered Georgette, rolling her eyes. "You definitely need us."

"What are you?" asked Emerald.

"We are Fae," said Monroe.

"What's Fae?" asked Emerald.

"We are descended of the Fairy folk," said Georgette. "The Ancient bloodline broke hundreds of generations ago, the Fae are of the warrior line."

"Fairies," said Maram in wonder. "Guinevere said there was others like me."

"We are not like you," said Monroe. "And we are not fairies."

"You said you're with the Commission," said Emerald. "Why are you here? What do you want? And what's an Ubel? Why did you ask about my grandfather? What's going on?"

The kitchen door creaked. Emerald turned and saw Guinevere walking in, then stall, her eyes locked on Monroe.

"What are you doing here?" the cat demanded.

"I am discussing that with Ms Wren and the Jinn," said Monroe. "It is none of your business"

"Until further notice it is precisely my business," said Guinevere, jumping onto the table and sitting firmly between Emerald and the two Fae women. "Does Nahla know you're here?"

"I'm sure she will in time," said Monroe, standing.

"Who's Nahla?" asked Emerald. "How do you know each other?"

Guinevere and Monroe both ignored the question. Emerald threw her hands in the air. What was happening?

"We will speak again," said Monroe, looking over Guinevere to Emerald.

"Oh, I, okay," stuttered Emerald. "Maybe next time I'll actually find out what we're talking about!"

Monroe and Georgette stepped together then in a whir of sparks and spinning air they vanished.

"Wow!" gasped Emerald.

"That was amazing!" gasped Maram.

"Show offs," grunted Guinevere.

"What was that about?" demanded Emerald, putting her amazement aside. "Who's Nahla? Why are they asking about my grandfather? How do you know her? What the hell is going on?"

"How did they know about me?" asked Maram. "We haven't told anyone."

"I have to go," said Guinevere.

"What?" asked Emerald. "Go where? What? Why? Don't you dare!"

The cat vanished with a pop.

"What the hell is happening here?" cried Emerald. "Did you know she could do that?"

"I am so confused!" wailed Maram.

They heard a tap at the door and turned to see Emerald's mum peering in. "I heard shouting and... oh, where's everyone gone?"

"Who bloody knows?" cried Emerald.

"Our list of stuff just got a whole lot longer..." said Maram, examining her finger nail.

"That looks sore," said Emerald's mum, taking Maram's hand and looking at it. "I'll get the Savlon." Emerald looked up at her mother pleadingly. "And the vodka."

ð

"The Vision has a report, Ms Hussain," said the young operative in front of Nahla's desk, shifting his feet nervously, and holding a file in his hands.

"And what report is that, Mr Mallory?" asked Nahla, looking at him impatiently. "I am rather busy, I assume this is nothing that couldn't wait?"

"Oh, erm,"

"Come on, Mr Mallory," said Nahla. "I don't have all day."

"There's been a change in the Ubel Project Ms Hussain," he squeaked. "Or not a change. An update. They said they're ready for you to have the next layer."

"The next layer?" demanded Nahla. "Hand me that and leave."

"Yes, Ms Hussain," he said, gratefully placing the folder on her desk then hastily retreating from the room.

Nahla opened the folder and scanned the printed words inside. Then she picked up the phone, hit a number and snapped, "Get me Wren."

Chapter Nineteen

"Why didn't they reveal this immediately?" demanded Stuart, pacing up and down Nahla's office. "We could have been prepared?"

"How?" asked Nahla.

"We could have prepared Monroe," he said. "Laid out an action plan."

"That's probably why they didn't then," said Nahla with a sigh. "If Monroe had been brought in sooner she could have prevented Hannah's death. Hannah had to die to motivate Monroe."

"I presume you will not be mentioning that to Monroe. We could have arranged for her to take on this fight anyway," said Stuart. "And ready. More equipped."

"Monroe would not engage in anything she had no personal investment in," said Nahla with a sigh, shaking her head. "The Fae are not blindly loyal to Commission orders."

"Do you not have authority over your people?" demanded Stuart.

"Do you over the Virilicae?" asked Nahla with a wry smile. "How's Balthasar Hamdani?"

"That is completely different," said Stuart gruffly. "Sometimes decisions must be reached."

"Yes well," said Nahla. "I am not dealing with the dangerous men of this world, Stuart. I am dealing with good people with cultures and loyalties of their own. People that deserve to be respected, not just managed."

"Respected so much we let their children die so they'll do what we want, rather than just telling them?" asked Stuart, raising an eyebrow.

Nahla shifted uncomfortably. "I see your point."

"Now games of moral superiority are aside, shall we move on and decide what we need to do?"

"Yes," agreed Nahla. "Guinevere is waiting."

"Let her wait," said Stuart.

"Respected, not managed," said Nahla sternly.

Standing, Stuart Wren straightened his tie and coughed sternly. "Let's go and see what the feline has to say," he said eventually.

Nahla led the way, Stuart following behind feeling irritable. He resented the lack of control in this project immeasurably, and the reliance on unpredictable Beings even more. The Virilicae could not be trusted, and were a proven danger, but he understood them. Motivated by power and the old teachings and customs of their tribe, it was far more simple than the masses of Beings Nahla dealt with, who all cared about different things for different reasons.

Nahla led them away from her office and down several corridors. Nervous administrative staff stood aside to allow them to pass and operatives nodded respectfully, occasionally greeting them by name.

"In here, Mr Wren," said Nahla, holding open a door.

Stuart entered and saw the tabby cat sitting primly on a plush sofa, a stern look on her face.

"Ms Hussain," greeted Guinevere. "Thank you for this meeting. Mr Wren, I don't believe we've met. I've been living and working closely with your granddaughter Emerald for several years now."

"Yes," said Stuart. "I am aware."

"Good," said Guinevere. "Then I am sure you know why I am here."

"Why don't you tell me," said Stuart, sitting on a leather arm chair on the other side of the coffee table, and leaning back.

"Monroe showed up at my house," she said. "I don't know how much she told Emerald before I intervened."

"Yes, we are aware," said Nahla.

"When I came back I was made aware of the secrecy insisted upon by The Vision," said Guinevere. "And I have maintained it."

"Thank you," said Nahla, nodding solemnly.

Stuart remained silent.

"How should I continue?" asked the cat.

"The Vision have recently brought us new information," said Nahla. "As of this moment proceed as you are. If Monroe returns, monitor her actions and report back. Do not interfere. Monroe and Fae being involved has been anticipated. Guide Emerald as you always have."

The cat nodded. "Very good."

"And whilst I have you here," said Nahla. "We have a new Potential for you."

The cat looked taken aback. "You do?"

"Obviously not yet," said Nahla. "But in due course."

"Oh," said Guinevere, nodding respectfully. "Of course. Yes."

"Very good," said Nahla, opening the door.

"Thank you for your time," said Guinevere.

Nahla thanked her in return and led Stuart from the room, closing the door behind them.

"She is loyal to my granddaughter," said Stuart.

"Yes," said Nahla. "But she is loyal to me too."

Stuart nodded. "You manage her brilliantly."

"I respect her completely," said Nahla, smiling.

ð

"Wolf?" asked Celeste, chewing on her lip.

"Oh yes," said Moira. "I find the form of a wolf to be the most powerful. Agile, fierce, fast."

Celeste stared at her, blinking. "Why do you need to be?" she asked, knowing the answer.

"Because there are dangerous men in the world, Celeste," said Moira. "Dangerous and wicked men who need to be removed."

"Oh..." said Celeste, her heart banging. "Of course"

The werewolf. The werewolf was here. The man killer.

"And now I'm training Lila to take my place," she said. "She is smart. Talented. But lacks backbone."

"You're a wolf too?" Celeste asked her.

Lila looked at her, her lip quivering. She couldn't look less like a wolf.

"I... I..." Lila stuttered. "I'm trying. I... I prefer a... I would like to be a bird. A sparrow. I can't yet. It's too small. I would like to fly. Away. But not yet. I can't yet."

"A sparrow," scoffed Moira, leaning back on her pillow and rolling her eyes. "Could you pick anything less worthy of your power? Archer would have thrown me from the organisation if she heard a descendent of mine speaking like that. And to think I was considering sending you for a formal education."

"I'm sorry," said Lila, visibly trembling.

"Have you been killing men?" asked Celeste, her voice barely above a breath. "Bad men?"

"Since 1941," said Moira, raising her chin with pride.

"Oh my God," whispered Celeste, gripping her crucifix and closing her eyes. "Why?"

"Did you not say your coven works to stop the evils of men as well?" asked Moira.

"Well, yes, we do," agreed Celeste.

"And you want the man who killed your friend to be put to death?"

Celeste hesitated. "Well, yes."

"Then don't ask stupid questions," said Moira, then she turned to look at Lila with a proud smile. "Lila here is working for our cause as well now. She's just had her first kill."

Moira spoke with such pride, smiling triumphantly at Lila who did not look like a killer. She looked like a frightened bird.

"I… I…" stuttered Lila. "I don't think… I…"

"Don't think what?" asked Moira.

"I don't think he… died. I don't think I killed him. Completely. I think… I think he survived… maybe."

"What?" demanded Moira, turning on her with fury in her eyes.

"There was blood," she stuttered, wide eyed and shaking violently. "Lots. Of blood. On the road and on the woman with him. Lots of blood. I thought at first… I thought he was… I tried. I did try. I thought he was dead but… but he… I ran away… he might not have been… he was…"

"Then what are you doing here?" demanded Moira. "Go back and finished the job!"

"I... I... I can't... he... he's going to be..."

"What?" demanded Moira. "He's going to be what?"

"Here," said Lila. "Hospital. Here."

A smile spread over Moira's lips. "Perfect."

ð

"I need to know what's going on," said Emerald's mother, slamming an empty shot glass onto the pine table top. "You've always protected me. Well, excluded me. But I need to know."

Emerald looked at her mother, then at Maram, then back to her mother. "We had to. Guinevere said..."

"I'm sure I can quite imagine what Guinevere said," said Emerald's mother. "And I am quite certain she is behind any spells of confusion I've felt over the years... and the reason for any missing memories. I'm not as stupid as you or your father seem to have thought. I may be mortal born, I may not be part of your world, but I am your mother and I am worthy of respect."

"I never said you weren't!" insisted Emerald.

"Then treat me like I am," said her mother. "Tell me the truth. I've kept out of it until now. I've kept quiet, not complained, out of respect for you. Now it's time to respect me. Tell me what's going on. What's a Jinn? Who were those women? How did Tig die and why isn't it on the news?"

"I'm a Jinn," said Maram, then poured another shot of vodka into her glass and shot it back. She grimaced. "I'm a genie. Those women were fairies. Tig was murdered by a man who is being given powers by somebody he thinks is God. It's not on the news because we're a coven of witches and deaths associated with magic are being erased by an organisation of people who are hiding evidence from mortals."

Emerald's mother sat back in her chair and nodded. "I see," she said. "Well that's pretty much what I expected. Hand over the bottle."

Maram slid the bottle across the table and Emerald's mother poured another. She paused for a moment then took the shot.

"Right," she said. "Where to start. Maram. You're a Genie?"

"Yes," she said. "I am."

"Where did you come from?"

"Granddad gave me a lamp," said Emerald.

"Granddad?" asked her mum, her face quizzical. "We haven't seen your grandfather since... wow... since you were eight? Is that why he came?"

"I guess," said Emerald. "He told me I'd know when to use it... I did it the night Daddy left."

Her mum looked stunned, tears sprung to her eyes. "Why?"

"To make him come home," she confessed.

"But..."

"Free will," said Maram. "She chose not to abuse the power."

"And you're a genie?"

"Yeah," said Maram. "I grant wishes, I serve my masters."

"Oh my god," she whispered. "How old are you?"

"I don't know," Maram admitted and Emerald wondered why she had never thought to ask. "I can't remember. I've served so many. Hundreds. Thousands."

"Thousands?" asked Emerald, her eyes wide.

"Maybe more," admitted Maram. "But this is the first time in my whole life I've actually experienced the world. This is the first time I've actually lived in thousands of years of being alive. I'm not a slave anymore."

Now Emerald's mother really was crying. "Oh Maram, my darling," she gasped. "Why didn't you tell me?"

Maram glanced at Emerald for a moment. "I was ashamed. I'm not human."

Emerald's mum stood and knelt on the floor in front of Maram's chair. "Maram, I love you like my own. You have nothing to be ashamed of. You're a wonderful woman and I am glad you're free."

Maram sniffed and rubbed her eyes. "Thank you."

Emerald's mum got back up, put a gentle hand on Maram's shoulder for a moment then sat back down. "So! Genies exist! Who knew? Let's move on... Tig's killer is being controlled by a non-God?"

"Yes," said Emerald. "He gets power from somewhere. And someone is telling him who to kill."

"Why would anyone want to hurt Tig?"

"He didn't," said Maram, then began to cry. "He wanted to kill me. Tig saved my life."

"And I didn't stop him," said Emerald. "I could. But I didn't. And now everyone's in hospital, Tig's dead. And we're alone."

"You're not alone," said a voice behind them. They turned and saw Guinevere sitting in the doorway looking serious. "I'm here. And Monroe and Georgette are with you too."

"The fairies..." said Emerald's mother, staring at the cat and looking a bit bleary eyed. "The large, wingless fairies..."

"Correct," said Guinevere.

"And I was impressed I adjusted to magic and a talking cat," she said, reaching for the vodka. "Now warrior Tinkerbell's been in my kitchen and my adopted daughter is a genie."

"Adopted daughter," Maram repeated, her voice barely audible.

"So you're cool with Monroe now?" asked Emerald, raising her eyesbrows. "You literally vanish, disappear somewhere mysterious, and now you're back with a total change of heart?"

"I took time to think," said Guinevere, climbing elegantly onto a chair and sitting down primly, her tail slightly flicking.

"Sure you did," said Emerald, crossing her arms. "I think my mum's not the only one being left out of the loop here. How do you know Monroe? She's Commission."

"You know I was Commission. Before." said Guinevere.

"What's Commission?" asked Emerald's mum.

"Secret society of assholes who let people die and hide the evidence," said Emerald.

"No," said Guinevere. "They're the magical authority. They maintain order, liaise between orders of magic and tribes of magical people. They stop evil from taking hold of the world, Emerald."

"Whatever," grunted Emerald, and chugged back the last of the vodka in her glass then refilled it. "So Monroe, what's the deal?"

"She could help," said Guinevere. "I'll make contact."

"How?" asked Maram. "You're retired."

"You're in a coven," said Emerald's mum, her voice hollow.

"Yes," said Emerald, surprised by the non sequitur.

"Your power came in," she said.

"Yes," said Emerald, a sick feeling suddenly falling over her. "Years ago."

"I mean, I knew," she said. "Of course I knew. I guess I knew. I hadn't really thought about it. You have power?"

"Yes," said Emerald.

"Like your father?"

"Nothing like her father!" spat Guinevere. "Her father is a pathetic weasel of a man who sniffs the edges of true power. His father had such hopes. But Eric Wren is nothing but a failure, an adulterer, and a weakling."

"You know his father?" asked Emerald's mother. "You know Stuart Wren?"

Guinevere looked startled for a moment. "Yes," she said. "I do."

"How?"

"He's the reason I was assigned to Emerald's case," she said, looking at her paws.

"My grandfather is in The Commission?" asked Emerald, fury bubbling in her chest.

Guinevere shifted slightly and looked deeply uncomfortable. "Yes, he is."

"Was he in The Commission when he gave me Maram's lamp?"

"Yes," said Guinevere.

"He did this," said Emerald, standing up so suddenly her chair flung over backwards. "He knew, didn't he? He gave me the lamp, he sent you to me. He knew this would happen. That's why the Commission are cleaning up after this guy. They knew. That's why Monroe came to me. That's why Tig is dead. Because of him. He did this. He did this! And you knew! You fucking knew and you let it happen!"

"Emerald..." started Guinevere.

"No!" she shouted. "I'm just a pawn! I'm just a puppet! This was all one big set up since I was 8 years old!"

Guinevere held up a paw. "If you'd just listen."

"To what?" demanded Emerald. "Some lecture about how I should be grateful that you believe in me? What about free will, Guinevere? Does The Commission believe in that? Does it occur to them that I might have had opinions on the subject? That I might have wanted to make my own choices about my life? That I might have wanted to be in control of my own life just a little bit? Does it even matter to them? They don't own me!"

"Excuse me," said Maram, standing up as well. "You know nothing about losing your free will. Nothing! I'm just desperately trying to experience any scratch of life before I'm banished back to that fucking lamp because I don't even really have a life to live! You've had choices your whole life and you just take them for granted. You want to know about being a puppet? Ask me. Ask me about the masters I've had, the things I've done, the choices I've never been allowed to make. Ask me about the wishes I've granted. About the people I've killed, the lives I've ruined. You're upset because people believe you can stop a possessed woman killer and are doing everything they can to help you make that happen? What about me? I was given to you as a gift so you could do it apparently! I'm not even a person, I'm your fucking possession! Craving free will are you? Try being a genie!"

Emerald blinked furiously. "Guinevere, are you with us?"

"Always."

"Mum, you in?"

"Damn right, I am."

"Right," said Emerald. "Guienvere, call Monroe. Let's get an army on this."

Chapter Twenty

It was late and the hospital was quiet. Fadius had moved as stealthily as possible through the corridors and stair cases, ducking into corners and keeping his head low. He was taking a big risk being there, but with his cap dipped low over his eyes and his confidence he could escape with speed of feet and strength of fist if necessary, he knew it was worth the risk. If he didn't work out their powers, their strengths, they could surprise him again and next time it could be fatal.

Standing quietly outside the room of one of the witch's, he listened at the slightly open door.

"Join us?" came a voice from inside. "But... but why?"

"She needs the strength of a unit," came another voice, older and more rasping.

"I don't believe I asked you," snapped the first voice angrily.

"I... I..." a timid voice said. "I just. I don't have any... one. Else. Except my grandma. I don't ... my father died.. my mother she... she works... she works away for this lady. Dead lady. She's busy."

"So why is that our problem?" asked the first voice again.

"You're down a witch, yes?" asked the older voice. "I will not be around for much longer. She's not strong enough to go alone. You need a witch, she needs a coven."

"She's right you know," came a male voice, he assumed belonged to the young man with the shaved head who had attempted to burn him with pathetically small fireballs. "There's only the six of us now. We can't do this with just six."

"THEY LIE," came the voice in Fadius's head. "SIX IN A COVEN. SIX. WHY ARE THEY LYING? THEY WERE AT FULL STRENGTH WHEN THE WITCH DIED. THEY MUST HAVE A REPLACEMENT ALREADY! THEY ARE LYING. THE WITCHES LIE."

"Excuse me sir?" came a voice in front of him, cutting through the ringing ache left by the voice in his head.

He looked up and saw an elderly man wearing a purple uniform and pushing an empty wheelchair. "What?"

"Are you lost?" he asked. "This isn't visiting hours, sir. Are you on your way to an appointment?"

"I'm just leaving," snarled Fadius, turning to go.

"Sir, are you on your way to an appointment?"

"No," said Fadius, pulling the cap low and walking down the corridor.

"Sir!" shouted the elderly man, and suddenly an alarm sounded overhead.

"RUN," commanded the voice.

Fadius felt a surge of heat and strength blast through his body, his blood was hot, his heart was racing. Ahead of him two security guards, each holding a heavy stick, stepped in his path as he ran towards them. Without a thought he knocked them against the walls and raced past.

He turned a corner then crashed into a stairwell. A doctor in a white jacket holding a clipboard was at the top of the stairs and looked up startled, then reached for his pocket but Fadius knocked him down with a punch and the man rolled backwards down the stairs, landing in a crumpled heap which Fadius leapt smoothly over, bouncing off the wall and heading down the next staircase.

Two women staggered back in shock as Fadius spun around the next corner, and a nurse ricocheted from his body as he charged past and smacked hard into a wall with a cry of pain, then he was on the ground floor.

"LEFT," the voice announced.

Fadius burst through the door. An old woman with a walker fell to the ground with a scream of pain and a horrible crunch, and Fadius ran to the left.

"RIGHT," came the voice.

Fadius ran through a door to the outside where two more security guards came running towards him. In the distance he heard the screams of sirens.

The security guards landed on the ground as he slammed them with his fists, then he dived down the path and into bushes at the side as police cars tore up the road towards the building. Several officers leapt out and, after the fallen security guards shouted to them, made chase into the bushes behind him.

Another blast of power and energy surged through Fadius' tiring limbs and he soon lost his pursuers, running through the wooded area that ran down the side of the hospital land then, cat like, he scaled a tree and perched still and silent in the branches overhead, barely breathing. The dark of the evening enveloped him like a blanket, masking him in the dark shadows of the tree.

Below he could hear police officers running around, barking instructions to one another.

"FIND OUT WHY THE WITCHES LIE," demanded the voice. "FIND OUT WHO THE THEIR SIXTH MEMBER IS. FIND OUT THEIR POWERS. WITH THEIR STRENGTH YOU HAVE THEIR WEAKNESS."

Fadius nodded silently, then stayed in the tree until long after the police had dispersed.

ð

In Abigail's room Dafydd Jones carefully checked her vitals and marked them down on a chart.

"Poor girl," he whispered, slotting the chart back into the file on the end of the bed and shaking his head sadly. He had been a nurse for over a decade and felt fairly confident this girl wasn't going to wake up.

He stepped towards the door when behind him he heard a piercing scream.

Spinning he saw Abi sitting up in bed, her mouth wide in a piercing and tortured scream, her face pale and her eyes hollow.

"Jesus Christ," he shouted, then hit an alarm on the wall and raced to her side.

Abi stopped screaming and turned to face him. "He's coming," she whispered, then fell back against the pillow unconscious.

ð

Celeste felt sorry for the nurse that stood awkwardly in front of them. She didn't envy her the job she was doing. But none of that compared to how frightened she felt to find out why the alarms had been sounding.

"What do you mean he was here?" demanded Carla.

The alarms had stopped and feet had stopped racing past the room. Celeste was still holding onto Ben's hand so tightly that his skin was turning purple but she was starting to calm down. Of course, the information they were being presented with wasn't helping.

"I'm sorry, Miss Martinez," said the nurse. "We have security officials stationed around the building but he must have got past."

"Shit," muttered Ben.

"I've got to get to Abi," said Carla. "She's in danger."

"He left the building," said the nurse. "Abi is safe."

"For now," said Ben. "But clearly this guy isn't done with us."

"Maram isn't even here. What the hell was he doing?" asked Carla.

"Listening," said Celeste, shifting uncomfortably. "He was out there, right? He was listening to us talk."

"That's disturbing," said Ben.

"I'm sure the detective will be coming to talk to you," said the nurse. "And extra security guards are being positioned."

"And we all know what a good job the guards are doing, don't we?" said Carla, folding her arms.

"Yes well... call if you need anything at all," said the nurse before backing out and carefully closing the door.

"You'd all be dead right now," said Moira, "if he'd wanted to come in. You, me, Lila. All dead by his hand."

"We aren't though, are we," said Carla, not looking at her.

"Because you were ready?" asked Moira. "Or because you were lucky?"

Celeste watched Carla's face turn from annoyed to worried then back to annoyed.

"We'll stop him," said Ben. "Don't worry."

"How?" asked Moira. "He got to you in here, and if he can get to you in here he can get to you out there. Are you ready?"

"We stopped him last time," said Carla. "We can stop him again."

"Oh I'm sorry." Said Moira, nodding. "You're right. You are referring to that hugely successful endeavour whilst left most of you wounded in hospital and one of you dead in the morgue. Well done to you. You clearly have him running scared."

"Well he didn't come in, did he?" said Carla. "If we are no threat why didn't he just bust in here and kill us?"

"He was listening," said Celeste, staring at Carla as her thoughts cleared. "He doesn't know what we can do. He was listening to us. Learning about us."

"Why?" asked Ben.

"So he can be sure to win next time," said Celeste. "He's never struggled before, has he? The women have always ended up dead. I know you were joking, Moira, but I think you were right. He is scared."

"You don't know that," said Carla.

"Then you explain it," said Celeste. "You tell me why he was out there. Why he didn't bust in? We're weak, we're hurt, we're isolated. We know if he'd come in we'd be dead. He didn't. He was hurt and he wasn't expecting to be. He's learning about us."

"Shit," whispered Ben. "He'll be following Emerald and Maram too. We need to warn them."

"Why?" demanded Carla. "They didn't warn us!"

"Come on, Carla!" demanded Celeste. "Let it go! They fucked up, okay? We know that. Tig knows that more than any of us. But what are we going to do? Just let him kill them? Try and find three new witches for a coven that took years to form in the first place? We need each other now more than ever or he really will win!"

Carla glared at her furiously. "I'm going to Abi," she said.

"Carla... please..." said Celeste.

"Do you want to die?" Moira asked Carla.

"Excuse me?" asked Carla.

"That's what this man wants," she said. "Me? I would rip his throat out with my teeth. I would drink his blood. I would feast on his intestines."

"Ew," whispered Celeste.

"What's your point?" asked Carla.

"You said yourselves it took years to form the coven you've patchworked together," said Moira. "I'm about to die. I know this. I have not accomplished everything I had hoped I could since her mother left her behind. I had high hopes that Lila could set out on her own; follow in my footsteps. But she is weak. Without me to guide her she will never reach her full potential. You need a witch. Lila needs a coven. She has learned a lot from me and she is ready to kill. You'd be an idiot to reject her."

Lila looked ill.

"No," said Carla. "I'm not changing my mind just because that lunatic got past security. We don't know her, but we do know you and you're crazy. We don't need her."

"Then you will die," said Moira.

"At least I won't have eaten anyone's intestines, you sicko," muttered Carla, then stormed out of the room and shut the door behind her.

"Foolish girl," muttered Moira.

"She's hurting," said Celeste. "And angry. But I think she's wrong."

"So do I," agreed Ben. "We've got a lot going for us, but we need all the help we can get."

"I agree," said Celeste.

"Carla will never agree to it," said Ben. "We can't go behind her back."

"She'll come around," said Celeste. "And I'm not ready to risk us all waiting for her."

"Smart girl," said Moira.

"Lila, would you join us?" Celeste asked the young girl.

"I, yes, I," stuttered Lila. "I don't want to... eat intestines."

Celeste smiled reassuringly. "I don't want you to eat intestines either."

"Give it time," said Moira, leaning back on her pillow and smiling. "Give it time."

ð

"Miss Martinez," said a doctor who was reading Abi's chart as Carla stepped into Abi's room. "There have been developments."

"What?" asked Carla, pushing past him and seeing Abi still unconscious on the bed. "What happened?"

"Miss Stone woke up," she said. "Only briefly. But she woke up and she communicated with one of our nurses."

"Oh my god!" Carla cried, her heart raced and she felt tears of joy spring to her eyes. She raced past him and put her hand gently on Abi's. "That's wonderful!"

"It doesn't necessarily mean anything huge," said the doctor, putting the chart down. "But she appears to be in a heavy sleep now, rather than a coma."

"Sleep?" asked Carla, a smile on her face so wide that her cheeks were hurting. "Sleep she can wake up from!"

"Potentially, yes," agreed the doctor, putting a hand on Carla's shoulder. "We're not out of the woods yet but it's definitely something to hold onto."

"That's wonderful, that's amazing," said Carla, stroking Abi's cheek as she sank into the chair by her pillow. "Thank you. Thank you so much."

"You're very welcome," said the doctor, setting the clipboard down in the end of the bed and turning to go.

"Wait," said Carla. "You said she communicated?"

"Yes, she spoke to the nurse who was in here," said the doctor.

"What did she say?"

"Oh, well, it's a little peculiar but it would make sense, she may still have been in a dream like state," said the doctor. "She said 'he's coming'."

"Who?" asked Carla, standing up. "The man who was outside our room? When was this? She was warning us?"

"No, no," said the doctor, her hands up. "I'm aware of your situation, Miss Martinez, and I know the man who attacked you was in the hospital and I know how frightened you must have been. But this incident with Miss Stone happened after the man had already been chased from the building. And anyway, she was unconscious. I promise, the two incidents are not related."

"He's coming," Carla repeated, then leant her head against the wall behind her.

ð

"Lord, why must I hide?" Fadius asked as he slunk through the darkness away from the hospital grounds.

He was confused, he was tired. The surge in strength he had experienced had subsided and his body was aching. His wounded eye was stinging and making his whole face throb. He needed sleep.

"NOTHING CAN INTERFERE WITH OUR PROGRESS," boomed the voice making his already aching head pound with pain. "WE ARE RUNNING OUT OF TIME."

"Lord, please," whispered Fadius as he collapsed to the ground behind a spike covered bush that scratched at his skin. "I just need to understand. I need to know why I'm doing this. Why can you not simply destroy her yourself?"

"YOU QUESTION YOUR LORD, FADIUS!" boomed the voice even louder than before. Fadius howled in pain and put his hands to his head. When he took them down again he saw blood. His nose was bleeding.

"No, Lord, no," he insisted. "I just don't understand. They seem... scared. They don't seem prepared. We could end it now. The witches in the hospital are hurt. The bearer of Beast and her ally are isolated. Surely now is the time to strike, Lord. Now is the time to end it."

"WE WERE SURPRISED BEFORE, FADIUS. I WILL NOT BE SURPRISED AGAIN. WE ARE RUNNING OUT OF TIME. I WILL NOT TAKE ANY CHANCES."

"Running out of time?" asked Fadius, questions banging around the pain of his head so hard they almost hurt more than the voice. What time? What was coming?

"FADIUS!" the voice roared. Fadius fell back onto the ground, his hands to his head as he curled in a ball crying in pain. "I CAN GIVE, BUT I CAN TAKE AWAY!"

Fadius felt pain through his body like nothing he had ever experienced. It felt like his blood was boiling, his limbs were dead weights. His chest was heavy and he struggled to breathe. Tears flooded his face from his remaining eye as he sobbed in agony and fear.

"I'm sorry, Lord," he wept. "I'm sorry. I'm so sorry. I'm so, so sorry. Please Lord, please."

The pain lessened and Fadius felt his body start to relax.

"NEVER QUESTION ME AGAIN, FADIUS."

"No Lord," Fadius promised. "Never again. I promise."

Chapter Twenty-One

True to her word, Guinevere had contacted the Fae and the following morning Emerald, Maram, Guinevere, Monroe and Georgette were sitting around the kitchen table in Emerald's mother's house. Despite Monroe's protestations, Emerald had insisted her mother remain present for the meeting, so she was busy preparing eggs and toast for everyone.

"We don't know as much as we would like," said Monroe, holding a mug of coffee and looking stern. "Unfortunately the Commission is very good at compartmentalising. But we know the Ubel Project has been running for many, many years."

"Why hasn't he been stopped yet?" asked Maram. "He's been killing women all over the world."

"No, he hasn't," said Georgette.

"Yes he has," insisted Emerald. "We tracked it."

"It wasn't all this man," said Georgette. "Other men have taken up the mantle of executioner. This man is the latest in a succession of men intent on murdering and maiming their way across the world to find you."

"As one dies, the next takes the challenge," said Monroe. "That much we do know."

"But... why hasn't the Commission stopped him?" asked Emerald.

"Because they can't," said Monroe. "They can stop the individual but not the whole endeavour. It's not about taking the head off the beast, it's about killing the beast."

Emerald put her head in her hands. "Great," she said miserably. "A whole organisation of powerful people can't stop him but they expect me to. Just great."

"So how are we doing it?" asked Maram.

"What is your power?" Georgette asked Emerald as Emerald's mother placed a plate of scrambled eggs on toast in front of her.

"I... Hulk out," said Emerald, embarrassed but not sure how else to describe it.

"You do what?" asked Emerald's mother.

"Hulk out," Georgette repeated, very slowly.

"What is hulking out?" asked Monroe.

"Like the Incredible Hulk," said Emerald. "But without the green. From the comic books."

"Hannah would have understood," said Monroe, sadness appearing on her face momentarily.

"She gets big and strong and angry," explained Maram. "Beats the shit out of anyone who gets in her way."

"Superb," said Monroe.

"You do that?" asked Emerald's mother, leaning on the kitchen counter.

"Yes, mum," said Emerald.

"Oh heavens," she gasped.

"And you, do the Jinn have any power beyond wish granting?"

"Not many, but I can sense if someone has power and sometimes I can feel emotions," said Maram. "And the magic works through me. The coven's strength affects me."

"That's useless to us," said Monroe dismissively.

Maram looked back at Monroe, irritated. "Okay, fairy, what's your power?"

"Fae," snapped Monroe. "We are not fairies."

"Fine," said Maram. "What are Fae powers?"

"We work spells," said Georgette. "The Speakers and Enchanters of your community are similar to our magic."

Guinevere's tail flicked. "What?" Emerald asked her.

A sound crunched outside the window and they started and looked around but nothing was there. Guinevere turned back to them.

"You'll need more than the Fae," said the cat. "This is... big. Bigger than I had initially anticipated. You'll need the strength of your coven."

"Well Abi's in a coma and Tig's dead," said Emerald. "And Carla, Ben and Celeste don't want anything to do with us. We're on our own. So I don't have that option."

"Well you're going to need to sort that out," said Georgette, not a flash of sympathy showing on her strong face. "Whatever petty squabbles you have going on are irrelevant in the face of this monster."

Emerald and Maram glanced at each other. "We'll try," said Maram. "I don't know if they'll be interested. They're scared and they're angry. They don't trust us."

"We have spells and an army of Fae ready to work with them," said Monroe. "That is not something to take lightly. That is something to be respected. I will not send my people in unless I know they will have everything they need to succeed. I will not sacrifice them for nothing. Hannah's death will be avenged."

"I understand," said Emerald, bobbing her head and feeling like she was being told off in school.

"We just need to find him," said Georgette.

"How do we do that?" asked Emerald.

"I don't know," said Monroe.

"He can't be far away," said Maram. "He was hurt and I'm still alive."

"We just have to find him before he finds us," said Emerald.

ð

Outside the window, Fadius watched the witch and the Bearer of the Beast in conversation with two small women. Were they the new coven members?

"GET CLOSER," the voice commanded.

"I can't," whispered Fadius.

"WE NEED TO KNOW THEIR POWERS."

Fadius crept closer to the window, stepping into a pebbled spot below the kitchen window with a loud crunch. He jumped and pressed himself back against the wall.

Inside the speaking stopped momentarily then started again.

"FAE," came the voice. "FAIRIES. PATHETIC."

"Fairies?" asked Fadius.

"THEY ARE DESPERATE IF THEY ARE BRINGING IN FAIRIES," the voice boomed in what was close to a laugh. "LET US PREPARE. THE TIME IS NEARLY UPON US. WE WILL DESTROY THEM."

"Them?" asked Fadius as he crept away from the house. "The Bearer of the Beast is the only one who needs to die."

"DO NOT QUESTION ME," the voice shrieked. "THEY ALL DESERVE TO DIE."

"Yes, Lord," agreed Fadius.

ð

Carla sat contorted on the plastic seat at Abi's bedside, her body curved onto the bed, her head resting on the blanket at Abi's side. She had tried many positions over the night but none were proving comfortable, but she missed lying at Abi's side so much that she was willing to endure the discomfort. The nurses had begged her to return to her own room for rest but when she had refused they had agreed to do her vitals there in Abi's room, and had prescribed painkillers she refused to take.

"I need to be alert," she had said. He could come back. She wouldn't leave Abi unprotected.

Her eyes felt heavy. She let them close for just a moment. Just a moment.

"Carla?"

Carla's eyes snapped open. She sat upright and stared. Was she dreaming. No, she wasn't. Abi was sitting up, staring at her through dark eyes. "Oh Abi! You're awake, oh I love you, I love you so much."

Carla flung her arms around Abi's fragile body and held her close, kissing her cheeks, her neck, her ears and her eyes, her hands in her hair and on her shoulders and her waist.

"Carla," Abi whispered, taking Carla's wrists and pushing her back. "Wait."

"Of course," said Carla, cupping Abi's face and resting her forehead against hers. "Of course my darling. Anything."

"She walks amongst us but all alone. Her life is real but not her own."

"I know," said Carla, sitting back and looking into Abi's eyes. "It's Maram."

"The eleventh moon rises, the eleventh night sky, the demon will rise, together they die," Abi went on.

"Wait, what?" asked Carla.

"I've heard nothing else," said Abi quietly, tears running down her cheeks. "Nothing but those words... and screaming. He's coming, Carla, he's coming. It's getting louder. He's coming. I saw his face. The demon. I saw his face. He's coming."

Carla pulled Abi into a hug and held her tightly, kissing her head. "Okay, honey. We'll figure it out. I promise. We'll figure it out."

"I'm frightened," said Abi, staring into Carla's eyes.

"I know baby, I know," said Carla. "We're safe now. He doesn't want us. We're safe."

"What?" asked Abi, sitting back. "What do you mean?"

"It's not us," said Carla, taking Abi's hand and kissing her fingers.

"I know," said Abi. "We thought it was Lara."

"Lara died," said Carla, remembering just how much Abi had missed. How much had happened. Then a sickness rose in her chest. "And... oh Abi, I'm so sorry... Tig's dead."

"Tig?" cried Abi, her face crumbling as huge heavy tears ran down her cheeks. "Are you sure?"

"Yes," said Carla, feeling tears streaming down her own cheeks. "She died. He killed her."

"The demon?"

"No, the fire guy, from your vision," said Carla. "He was coming for Maram and Tig saved her."

Abi broke down and cried. Huge gut wrenching sobs that shook her whole body.

A nurse came running in and when she saw Abi she cried out in surprise. "Doctor!" the nurse shouted. "Get me a doctor in here!"

"We have to stop him," Abi said, staring at Carla as the nurse frantically started strapping things to her.

"No, we don't," said Carla.

"Lie down, please," said the nurse.

Abi obeyed but didn't take her eyes off Carla. "Why not? Didn't you hear what I said?"

"I heard you," said Carla. "But it's not our problem anymore. He doesn't want us. We're going to be fine."

Abi sat back up, startling the nurse who took a step back, letting her speak. "What are you talking about?" she cried. "Of course it is! Of course it's our problem! What are you talking about? You said he's after Maram!"

"It's complicated," said Carla. "But we're going to go away. You and me. We aren't responsible for Maram. I'm going to keep you safe far away from here."

"Please," said the nurse. "I know you need to catch up, I know this is important, but please. I need you to lie down. I need to make sure you're safe."

Abi lay down and turned her face away. The doctor ran in and started talking to the nurse and to Abi, asking her questions and jotting down notes.

"Abi..." said Carla, reaching for her hand, but Abi pulled it away.

"You're not who I thought you were," she said, tears running down her cheeks.

"Can you wait outside for a moment please, Miss Martinez?" asked the nurse, putting a gentle hand on Carla's shoulder.

Carla looked up at her and tried to stand but couldn't. She felt weak. Dizzy. Looking again at Abi who was talking to the doctor quietly, describing how she felt and what she remembered, Carla forced herself to her feet and followed the nurse outside.

"Will she be okay?" Carla asked her, her voice trembling.

"We don't know just yet," said the nurse. "But we need her not to be stressed right now. She's been through a trauma. She needs some quiet."

Carla nodded, tears flooding her cheeks. As the nurse slipped back into the room, pulling the door closed behind her, Carla sank into one of the plastic seats that lined the wall and sobbed.

ð

"I'd advise you to go home," said the doctor who Celeste didn't recognise. "In my opinion, you'd be perfectly safe there. Given the incident last night you may even be safer at home than here."

"Oh..." said Celeste, surprised. "I see."

"Would you like to go home?" he asked, leaning in.

"I would," said Celeste. She didn't want to go home, but she did want to go to Emerald and Maram and warn them.

"Excellent," he said, closing the folder in his lap and smiling broadly. "Good to know. Well then, you're free to leave. I'll be speaking with your friends as well in due course."

"Really?" asked Celeste. Her ribs were broken, her body bruised, her head wounded. She was still wired to machines, still being given pain killers and antibiotics via a drip. "I was told I'd be here a while. It's only been a couple of days. Is it really safe to go?"

"I know it has been very hard but we are very impressed with your recovery," he said, earnestly.

"We've got broken bones..." said Celeste.

"Miss Williams," said the doctor, tilting his head to the side. "I think you're stronger than you think you are. I also think that you'll do better out there than you will in here. There's a lot of healing that can be done in the comfort of your normal life."

"Right," said Celeste. "I see."

The doctor stood. "I've signed your discharge notes, you can leave as soon as you're ready!"

"Erm, thank you, Dr Tribble," said Celeste.

The doctor pulled open the curtain around her bed and went to leave.

"Excuse me, doctor," called Moira from her bed.

"Yes? Mrs erm.."

"Miss," said Moira.

"Miss, sorry," said the doctor, glancing to the door.

"Where did you qualify?"

"Excuse me?" he asked, staring at her with a confused face.

"To be a doctor," she asked him. "Where did you qualify?"

"Birmingham," he said.

"When?"

"1983," he said.

"I see. You were under Dr Gibson then, I presume?"

"Dr Gibson?" he asked, cocking his head and frowning at her in utter bewilderment before straightening himself out.

"Yes," said the Moira. "Dr Gibson was resident in Birmingham at that time, wasn't he?"

"Yes," he said. "Yes he was. Right, I'll be on my way. Good day, ladies."

After he'd left and closed the door, Celeste swung her legs and put her feet on the floor. Her head pounded.

"Who's Dr Gibson?" she asked Moira after the pain had stopped throbbing so intensely.

"I have no idea," said Moira.

Celeste gave her a look as bewildered as the doctor had just made. "What?"

"He's a fraud," she said. "One of them. That murderer is not the only one watching you, my girl. And quite frankly I don't know who I'd sooner pit my teeth against."

"One of them?" asked Celeste, glancing nervously at the door, then wincing as her head banged.

"Commission," she said. "Interfering bastards who think they rule the planet."

"Oh..." she fiddled nervously with her necklace.

"Call Lila," said Moira, sternly. "Deal with the man, and watch your back. If they're involved it cannot mean anything good, and if they want you out of here there's a reason for it. And for God's sake get yourself a Healer. I'm trusting you with my granddaughter and I don't know how you expect to do what you're doing without a good Healer."

Chapter Twenty-Two

"They're not going to go for it," said Maram as they walked along the path past the woodlands, the cold air dry and bright as the late morning sun sat high in the sky. It was the first day in a while with no rain.

"They might," said Emerald, a sinking feeling in her heart.

"Dibs you tell Monroe when they don't," said Maram.

"Get lost! She's terrifying, you do it!"

"Not a chance," said Maram.

"What scares you more," said Emerald. "Telling Monroe they're not joining us, or asking them to join us in the first place?"

"Erm..."

"I'm about equal on both, so you pick and I'll do the other," said Emerald as they approached the doors of the hospital.

"You tell Monroe," said Maram as the doors to the hospital opened with a swoosh and they stepped into the foyer.

"Deal," said Emerald.

Sitting together in a huddle in the corner of the room were Carla, Ben, Celeste, Abi and a strange girl Emerald didn't recognise. They turned their faces and stared at

them as they stepped inside. Emerald and Maram froze.
"Shit," said Maram. "I change my mind. I'll tell Monroe."

"Fuck off!" hissed Emerald. "You made your choice!"

"Goddammit!"

"What are you doing here?" asked Carla, standing up. Several people in the foyer stopped and stared. At her side Celeste tried to get Carla to sit back down but she shook her off.

Emerald led them towards the group, avoiding a woman with a cleaning trolley and an old couple with sticks. As they reached the corner, five faces stared up at them, including one Emerald didn't know but thought, vaguely, she recognised.

"We... wanted to..." stuttered Maram. "I mean Emerald thought..."

Emerald elbowed her hard in the ribs and Maram yelped.

"What?" asked Carla. "You want to apologise again?"

"Carla," said Abi, her voice more serious than Emerald could ever remember hearing it. "Stop it."

Carla looked round at her then sat down. "Sorry," she said.

"Maybe you can do Monroe," whispered Maram.

Abi stood up and beckoned them to sit. "Please," she said. "This is important. You need to be involved."

Emerald caught Maram's eye and shrugged. Whatever she expected it wasn't this. Not knowing what else to do, she lowered herself into the empty chair beside Ben, who smiled a half smile at her, and Maram sat on her other side next to a girl Emerald didn't know and who was busy twisting her fingers in her lap nervously.

"So... you're awake Abi!" said Emerald. "That's great!"

"I've been told what happened," said Abi, a calm strength radiating from her that Emerald was struggling to get used to. By the look on Carla's face it was taking her by surprise too.

"I'm sorry," said Maram.

"Now isn't the time," said Abi, holding up a hand.

"Oh," said Maram, raising her eyebrows and looking at Emerald who shrugged.

"She walks amongst us but all alone, her life is real but not her own," said Abi. "The eleventh moon rises, the eleventh night sky, the demon will rise, together they die."

"What?" asked Emerald.

"The rest of the prophecy," said Abi. "Now we know the first part is about you, Maram, we can assume the rest is. Which means time is of the essence."

"It is?" asked Maram.

"Tomorrow night you will come together and you will both die," said Abi, her voice was unnervingly calm, her face unemotional.

"What?" asked Emerald. "What are you talking about?"

"If we want to stop the prophecy we need to kill him before tomorrow night," said Abi.

"Or I'll die..." said Maram.

"Yes," said Abi.

Maram nodded, tears starting to trickle down her cheeks. "I guess that makes sense," she said. "I should have known it couldn't last forever."

"This is bullshit!" shouted Emerald. "What do you mean she's going to die? Why?"

"Why is her life real but not her own?" asked Carla.

Emerald looked at Maram who was quietly weeping. "Because she's a genie."

"A what?" asked Ben.

"A genie," Maram said, then began to sob.

"I don't understand," whispered Celeste.

"An actual genie?" asked Ben. "As in lives in a lamp and grants wishes type genie? Like in Aladdin?"

Next to Emerald, Maram was nodding miserably. There were shocked looks exchanged around the group.

"She's a... she's a slave..." said the strange girl. "Someone else owns her life. That's why it's not her own."

"Who are you?" demanded Emerald, peering at her. She was so familiar. But where from?

"L... Lila... Lila Berry," said the girl, tucking some of her dark curls behind her left ear and staring at her feet.

"Why are you here?" asked Emerald.

"She's here because I invited her," said Abi. "Because Tig is dead. Because we need a seventh."

"Or, perhaps we just need a sixth," said Celeste looking crestfallen. "Given that Maram is apparently not actually a witch."

"You're such a liar," growled Carla, staring at Maram.

"Back off," snapped Emerald.

"Why?" demanded Carla.

Abi stood. "We are a coven of seven," she said. "Maram is our sister witch and has fought at our side time and time again. Tig did not die for nothing, she died for Maram. She died for us. We could all be dead now if she hadn't sacrificed herself, and to walk away from that now is the ultimate insult to the woman she was."

Emerald watched Abi speak in amazement. Everyone stared at her, captivated, listening. She was leading them in a way Emerald had always been expected to do but had always fallen short of. What had happened to her in that coma?

"Emerald, Maram," Abi said, sitting down. "We are all together on this, are you with us?"

"Yes," said Emerald.

"Yes," said Maram.

"Then let's join hands," said Abi, holding out her hands to Lila on her left and Carla on her right.

Hesitantly Maram placed her hand in Lila's. Emerald took her other, then took Ben's who took Celeste's. As the circle was completed the heat began to surge through them. Reconnected now for the first time since before Tig's death, Emerald felt the power swell inside her like an instant relief from the tired weight of life. She breathed deeply, the golden light filling her.

When they let go, Emerald turned to Maram who was smiling and crying and gave her a hug.

"We can do this," she promised her.

Maram nodded but the sadness in her eyes was back and Emerald knew she didn't believe her.

"Emerald, what's your plan?" asked Abi.

"Erm, I don't really have one," Emerald admitted. "But I do have a fairy warrior and her very angry daughter in the kitchen at home having lunch with my mum."

Everyone was silent for a moment then Celeste started to laugh. The tension broke and everyone else started to laugh too, even Carla.

"I'm serious!" insisted Emerald. "Her name's Monroe and she's the most terrifying person I've ever met in my life!"

"That's because you've never met my grandma," said Lila.

"She's got a point there," said Celeste.

"We have a lot to talk about," said Abi. "Shall we go to your fairy warrior and start making plans?"

Emerald blinked. This new Abi confusing her and impressing her in equal measure.

"Yeah," she said. "Let's go."

As the seven women walked out of the hospital Maram leaned into Emerald. "I never thought this would happen you know," she said quietly.

"Me neither," Emerald replied.

"Hey, I'll do you a favour," said Maram. "I'll tell Monroe."

ð

As the seven of them walked into the kitchen at Emerald's mother's house, a rather shaken Olivia Wren stood up and relinquished her seat. Monroe and Georgette also stood, no surprise on their face nor even pleasure. It was as if they had simply expected it. Guinevere remained seated, her eyes narrow.

"Are we ready to begin?" asked Monroe.

"Erm, yes," said Emerald. "Yes we are. This is Abi, she's a Seer, Carla who's a bone breaker. This is Ben who's a Firestarter and Celeste who's telekinetic. And this is Lila who... is... new..."

"I'm a... a... sh.... sh... shapeshifter," said Lila, looking at the floor.

"Oh right," said Emerald, frowning. Something was nagging at her brain and she couldn't work out what.

"I change into animals," said Lila.

"Well," said Monroe. "With witches, a genie, and an army of Fae, I think we have something we can work with."

ð

"So now we know," whispered Fadius.

"NOW WE PREPARE. WE STRIKE BEFORE SUNDOWN TOMORROW NIGHT."

ð

"Hello again, Guinevere," said Nahla as the cat was ushered in. "Do we have some progress?"

"Are you aware of the second part of the prophecy?" the cat asked.

"Yes," said Nahla. "The Vision reported it to us recently. We made moves to enable the coven to assemble for battle."

The cat nodded. "Of course."

"Anything more?"

"Does Mr Wren need to be present if it pertains to his granddaughter?"

Nahla sighed and picked up the phone. "Get me Wren."

A moment later the door behind Guinevere opened and Stuart Wren walked in. "You rang?"

"You knocked?" Nahla asked, raising her eyebrows.

Stuart Wren wrapped his knuckles on the open door, then came in and sat on one of the plush leather chairs. "Where are we up to?"

"The Coven has reassembled," Guinevere reported. "Agatha Moss has been replaced by Lila Berry, a young shape shifter. Her mother left her for the Power movement and she has been raised by her grandmother,

Moira. By all accounts the grandmother appears to be a serial killer but she only murdered mortal men so is unlikely to have shown up on your radar."

"And Monroe?" asked Nahla.

"She's in place. She and Georgette have pledged twenty Fae to the battle," said Guinevere.

"Only twenty?" asked Stuart, raising his eyebrows. "I thought she was bringing an army."

"The Fae are dying out," said Nahla in an irritated growl. "For Monroe to be both risking and able to find twenty of her people willing to take on an unknown monster to avenge the death of her daughter you can be sure this is taken seriously."

"It'll be over by nightfall tomorrow night," confirmed Guinevere. "If the prophecy is correct the problem will be neutralised."

"It's a shame to lose a Genie," said Nahla. "Especially one I could have brought in. They're never available long enough before being moved on." She sighed and shook her head momentarily. "Such is life I suppose."

"And Emerald?" asked Stuart. "Is she in place for the next phase?"

Guinevere hesitated. "That could be a little trickier, Mr Wren,"

"Then it's time to make it simpler, isn't it?" said Stuart.

"Yes, Mr Wren," Guinevere agreed.

"Thank you, Guinevere," said Nahla.

Guinevere stood, nodded respectfully to both, then left the room.

For a moment the two stood in silence.

"Our time together will be over again soon, old friend," said Stuart, sitting casually on the edge of Nahla's desk.

"Get your ass off my desk," said Nahla, smacking at him with a hand.

The man laughed and slid off then walked to the door. "The next few hours will be interesting," he said.

"Aren't they all?" asked Nahla.

"Some more than others," said Stuart, then stepped out and closed the door behind him.

Chapter Twenty-Three

The rain was heavy and the trees were thick, so any light from the setting sun was covered by clouds and leaves before it reached Fadius. He stumbled through the woods outside the town, his legs aching from the five hour walk he had been sent on.

"FURTHER," the voice in his head boomed.

"Yes Lord," muttered Fadius. His legs ached, his back ached. The dark of the woods was oppressive and he kept tripping on sticks and rocks underfoot.

Something moved at his left, a scurrying crunching noise. He startled and looked around, peering through the gloom but seeing only the shadows of trees and plants as the rain masked any clarity he would be able to achieve.

He shivered.

Stumbling on a rock he fell to the ground, his hands landing heavily in the wet earth, slime and leaves sticking to him. He cried out in pain and disgust as he tried to push himself up.

Something cold touched the back of his neck. Fadius howled, spinning on the spot and putting his hands out trying to feel what was there, the darkness seeming blacker than before.

"Who's there?" he cried out, pushing himself backwards through the dirt, skidding on the mud as sticks and rocks cut his hands and back.

"GET UP, FADIUS," the voice boomed.

Breathing hard and shaking with cold and fear, Fadius staggered to his feet, wiping the cold sweat from his brow and staring around wildly.

The air felt thick and wet, like syrup. It stuck in his throat and glooped into his lungs.

He kept walking, glancing around in fear, until before him an enormous building loomed in a clearing.

It was old and brick, with a broken roof and no windows, just a large, shabby wooden door sitting loosely in a frame. It looked abandoned and derelict. And dark. So dark.

What was he supposed to do? Knock?

The wind whipped the rain hard into his face, eyes and ears and he was soaked through, coated in mud, and scratched all over. Outside was pain and cold, inside would at least be dry.

Of course, what was in there he didn't know. Why had he been sent here? What waited inside that he could use to take on the witches? His energy was drained, his body battered. If it was a weapon, could he lift it? If it was some kind of monster, could he restrain it?

"OPEN THE DOOR FADIUS," the voice boomed ominously in his head.

His filthy, bleeding hand shook violently as he raised it to the door. Pressing his hand against the rotting wood he pushed. It swung open with a painful creak and bumped against the wall of a dark corridor behind.

Fadius stared into the pitch black ahead of him. Looking back over his shoulder the grey gloom of the wood behind him suddenly felt welcoming and inviting.

"GO IN, FADIUS, NOW," the voice ordered.

Hesitantly, Fadius placed a foot on the stone floor of the corridor. As soon as he stepped inside, the sound of the rain, the noise of the woods outside, vanished. It was like stepping into a vacuum. Silence fell like a deafening blanket, smothering everything around him.

His heart raced.

Walking forwards he kept his right hand against the wall to guide him, taking slow, nervous steps, feeling for a drop or obstacles before him with each movement of his foot. There was no light at all. No sound.

He walked on and on. The path didn't rise or fall, it didn't turn or curve. Straight, dark, silence surrounded him for so long he wondered if he'd imagined noise ever really existed at all, for so long that his feet were starting to lose the ability to support his weight. He felt dizzy and sick. Had he been walking for hours? Days?

Then the path came to a stop.

He felt in front of him and there was the same brick as the wall he'd been touching. He reached out with his left hand but the other wall was still there too. It was a dead end. Panicked, exhausted and desperate, Fadius felt around frantically, running his hands over the rough brick looking for some kind of door or opening but there was nothing.

Falling to his knees he began to sob. "Help me, Lord, please..." he begged but the voice was silent.

What was he supposed to do? Go back? Wait? What was happening? He'd walked so far. His body ached. He stank of old blood and old sweat and old filth, mixed with the mud and grime of the woods outside. He sobbed. The passage felt like it was miles long and the walk back to yet more walking in the cold and the rain felt like an impossible task. Filled with self loathing, misery and exhaustion, Fadius curled up on the floor and cried.

After a few minutes, possibly an hour it was almost impossible to tell, Fadius started to hear the sound of cello music.

He opened his eyes and startled then threw himself backwards. He was no longer in the pitch dark alley, but a warmly lit living room with a roaring fire and a fluffy rug, vases of fresh flowers and lots of knitted cushions and blankets adorning every surface. A woman with grey curls, pink rimmed glasses and a pair of sensible trousers sat at a small table knitting in rich turquoise wool.

"Hello there, deary," she greeted Fadius. "You certainly took a long time getting here. Do shut the door, will you? I'm not paying to heat the forest."

Fadius stared at her, his mouth hanging open, then turned to look behind him. The rotten, rickety door was directly behind him, still ajar as he had left it, and looking out onto the dark, rainy woodlands he had left so many hours before.

"What?" he eventually managed to ask.

"Oh come now," she tutted, putting the knitting down carefully then standing up.

She was small, and plump, with a gentle face and kind eyes. She moved slowly with a slight limp, and when she stepped past him to close the door he got the scent of some floral perfume.

"Where am I?" Fadius asked. "Who are you? Why am I here?"

"Well," said the woman, walking back to her seat and picking up her knitting again. "I'm known by a few names in a few circles. I suppose it depends who sent you here. I'm known as Aglorion to some. The Deleterious to others."

"The what?" asked Fadius, utterly confused and starting to wonder if he was dreaming.

"Deleterious, dear," said the woman as though that made it clearer.

"Oh," said Fadius, rubbing his head. Where was his Lord? Why did he feel like he was alone all of a sudden? Why had he been sent to this insane woman? He stood up from the floor and then wondered if he was permitted to sit on the sofa, but felt too shy to ask.

"For a brief while there was a tribe in Taiwan who named me the Goddess of Ruin, though I didn't much care for that one," she said, her knitting needles clacking together as soft violin music strummed from a sound system somewhere in the room. "Far too grand."

"Oh," said Fadius.

The woman looked at him and put her knitting down. "My mother named me Jenny," she said. "Jennifer Archer. And you?"

"Erm, Fadius Kalm," said Fadius.

"And I thought Goddess of Ruin was grand," said Jenny, raising her eyebrows. "So, Mister Kalm, why don't you tell me why you're here and I'll see if I'm able to help you."

"I was sent here," he said. "by God."

Laughter erupted from Jenny. She laughed so hard she had to put down her knitting and wipe her eyes. Eventually, when she was able to, she said, "Of course you were! Oh dear, of course."

Fadius frowned. He felt like he was being mocked though couldn't work out why.

"Yes," he said eventually, and in a voice more petulant than he had intended. "He sent me here to get what I need to fight a coven of witches, a genie, and an army of Fae."

"Oh he did, did he?" she said. "I assume he told you there will be a price."

"Erm, okay," said Fadius, desperately wishing the voice would come back.

"Are these witches born of power?" she asked him, picking up a notebook and pen from the table beside her.

"I... I assume so," said Fadius.

"Are you certain? These are not Virilicae?"

"Virili-what?" asked Fadius, his head hurting. What was happening?

The woman rolled her eyes. "If your *God* wasn't such a coward he could have told me all this himself. Why he's sent me a rube I do not know."

"I... am..." Fadius stammered. "Helping."

"Of course you are, dear," she said, nodding in an annoyingly patronising way. "Are they men or women?"

"Five women, one man," he said.

"Born of power then," she said. "The Virilicae are a dreadfully patriarchal lot. I don't enjoy my encounters with them at all."

Fadius stared at her. He towered over her. He was strong, and fit, and covered in so much mud and blood that he must have made a terrible sight. But the woman spoke to him and made him feel like he was a little boy asking a teacher if he was allowed to go to the toilet.

"So," she said. "Why don't you take a seat and tell me what we're dealing with. And don't look so frightened, deary, I'm not that scary."

Fadius opened and closed his mouth like a goldfish, then obediently sat. Whatever was happening he was here, he might as well do his job.

ð

Turning over in her childhood bed, Emerald spotted Maram sitting in the window staring out.

"Hey," she said quietly.

For a moment Maram didn't move, then she turned to Emerald. Her face was blotchy and gaunt, and the moonlight of the early hours made her look grey and frail. "Hi," she said, then sniffed heavily and wiped her nose with the back of her hand.

"You alright?"

"No."

Emerald nodded, she felt stupid. "I'm sorry," she said.

"Not your fault," said Maram with a shrug, gazing back out of the window. "I'm just so stupid."

"You're not stupid," said Emerald, slipping out of bed and sitting down next to Maram.

"I'm going to die, Em," she said. "Actually die."

"You don't know that," said Emerald. "We're going to find him, we're going to stop him."

"Foolish thing is," Maram went on as if she hadn't heard her. "I've wanted to die so many times. Wished for death. And now... in this life... I've felt like I'll actually get the opportunity to die but a good death. I wanted to die at the end of a long life, as an old lady with a lifetime of memories behind me."

"It can still happen!" insisted Emerald.

"You heard Abi," said Maram. "Together they die. We know it's about me. I'm going to die to stop him."

"Let's leave," said Emerald, taking Maram's hands. "We don't have to stay. Let's just go. Get a bus or a train and just leave."

"Leave everyone to die?" asked Maram.

"You don't know that'll happen," whispered Emerald, her eyes dropping.

"Tig died because I was a coward," said Maram. "It explains why he's coming for me, doesn't it? He knows I'm the only one who can kill him otherwise he wouldn't bother. I can't run away. Not again. Nobody else is going to die so I can live, Em."

"You're so brave," said Emerald, tears slipping down her cheeks.

Maram shrugged. "I'm not," she said. "I'm terrified. I love this life, Emerald. I love it more than I can ever tell you. I can remember every single second of my time with you. Every single one. I've lived a thousand lives and not one even comes close to the magic of this one. And I'm absolutely petrified of dying."

"I'll be with you," Emerald promised, crying hard.

"I know," she said. "You always have been."

"I always will."

The two girls sat in the window of the room where they had first met and gazed out. The moon was dropping and the grey of the clouds overhead was turning from a dirty charcoal to a cold steel and a fierce rain battered the window. It was November 11th, the day Maram was destined to die.

Chapter Twenty-Four

When Fadius finally made his way back to the town it was dawn, the light was cool and grey, and a miserable drizzle fell all around him. He was filthy, sweating and exhausted, and utterly confused. He had not heard the Voice since before he met Jenny. He looked at the list in his hand and assumed he just had to carry on and do as the woman had said, gather what she needed and then return.

But without the Voice, did he really have to? Could he just find somewhere to sleep? A shelter? Anything? If the Voice was gone, perhaps his servitude was finished.

But what if it came back and he hadn't performed his duties? Where can you go to hide from a voice in your head?

First on the list was a laburnum.

Folding the list and stuffing it into his pocket, Fadius set off on his raw aching feet for the market, not sure if he hoped the voice would return to make his work justified, or if it would stay gone so he could finally get some peace.

ð

As the coven emerged from various bedrooms in Emerald's mother's house, they found Emerald's mother,

Guinevere, Monroe and Georgette in the kitchen. The room smelled of cooking eggs, hot buttered toast, and strong coffee. Monroe was sipping from a mug, Georgette was furiously writing on a piece of paper. Guinevere sat on the kitchen counter licking a paw, watching the Fae through narrowed eyes.

The night before, they had shared as much information as possible, but emotions had been fraught and they had all been exhausted. Emerald saw that whilst she and the others had been sleeping, the Fae had been working. A stack of paper covered in words sat beside Georgette, and when she got to the bottom of the one she was working on she added it to the stack and started on the next.

"Good morning," Monroe greeted.

"Hello all!" said Emerald's mother with a cheery wave and a huge smile which didn't meet her eyes. Emerald wondered how long she'd been awake. And why she was wearing her smart clothes not her pyjamas like all sensible people were at seven in the morning. Then she noticed Monroe and Georgette were pristine. Suddenly her fluffy sheep print pyjamas felt quite ridiculous.

"Coffee," muttered Maram, apparently less perturbed by her own Minion pyjamas in the presence of the Fae. She sat down heavily on a chair and poured a mug from the pot that was in the middle of the table.

The others nervously sat round the table, all dressed in pyjamas that Emerald and Maram had left in their old bedroom due to the unanticipated sleepover. Ben and Carla were both far too tall, their ankle bones fully on show, while Abi had rolled up the legs and sleeves of hers.

Maram poured coffee into the waiting mugs and Emerald fetched milk and sugar and set them on the table, but took her own mug with the coffee black and sipped it like it was the elixir of life. The last few days were catching up on her. She felt utterly drained. She had nothing left to give but what choice did she have?

Emerald's mum stepped over with a bowl of scrambled eggs and a toast rack laden with thick white toast. "I'll give you all some space," she said. "If you need anything at all you call me, okay?"

"Are you okay with that?" Emerald asked her.

"Of course," she said. "I will be here as soon as there's anything I can help with, you know that. But I can't help with this. It's just not my world. I trust you though. You can do this."

"Hey mum," said Emerald putting a hand on her arm. "I'm sorry about this. Thank you for everything."

Emerald's mum frowned for a moment, a heavy sadness in her eyes, then leaned down and kissed her daughter's cheek. "I love you, Emerald Wren," she whispered quietly in her ear. "You never need to be sorry. Not with me. Not ever." She squeezed Emerald's shoulder then stepped out, closing the kitchen door behind her.

"Your mum's lovely," said Ben, spooning eggs onto his plate.

"I hope you're all well rested," said Monroe, cutting him off and standing up. "We have work to do today. You are woefully ill prepared for battle. Your weapons creator is dead, you don't have a healer, and you have a new member who is unfamiliar with your process. If I am sending my people to war at your side, I need to be certain you're ready. Ubel must pay!" She slammed a fist down on the table making the plates and cups rattle.

Emerald peered at the slopped coffee and took a bite of her toast. "Is Ubel the guy or the God?"

"The God," said Carla through a mouthful of eggs.

"He's not a God," protested Celeste. "Didn't we decide that?"

Monroe huffed, running her hand through her hair. "You're unfocused."

"I'm hungry," said Maram.

"For fuck's sake!" cried Georgette. "This monster murdered my little sister! He's murdered humans, witches and more for years, all while he's been looking for you! And he's murdered one of your own sister witches. How many more have to die before you'll start taking this seriously? Do Hannah and Agatha's deaths mean so little? Do you even want to stop him?"

Maram shoved back her chair then left the room, slamming the kitchen door behind her.

"Now is not the time for hurt feelings," said Monroe.

"She's going to die tonight," said Emerald. "Do you really think she needs to take this more seriously? Do you really think she doesn't care?"

"We won't let her die," said Ben.

"Tonight they will both die," said Abi. "There's no stopping it."

"Unless we take him out before sundown," said Carla. "That's what we decided, right?"

Monroe's eyes dropped momentarily, then she looked back up. "The sooner we take him down the more chance we all have of surviving. After the body of the man he controls dies he will take another body, and another, and another. He will keep taking bodies from now until the end of time if we don't stop him. Any collateral damage in that cause is worth it."

"Collateral damage?" asked Emerald, screwing up her face and standing up. "Seriously? Collateral damage? I'm going after Maram. We'll be back soon to sort out how to try and save her life. Collateral damage, my arse. Tinkerbell is just one bloody massive lie, isn't she?"

Emerald left the room and shut the door with a slam. She found Maram crying on the stairs, wrapped in Emerald's mother's arms.

"You won't let her die," said Emerald's mother.

"We are going to stop it happening," said Emerald. "If we can."

"If?" asked Emerald's mother. "What if?"

Maram's face, blotchy and red, turned up to Emerald's mum. "If I don't die, everyone will. Including Emerald."

Emerald's mother blinked. Emerald knew in her heart that her mother would throw anybody to the wolves to save her daughter, including Maram. And that reality was hurting her mother as much as it was hurting Maram, who sat at her side sobbing. But what was she supposed to do?

"Hey, let's go out for a bit," said Emerald. "It's early. We'll go for a walk. Leave everyone else working. Get some air, yeah?"

Maram nodded. "Guess I might as well enjoy my last day, right?"

Emerald didn't know what to say. So she said nothing. They found their coats and bags and slipped out into the grey drizzle of the morning.

ð

The market was busy. People bustled about putting the last items on their stalls before the first morning shoppers arrived. A man stood at a flower stall setting out a display of crocuses.

"Excuse me," said Fadius.

The man looked up and startled. Fadius knew he looked an absolute ruin with the mud and blood running in trickles down his face in the rain, and his blooded eye wound goopy with crusted blood. "Are you okay there?"

"Do you have any laburnum?" he asked, ignoring the man's question.

"Aye, I do," he said, eyeing Fadius suspiciously, the mud and blood that caked his clothes made him quite a sight. The man's eyes lingered on the dried up mess of gunge where Fadius' now destroyed eye used to be. "A couple of small tubs of them over there, ready for planting. You don't strike me as a gardener, however, and you don't look to be carrying any money."

The man was right. He had no money.

What should he do? He had things far more challenging to try and gather. A simple flower was the easy one. He'd have to steal it. But how? The flower seller was staring at him.

He took steps backwards, then turned away. If he'd found it once he'd find it again.

"KILL HIM," the voice boomed into his head.

Fadius cried out, clutching at his head and bending over double. The silence in his head had him ill prepared for the agonising cacophony the voice thundered in.

"Hey, you alright there, my man?" asked the flower seller, stepping out from behind his stall. "You want a sit down?"

Fadius looked up at him and nodded. "Yes... please..." he stuttered.

"Come on," said the flower seller, leading him around the back of the stall. "You can't have my plants, but I'm not without a heart. I see you're in a bad way. Is there anybody I can call for you?"

He opened the door of the large green van behind his stall and helped Fadius lower himself into the driver's seat.

"Thank you," Fadius grunted.

"Here now," said the flower seller. "How about a sip of water. How's the head now, man?"

He went to lean past Fadius to retrieve a plastic bottle that was lying on the dashboard.

"NOW," the voice roared.

Almost on auto pilot, Fadius raised his arms, gripped the man's head and twisted it before the flower seller even realised what was happening. Smoothly, Fadius slipped from the van, and boosted the flower seller's body into a crumpled heap across the front seats of the van.

Shutting the door, Fadius stepped out from between the vehicles, picked up the yellow flowering shrub and made his way between the slowly growing crowds of people that moved through the market. He had done so little with his life, until now. Struggle though he may with the idea of killing, he still could not deny the rush he felt when he knew life had been ended by his hands alone. As he moved amongst the people of the market and they stepped out of his way, fearful looks on their faces, he smiled a little. They were right to be afraid. Finally, people were right to be afraid.

ð

Emerald and Maram walked the thirty minutes from Emerald's mother's house to the centre of town in silence, then began to walk up the high street. It was quiet but slowly starting to fill. Market day was always a little busier. The market square was ahead of them, and the colourful awnings over the stalls provided shelter from the slowly increasing rain to the people below.

"It just feels so weird," said Maram after a moment.

"What does?" asked Emerald.

"This. Everything. This is the last time I'm going to see this place," she said. "I've seen it hundreds of times but... it looks different now."

"Yeah," said Emerald, stopping and looking around. The grey streets, the shop signs, the drizzling rain. It looked the same as it always had. But Maram was right. It was different. "Hey, let's get some coffee. It's freezing."

Maram gave her a half-hearted smile of agreement and Emerald directed them into the bakery on the corner.

"Morning ladies," said the young man on the counter as they stepped in out of the rain. He was smiling broadly at them but Emerald noted with irritation that his eyes were lingering on Maram. As if now was an appropriate time for some idiot to be flirting with her. "Normally it's the old dears up this early for the market."

On a pinhead Maram changed her demeanour entirely. Her eyes became wider and she swung her head, flicking her long hair over her shoulder. "Hey," she said.

Emerald scowled. "Coffees," she said, through gritted teeth. "Two of them. Black. Large as you've got."

"Up late?" asked the boy, not moving to get their order.

"All night," answered Maram in a tone that irritated Emerald deeply. What was she doing? They didn't have time for this. What was the point? What the hell was she thinking?

"Coffees," Emerald snapped at him.

"No problem," said the boy. "I'll write your names on the cups. So... what are they?"

"She's Emerald, and I'm Maram," said Maram, smiling coyly and looking doe eyed.

"Fuck's sake," Emerald muttered under her breath. This charade was annoying at the best of times.

"Maram, eh?" he said, picking up a white cardboard cup. "And how am I spelling that?"

"M A R A M," spelled Maram, leaning forward on the counter, watching as he wrote it.

"And your phone number?" he asked, pen poised.

"Fuck's sake!" said Emerald out loud this time as Maram giggled.

"Alright, alright," said the boy. "I'll make your drinks. I'm Oli, by the way."

"Thanks Oli," said Maram, smiling her best smile.

Oli turned away and went to the machine behind him, and started sorting out their drinks.

"What are you doing?" Emerald hissed.

Maram looked at her innocently. "What?" she asked, then turned away, pointedly not looking back at Emerald.

"Here you are," said Oli, placing the steaming cups on the glass counter top and clicking plastic tops on the top. "That'll be seven pounds and fifty two pence."

Emerald handed him a ten pound note and accepted the change whilst Maram and Oli smiled at each other and ignored her.

"Don't be a stranger," said Oli. "I work mornings. Be a pleasure to service you."

"Fuck's sake!" Emerald cried whilst Maram laughed.

Emerald walked out with a stomp.

"What's your problem?" demanded Maram, catching up to her.

"My problem?" cried Emerald, turning round and glaring at her. "What's your problem? What the hell are you doing?"

"What?" asked Maram. "Talking! Being normal!"

"It's bad enough normally, but don't you think we've got enough going on already for you to be flirting with some bakery bonehead?"

"Bad enough normally?" demanded Maram. "What the hell does that mean?"

"Oh come on, Maram," said Emerald, walking away from her. "You know what I mean."

"No, I don't actually," Maram said, following her.

"Yes you do!" said Emerald, turning back to her and waving an arm in exasperation. "You know exactly what I mean. All these idiot boys. You have this horrible past, the worst of the worst, but you're such a..."

"A what?" shouted Maram. "Go on, Em, why don't you tell me what I am."

"Nothing," muttered Emerald, suddenly feeling horrible and looking down at the hot coffee in her hand that didn't have her name on it. "It doesn't matter."

"No?" asked Maram, storming towards her. "Sure? Sure it doesn't matter? You were going to call me a slut, Emerald. A slut. I think that matters."

"You're not a slut," said Emerald quietly, guilt surging through her because that was exactly what she was going to call her. And it was a word she had never considered using. Not since the night her father had left.

"Then what's the problem?" she asked. "Because you choose to live like a freaking nun the rest of us have to as well?"

"I'm not a nun!"

"Sure you are, Emerald," said Maram, putting a hand on her hip. "Ben's right there, under your nose, begging you to so much as look at him and nothing. You're sealed shut!"

"I am not!" protested Emerald hotly as the guilt left her and defensive fury started kicking in. "I'm just picky! Unlike some of us."

"See! You do think I'm a slut!"

"I do not! I just don't get what the hell is wrong with you!"

Maram stared at her in silence, fury all over her face. "You don't get what the hell is wrong with me?"

Emerald faltered slightly. Maram looked scary. "I mean..."

"What?"

"Just..."

"What?" Maram screamed.

"You might die tonight... why are you picking up some loser guy when this could be your last day?"

Emerald looked into Maram's eyes and saw an extraordinary amount of pain in them. So much hurt, so much betrayal, the haunting of so many memories all seemed to play across those deep brown eyes that she had looked into so many times since they were children. So much life and laughter had played out in those eyes, but never so much that the deep desperate sadness was completely hidden. Emerald knew in that moment that whilst her mother might not be willing to sacrifice Emerald to save Maram, Emerald knew she would willingly die for her in an instant.

Overhead the rain was picking up pace now. Around them people were ducking under shop doorways and hurrying past under umbrellas, their heads down. Emerald and Maram stood facing each other, the rain plastering their hair to their faces.

"Because I can," said Maram quietly. "Because my whole life I never got to live. I never got to experience an actual life because I was an object. By some shitty luck I got to be a female genie so I was stuck in this body with men who owned me and could do anything they wanted to me. I just want to belong to myself! Do you understand?"

Emerald remembered their fight on the bus, the day they'd met Ben. The first time they'd ever used their powers to save someone. "Yes."

"It makes me feel alive," she said. "To have that freedom. And oh my god right now I just need to feel alive! This is my last chance to feel anything at all."

"I'm sorry," said Emerald. "I really am. I was a cow."

"You're not a cow," said Maram, shrugging. "You're not a nun either."

"Come on," said Emerald as the wind whipped rain into her cheek. "I'm freezing."

Emerald sipped her coffee as they walked. It was still scolding hot but the familiar comfort of the bitter heat soothed her.

Maram was about to say something when she flung an arm across Emerald's chest. "Oh my god," she hissed, then dragged Emerald off the street and into the doorway of a hairdressers.

"What?" asked Emerald.

"It's him," she whispered.

Emerald peered out and saw him. Walking across the street not forty yards ahead of them, with a black dried up pulp where his eye used to be, and grime caked to his enormous body, walked the man who had attacked them.

The man who had killed Tig. The man who was going to kill Maram.

And he was very carefully carrying a plant covered in pretty yellow flowers.

"You know how I thought this place looked weird?" asked Maram, leaning back against the wall.

"Yeah," said Emerald.

"I didn't know what the hell I was talking about."

Chapter Twenty-Five

Moira swung her legs out of the bed and placed her gnarled feet on the floor of the room.

Her new roommate, an old woman with a blue rinse and a distinct odour, was snoring. Moira carefully, and silently, slipped past her, pulled open the door and peered out into the corridor.

Two nurses were deep in conversation over some paperwork in one direction, and a cleaner was mopping the floor in the other. She took her chances with the cleaner.

"Hello there, dear," he said as she approached. "Are you a bit lost, love?"

Moira narrowed her eyes. "No," she said, and kept walking.

"Hang on, there darlin'," he said, leaning the mop against the wall and putting a hand on Moira's arm.

Without hesitation, her arm shot out and she pinned the man against the wall by his throat. "Never. Touch me. Again." She snarled, her face contorting into that of a wolf, her hot, wet breath against his face.

The man's eyes widened in horrified panic as he struggled against the arm that held him. Looking at her face, the huge fangs reflected in his eyes, he fainted. Moira wasn't sure if it was the lack of oxygen from the choke hold or the terrible sight she presented before him that had caused it, but it didn't really matter either way.

Returning to her normal form, Moira glanced over her shoulder and saw the nurses hadn't looked up from their paperwork. She slowly allowed the man's unconscious body to fall to the floor, then quickly stepped over him and slipped through a door into the stair well.

Cursing under her breath, Moira lent against the wall for a moment. She was old and she was dying, and taking form was becoming harder and more draining every single time. She felt battered. But there was a job to be done, and if nothing else she was going to ensure her legacy was not tarnished.

Moira started down the stairs as quietly as she could.

ð

Returning once more to the hospital, Fadius started through the woodland. He shouldn't be there. He had appealed to the voice in his head, begged for there to be some other option but no answer had come. Since the incident at the market the voice had stayed away.

He knew of no other option. He needed the blood of someone who has touched a shape shifter, and this was the only place he was sure he could get it.

ð

The hospital was starting to get busy now. Patients were waking, doctors were starting rounds, porters with trolleys were beginning to distribute cups of tea and hot buttered toast to the patients. Ward seventeen was large and Moira kept her head down, hoping those around her would assume she was just another patient on her way to use the bathroom. The staff were all so busy that a woman in a hospital gown walking past and not causing any drama or needing any help was immaterial, and she was able to make her way to room fifteen with ease.

Stepping inside, she quietly closed the door. Four beds, two on each side lined the walls, each with lilac patterned curtains surrounding them.

"Barry?" she called out. "Barry Matthews?"

"Yes?" came a voice from the bed by the window.

Moira smiled and walked over, stepping between the curtains.

ð

The ward was on the ground floor which made Fadius' task far more simple than had he had to ascend higher into the workings of the hospital. He moved through the grounds as inconspicuously as he could until he came to the window that sat slightly open, just enough to allow a cool breeze into the cramped room.

ð

"Who are you?" asked Barry, peering through his swollen eyes.

Moira smiled. Lila may have failed to perform the final kill, but she had certainly left him in a bad way. Bandages wound around his body, his face was mottled with bruising and blood.

"Do you know why you're here, Mr Matthews?" Moira asked him.

"Of course I bloody do," said Barry, looking down at himself. "I don't know why you are though! Are you lost? Crazy old bint."

"You're here because you're a misogynist," said Moira, stepping towards him. "An abuser. A danger to women."

Barry started to look nervous and began fumbling around for the alarm for the nurse.

ð

Fadius pulled the window further open as quietly as he could, then hoisted himself up into the frame.

ð

Moira reached out quickly and pulled the switch away. "Oh no," she said. "Nobody is coming to help you. You're all alone, Barry. Just like the women you took advantage of."

Watching Barry's face begin to contort in fear and horror, Moira began to slowly change into her wolf form.

ð

Fadius ripped open the curtain and cried out in surprise. A half woman, half wolf, stood over the man, ready to pounce.

"No!" shouted Fadius, he needed the man alive or the blood would be no good. And he had no other option. Without this man's blood he would fail, and the consequences could be dire.

The woman looked up, stunned, her elongated jaw full of fangs as sharp as knives open and ready to bite.

Fadius stepped towards her, his fist raised.

ð

Moira panicked. The man was huge, he was strong, and everything she had left was going into taking wolf form. She stumbled backwards and the change fell away. She became just a frightened old lady cowering before a powerful man, and she was furious about it.

ð

Fadius swung his fist hard into the side of her head. She smashed into the cabinet by the man's bed and fell to the ground in a heap.

"Oh man," cried Barry. "Thank you so much, dude. Jesus that was crazy!"

Around the room from behind the curtains, Fadius could hear male voices starting to shout. Even without seeing it, there was obviously some danger in the room and panic was starting. Fadius could not afford any further interruption to his task.

Fadius turned to the man and approached him.

"Thanks man," said the man again. "Seriously. What do I owe you?"

Fadius put a hand squarely on his shoulder, gripped his forearm with the other and pulled. "Just this," he said as the arm ripped from the socket.

Screams followed Fadius as he leapt through the window and raced through the grounds of the hospital towards the wooded area, carrying the man's arm and leaving a trail of blood behind him.

ð

Maram carefully sketched the plant in as much detail as she could remember, whilst the coven, the Fae, Guinevere and Emerald's mother watched on.

"Was it yellow?" asked Emerald's mum.

"Yes," said Emerald, looking up at her.

"It's a laburnum," she said. "We had one out front before you were born but I had it ripped out whilst you were a baby."

"Why?" asked Emerald.

"They're dreadfully poisonous," she said.

"Poison?" asked Monroe, frowning. "That seems a peculiar method of attack."

"He'd never get close enough to make us swallow poison," said Carla. "What's he playing at?"

"What does it do?" asked Maram. "What are the effects?"

"Well it can be death," said Emerald's mum. "But it can put you into a coma or cause extreme tiredness, amongst other things."

Monroe leant against the wall. "He's not going to be trying to poison you," she said. "In this type of combat, poison is too hard to administer. And with time running out it makes no sense."

"I can try and summons a vision," said Abi.

"No!" insisted Carla. "No, you can't."

"What other choice do we have?" asked Abi. "He's doing something isn't he? He's not just going to barrel up here with his fists flying and hoping for the best. We know he's been watching us, now we're just sitting ducks whilst he's preparing something we don't understand!"

"But..." started Carla.

"But nothing, Car," said Abi, shaking her head. "This is my job. It's why I'm here. And if I can save Maram, and anybody else, then I have to do it."

"But last time... Abs... Abi I can't lose you," said Carla, resting her forehead against Abi's and cupping her face. "Please. Don't."

"The Seer is right," said Georgette.

"The Seer has a name!" snapped Carla, turning on her.

Abi held up a hand. "Stop," she said. "I'm going to do this. Let's join first. I need all the help I can get."

The seven witches gathered around and sat on the floor in a circle. Emerald's mother watched on, clearly fascinated. They took hands and the warmth and strength began to fill Emerald, she felt empowered. Opening her eyes she saw Abi sat with hers closed, seeking a vision.

"I know what to target," Abi said quietly. "I know what I'm looking for. I just need to make the connection."

Carla looked terrified. Abi looked strong and calm, in control and confident.

Abi's back stiffened. She dropped Carla's and Ben's hands on either side and held her hands to the sides of her head. She sat absolutely still. There was no thrashing or crying, no fear or pain.

"I see him," said Abi.

"As in... right now?" asked Celeste, staring at her.

"Right now," said Abi.

"Are you sure?" asked Emerald, starting to doubt this new found confidence Abi was displaying. Perhaps the coma had messed her up.

"He's... in a kitchen," said Abi. "A big kitchen. Restaurant kitchen."

Emerald felt her stomach start to plummet. "Which restaurant?"

"I can't tell," said Abi, frowning. "He's by a big oven. Picking up... coals..."

Maram's head snapped round to Emerald, her mouth open and her eyes wide. "Coal?" she asked.

"I'm losing... he's..." Abi opened her eyes and looked around at them all, then her eyes rolled back in her head and she collapsed.

As Carla hurried to Abi's side, Emerald raced to her bag and fumbled round, pulling out her phone. She quickly unlocked the screen and hit the speed dial.

"Nobody's answering," she said, looking at Maram.

"Let's go," said Emerald, grabbing her coat. "If he's hurt Vinnie..."

Maram stood up and grabbed her own coat. "Don't..." she said, shaking her head. "I can't deal with that."

They hesitated for a moment, looking into each other's eyes. Emerald could feel Maram's fear as strongly as her own.

"How long will you be gone for?" asked Georgette, crossing her arms.

"I don't know," said Emerald. "As long as we need to be."

Before she could argue, Emerald and Maram turned and left, closing the door behind them.

ð

Emerald's mother crouched down at Abi's side and put her fingers onto her neck to check her pulse whilst Guinevere peered over them from the armchair, her tail flicking.

"She's okay," said Emerald's mum.

"Oh thank goodness," whispered the cat under her breath.

Carla nodded, choking back tears.

"Your supposed leader is completely irrational," said Monroe. "And the Genie! She's going to be sacrificing herself to save the world! What are they running off for? He's planning your doom and you treat it like it's irrelevant!"

"Help me get her to the sofa," said Carla ignoring Monroe and carefully lifting Abi's head and shoulders.

Emerald's mother carefully took her legs and together they carefully lifted her then set her down on the sofa, Carla gently pushing a cushion under her head, then gently kissed her cheek.

"You should all be focussing!" said Monroe behind them.

Ben put a hand on Carla's arm. "You okay?" he asked her.

"No," said Carla, smiling a sad half smile.

"Shall I put the kettle on?" suggested Emerald's mum.

"Thanks," said Carla. "I'd appreciate it."

"You've lost your leader and Genie," said Georgette, standing at her mother's side. "Now your Seer's unconscious *again*! You're down to four functioning members, it's time to concentrate!"

"We are concentrating," said Celeste. "On our four functioning members."

Carla was about to turn her frustration on Monroe when she heard a phone start to ring. "What's ringing?" she asked.

"It's m.... m.... mine," said Lila, awkwardly standing up and shuffling off to her bag, visibly cowering under Monroe's furious gaze.

"What now?" asked Georgette, exasperated.

Lila turned away, answering the phone in the corner, making herself as small as possible.

"Yes, this is Lila," she said. "Oh, oh my God, oh no..."

Carla caught Celeste's eye and shrugged, feeling nervous. What now, indeed?

"I'll be there," said Lila, then hung up the phone. She stayed in the corner, staring at the wall, her whole body shaking.

"Lila?" said Celeste, approaching her quietly. She put a hand out and touched Lila's shoulder. Lila jumped, spinning around and staring at her. "What happened?"

"My... grandma..." she said, her bottom lip trembling. "She's... she... she's dead."

"Oh Lila," said Celeste, pulling her into a hug. "I'm so sorry."

"I need to go," she said, grabbing her bag.

"Why?" demanded Monroe.

"Wh... wh... because... she's dead," stuttered Lila.

“Exactly,” said Georgette. “She’s dead. There’s nothing to be done. Humans die at a remarkably young age. It’s normal.”

“But… but I… I…” Lila looked frantically back and forth.

“I’ll drive you,” said Ben. “Come on.”

Monroe and Georgette stared in fury as Ben and Lila left the room and went outside to Ben’s car.

“And then there were two,” said Carla.

“Oh my God!” Guinevere suddenly cried. “I’ve got to go.”

With a peculiar pop, the cat suddenly vanished.

Carla and Celeste stared at each other. “Did you know she could do that?” Carla asked.

“No!”

“And this is the team they are trusting to deal with Ubel,” said Georgette, shaking her head. “We’re doomed.”

Chapter Twenty-Six

The bag at Fadius' side moved and jostled as its content struggled and squeaked. Now he was away from the town and the suspicious eyes, Fadius ignored it and trudged on. He ached so much that each step was agony. He felt dizzy and sick. His bloodied eye burned and itched, but every time he touched it to relieve the itching he felt a stabbing pain through his head so agonising he feared he'd lose consciousness.

When he had felt so broken doing his work before, his lord had granted him release, had given him strength and power when he so desperately needed it. Now he was alone, fighting on with no guarantee of ever feeling whole again.

"Where are you?" he asked out loud, stopping and staring at the sky as if he might see the face of his master looking down. "Why have you left me?"

No answer.

"I know you can hear me!" he shouted into the rain. "I know you can! Why are you ignoring me?"

No answer. He put his head in his hand and remembered Jenny's words.

"What are you afraid of?" he asked. "Why are you afraid of an old woman?"

"I AM NOT AFRAID," the voice boomed, louder than he remembered it ever being. He fell to his knees in pain, his hands clutched to his head to prevent his skull from splintering.

"Lord!" howled Fadius. "Please. Stay with me! I am weak! I am tired! I am in pain! Please, Lord! Please! Help me!"

"NOT UNTIL THE JOB IS DONE," the voice said.

"I can't," Fadius sobbed. "I can't."

"DO IT AND YOU WILL BE REWARDED!" the voice boomed.

Rewarded. Strength. Freedom from pain. Fadius held the struggling bag to his side, gritted his teeth, and forced himself back to his feet. For the reward he could do it. He put one foot in front of the other and forced his weary body on.

ઠ

"This is lunacy," said Georgette, stomping up and down, her small feet making an impressively loud sound. "This is when we are supposed to be all together! Have you girls never fought a battle before? Do you not know how this is supposed to work? I've never worked with such amateurs! Mother, this is a mistake. It must be a mistake! They've got it wrong. Tell Wren he's wrong!"

"Wren?" asked Carla, looking up.

"The Vision agreed," said Monroe, ignoring Carla. "This is the only way."

Georgette flung her arms in the air. "Then where are they? It's nearly noon! This is ridiculous!"

Next to Carla Abi groaned.

"Abi?" Carla said, turning to her and gently stroking her face. "Babe?"

"They'll be home soon," said Abi in a quiet voice.

"Who will?" demanded Monroe.

"Everyone," said Abi. "They're coming. Now."

They heard the kitchen door open and the sound of Emerald and Maram stomping in.

ð

Emerald stormed into the living room and found them all staring at her. Emerald gulped. They looked expectant. They wanted her to say or do something.

"What?" she asked.

"Nothing," said Carla, but looked at Abi with a wonder in her eyes.

Behind them the kitchen door went again as Ben and Lila came in.

"Vinnie's alive," Emerald said as they came in. "Shaken, but alive. The douchebag scared him half to death but after he'd stolen the coals he left him be."

"My grandma's dead," Lila said, her arms wrapped about herself and a look of absolute despair on her face.

"Oh my god," gasped Maram. "I'm so sorry, Lila!"

"What happened?" asked Emerald.

"I don't know," said Lila. "They wouldn't tell us much. There was a detective guy, Tribble or Trubble or something, and they said they were investigating and not to worry. But my grandma's dead! She's all I had. I don't know what to do now." She started to cry, huge tears running down her cheeks as she gasped in anguish.

Emerald's mother rushed to the crying girl and held her in a hug, making gentle soothing noises as she wept.

"Tribble?" asked Celeste after a moment.

"Yes," said Lila, choking on the words and looking up from Emerald's mother with a face blotchy and red. "Something like that."

"He's Commission," said Celeste.

"Really?" asked Lila, her eyes wide as she rubbed her eyes with the back of her sleeve.

"According to your grandmother!" said Celeste. "He's the one who got me discharged, only he was Dr Tribble then."

"Commission were at Vincenzo's too," said Emerald. "Or at least Detective Raza was. He's who I spoke to at the hospital and I think who covered up Tig's death. Lied right to my face, acted like he didn't know what was what. They think we're stupid."

"So Commission crawling all over this, huh?" said Ben, crossing his arms.

"You are fools," spat Monroe.

"Excuse me?" asked Emerald, turning to her.

"Of course the Commission are involved. How uneducated are you? How do you expect to accomplish this task when you're so fixated on irrelevant minutia?"

"What exactly do you mean by minutia?" asked Emerald, narrowing her eyes.

"Your friend died fighting, that is an honourable death," said Georgette. "Your grandmother was old, that is an irrelevant death. Your boss is alive, so that doesn't even need considering! My sister is an innocent death by his hand, yet you don't see us fixating on that. The battle should be the focus! The fight! You're distracted by things that do not matter when we don't even have a plan of action!"

"We'll get there," said Emerald.

"How?" demanded Georgette. "When? You're the leader but you do nothing! Would we even be safe to follow a plan you made? Why should we be following your lead when you are so inept?"

It stung. Emerald felt inept. She had never felt cut out to lead yet it was a job that had fallen to her and everyone expected her to perform accordingly. Now presented with accusations that she wasn't able to be what they needed her to be, Emerald felt incredibly defensive. This was her coven, her friends. They needed her to lead them and lead them she would.

"We'll make a plan," Emerald said. "We always come up with a plan."

"We are warriors," said Monroe. "We know how to fight, how to work. Sitting around drinking cups of tea and worrying about irrelevant gossip is how you get yourself killed. We know that. This is why the Fae are far better suited to leadership than any witches!"

"Yet you're the species that's dying out," said Ben under his breath.

Emerald flashed a mischievous grin at him and his eyes lit up.

"This is ridiculous!" shouted Monroe. "You're unprepared. You're unprofessional..."

"We're here!" Celeste shouted, standing up and interrupting Monroe with a ferocious look on her face. "We are here and we are fighting and we are doing it! Nobody forced you to be here. Nobody! You came to us, remember? And that *minutia* is the reason we are doing it! The reason we are invested! Because they're not minutia they are people and they are important! The fight isn't the focus because the focus is the people we love, and if we didn't have them we would have no reason to fight! So either get on board, listen to us and follow us, or fuck off, because you're doing nothing right now except pissing me off!"

Everyone stared silently at the two women, Celeste staring down Monroe who, for once, looked almost humble.

Emerald looked around, unsure what to say or do, the silence in the room drowning out even the sound of breathing when suddenly a loud POP noise burst the bubble and Guinevere appeared in the middle of the room.

"I know what he's doing," said the cat. "He's making potions tailored to each of your powers. The laburnum slows Celeste's movements, the coal releases carbon monoxide to put out Ben's fire. I don't know who he's got doing it but these things he's collecting are ingredients. We need to start thinking of new ways to fight him or he's going to win."

Everyone stared at her. The sudden influx of information sat oddly on the intensity in the air.

Guinevere looked around in confusion as nobody spoke.

"Right," said Monroe after a moment. "Let's get down to business. Emerald, what's your plan?"

ð

Fadius stared up at the building that loomed ahead of him. Even though the sun was now at its highest and the rain had lightened up to just an irritating spatter, it still felt foreboding and dark in the shadow of the witch's home.

He looked at the door. Was he going to be trapped in the dark for untold hours again?

The bag moved and squeaked and he was fed up of carrying it so he gritted his teeth and approached the old wooden door. Opening it he was met by warm firelight and the sound of cello music coming from hidden speakers.

"Good afternoon, Fadius," greeted Jenny, who was carefully pouring tea into a china cup on a wooden sewing table. "Do you have everything I need?"

"I do," said Fadius, lifting the bag, still squeaking and moving about though with less gusto now.

"Ah, nice and fresh I see," said Jenny smiling, then took a sip of the tea.

"Where should I put it?"

"Give it here," said Jenny, setting the teacup down gently and reaching out for the bag.

Fadius handed it over and Jenny reached inside, and with one hand she pulled out the wriggling, squealing piglet who seemed to have regained its enthusiasm for the protest. She cooed and fussed it, stroking its head and holding it securely against her chest. The piglet seemed to calm down and allowed Jenny to hold it close, gazing up at her out of big brown eyes.

"Excellent. Lovely little thing. We'll look after you first I think. I think I'll call you Tiddles," she said to the piglet. With a cursory glance into the rest of the bag, she nodded slightly, then set it down on the table and carried the piglet to a door in the corner. "Come on then, Fadius."

Fadius followed the old woman across the fluffy rug and to the door. She opened it and stepped through into darkness. Fadius followed, regretfully leaving behind the soft warmth of the living room, and stepping into the darkness beyond.

For a moment he heard nothing. A vacuum of silence and darkness seemed to blot out any noise or light from the room behind, and he could neither hear nor sense the presence of Jenny anywhere.

"Hello?" he called out.

He heard a grunt and a snuffle, then a fire suddenly lit up, casting an orange glow. Fadius shuddered. Whereas the warm light of the fire in the living room had been comforting and soft, in here it cast ominous shadows across book cases, jars and cabinets that lined the walls. The fire was below a large, black cauldron. He was surprised. It looked like something from a storybook.

"Come here, Fadius," said Jenny. He looked about and spotted her standing at one of the bookcases, the piglet in her arm watching what she was doing. "Fetch me the jar labelled scales would you?" she asked, pointing to a row of jars filled with strange silver substances on a shelf to her left.

Fadius nodded and fetched the jar as Jenny pulled a book down from the shelf, cooing tenderly to the piglet as she did it. "What are these?" asked Fadius, looking into the jar. They looked like fish scales but much larger, and they seemed to glow with a luminescence that seemed other worldly.

"Scales from the tail of some unfortunate mermaid," said Jenny. "The poor dear was Harvested."

Fadius balked. "Mermaid?" he asked.

"Yes, dear," she said, taking the jar from him and setting it on a worktop.

"Now, if you'll just hold Tiddles here," she said, handing him the piglet who eyed him warily but didn't protest as he took him from Jenny's arms.

Fadius watched with curiosity as, using a pair of very fine tweezers, Jenny extracted one of the scales from the jar and placed it on a chopping board. She carefully screwed the lid back on the jar and set it on the worktop, then picked up a fiendishly sharp looking knife.

Very delicately, she sliced the scale into millimetre thick strips. Leaving the scale slices on the side, she went to the cauldron and stirred it. Bubbles began to pop from inside and he nodded, then went to another shelf and picked several pots off. They looked like herb jars from a supermarket with perforated lids. Deftly she sprinkled the contents into the cauldron a bit at a time, stirring and sniffing as she went. After a few shakes she returned to the table, lifted the chopping board and carefully slid the scale slices into the water. It hissed and fizzed, a rich turquoise smoke erupting in a glistening plume from inside.

"Perfect," she said, with a satisfied nod. "Hand me Tiddles, would you?"

Fadius handed the contented little piglet over to her. It seemed grateful to be returned to the woman and nestled into her. "Hello, darling," she said, and patted him on the head, then dropped him straight into the boiling water where a panicked squeal erupted. She pushed the piglet under the water with the spoon for a moment, then stirred it. Fadius staggered backwards. "All done," she said. "This is the Osseineous Brittlety."

"The Ossei what?" asked Fadius, still too haunted by what had just happened to Tiddles to process what he was being told.

"The Osseineous Brittlety," said Jenny, carefully spooning some of the liquid into a glass jar. "Drink it and it'll strengthen your bones against the bone breaker, and each attack she makes on you will weaken her own bones instead."

"Wow," said Fadius, accepting the jar she handed to him and looking at the glistening silver liquid inside. "How does that work then?"

"Magic, my dear boy," she said, tutting cheerfully. "But it'll only last for ten minutes. So don't use it until you have to. I'd give you more but it's valuable and I don't care to waste it on your boss. Now, what should we tackle next? How about the shapeshifter. I presume that man's arm is the blood you brought me?"

"Yes," said Fadius.

"Super," she said. "And this man, any chance he was a murderer or a thief?"

"A thief perhaps," said Fadius.

"Lovely," she said. "I have an excellent recipe that calls for the fingernails of a thief. I do like a man who goes above and beyond requirements. Now, dear, run along and fetch the arm for me, would you?"

Fadius blinked then obeyed. He didn't know whether he was just used to obeying now or whether it was the ice cold fear he felt in his chest whenever Jenny made eye contact with him, but there was no way he was going to ignore her instructions. He hurried away to retrieve the severed arm, leaving Jenny decanting the piglet potion into a series of glass jars behind him.

Chapter Twenty-Seven

"What potions?" asked Emerald. "Do you mean Fadius is a witch?"

"He's not a witch," said Celeste. "He was surprised by our magic."

"No, he's not a witch," said Guinevere. "But he is working with one."

"A witch who'd turn on her own?" said Monroe, raising an eyebrow.

"Unfortunately yes," said Guinevere. "They tend to operate under the radar. The Commission keep tabs where possible but usually they're operating under a complex network of enchantments and living in isolation. There are a few larger organisations, though before they cause too much damage they're usually taken care of."

"Why would they do it?" asked Emerald.

"Power," said Guinevere.

"Put we have power," said Celeste. "That's how we're born."

"Yes," said Guinevere. "But you could have more."

"How?" asked Carla, sitting up a little.

"If you were willing to sacrifice part of your humanity," said Guinevere, fixing Carla with a serious look.

"Yeah, but... how?" asked Carla again, ignoring the piercing look the cat was giving her. "I mean if he's teamed up with some badass witch who's powerful and is arming him against us then shouldn't we be supercharging up to match him?"

"Yes," said Georgette. "She's right."

"No she isn't," said Monroe, turning to her daughter.

"What?" asked Georgette, staring at her mother in shock. "You think they should take this on whilst they're weak?"

"We're not weak," said Emerald.

"Compared to him you are!" protested Georgette.

"Would you turn on the Fae so easily?" asked Monroe.

"What?" asked Goergette.

"Would you act in a way that harms us just so you could be stronger?"

"No!" protested Georgette.

"Would you take the life of a Fae to save your own?"

"No... I..."

"Would you kill a witch or a mermaid? Even a mortal?" asked Monroe.

"No," said Georgette, her eyes dropping.

"That's what these witches do," said Guinevere. "And this witch who Fadius has gone to isn't only willing to sacrifice others for her own power, but she's willing to create weapons against her own kind to boost the strength in our enemies as well. She has gone far down that rabbit hole. Further than most driven by power."

"But what do we do then?" asked Carla.

"Erm..." said Emerald, looking around nervously. "I haven't actually figured that part out yet."

"Well then," said Monroe. "Let's get to work. We've got less than four hours to get our shit together."

ð

"And finally," said Jenny, handing Fadius a long thin vile of purple liquid. "Tetanai."

"Tetanai," Fadius repeated, looking down at the line of jars and bottles at his side, hoping he would remember them all and doubting himself.

"This needs to come into contact with her skin," said Jenny. "Any part of her skin. It'll absorb immediately and her muscles will break down. The bigger she gets, the weaker she'll become. If she's foolish and tries anyway, her muscles will waste away completely and she will die, but I expect she won't care about any of this enough to risk it. Still, she'll be weakened enough that you can dispose of her with ease before it matters."

"Okay," said Fadius, and bent down to start collecting the potions.

"Wait, wait, wait," said Jenny. "You and I are not through yet, Fadius dear."

"Oh," said Fadius, looking up nervously.

The woman smiled a warm smile, full of gentle kindness. His blood ran cold. "The price still needs to be paid. I do not work for free, remember, dear."

"Oh," said Fadius, nervously watching her. "What do you want?"

Jenny walked to a chest of drawers and took out a long tapered silver knife with a fiercely sharp point. Fadius gulped.

I'm bigger than her, he said to himself. I'm stronger. I have killed women with ease. I shouldn't be afraid. I could kill her with one fist to the face. But the sight of Jenny with that knife was terrifying. The light from the fire glinted off the blade, flashing across her face. She no longer looked old and sweet, she looked horrific. She looked demonic.

"Few people live to have as close proximity to a... God... as you have," said Jenny. She lingered over the word God with a smirk. A feeling of lead sunk into Fadius' chest. "It changes a man. It changes your make up. You've felt his presence in your blood?"

Fadius thought of the strength and power that had surged through him. The feeling he longed for, craved. The sensation he knew he would kill for if he could only feel it again. "Yes," he said.

"Yes," she said, smiling. "I'm familiar with how these... *Gods*... work..."

Gods. Again with the smirk. Now plural. Fadius hurt inside so deeply.

Jenny went to a shelf and got an empty jar. Then to a cupboard and pulled out a bottle of green liquid. She held it up to the firelight and shook it, peering into it, and blue bubbles appeared as she shook the liquid and hovered inside.

"Hold out your hand, Fadius," Jenny commanded. "And come over here."

Fadius did as he was told.

Jenny set the bottle on the counter top and took a cork from the top. The blue bubbles stayed motionless in the water.

Jenny took his wrist firmly in her wrinkled hand, took the knife in her other, and held it over his hand. Fadius watched in horror. Terrified. He couldn't fight her off. He didn't know why. But even if he had wanted to he knew he would be powerless and now he was too frozen in fear to even try.

The long blade, at least as long as Jenny's forearm, waited over his arm. Jenny watched his eyes for a moment, then quick as a flash stuck the tip of the blade firmly into the pad of his thumb.

Fadius yelped in surprise as a round balloon of blood boiled out from his skin. Jenny set the knife down, then lifted the bottle and held it below his thumb. She very carefully squeezed and three round globules dropped into the potion below. Each drop landed with a hiss and a sizzle, then the blood dispersed through the liquid and formed a film across the top of each bubble, turning them from blue to red.

Jenny shook the bottle again and this time the red bubbles moved, colliding into one another and ricocheting with a peculiar clinking sound, like glass in a cabinet.

"Excellent," said Jenny.

"What is it?" asked Fadius, taking his hand back.

"It's the first ingredient in a curse, dear," she said, her face back to the warmth he remembered, soft and old, like a kindly nun. He didn't like it. He had seen beneath the mask now.

"What are the other ingredients?" Fadius asked.

"Oh, I won't be able to collect those for a while," she said. "But I'll be in touch.

"With me?" he asked.

"Yes, dear," she said. "I'm afraid this is a price you'll be paying for quite some time. I hope your God is worth it."

"For how long?" asked Fadius, looking at his finger as it began to sting, the wound turning a strange blue colour as the burning sensation began to spread to his hand and arm.

"Eternity, dear," she said.

"What?" asked Fadius.

"Yes, dear," she said. "And don't think of escape. There is nothing you can do. Once you're ready, I shall come. You're marked now, dear."

He looked at his finger, the blue spreading from the wound, tracking outwards like an anemone.

Fadius stumbled backwards. He gathered up the six potions she had made him and hurried for the door. Jenny watched him for a moment then turned her back, busying herself with the curse bottle. He stumbled through the living room, the cello music escorting him with a haunting tune of sorrow, and out through the door into the late afternoon grey light of autumn.

"WELL DONE FADIUS," the voice boomed in his head. Fadius cried out in agony and surprise. He fell to his knees, the potions landing on the soft ground in front of him. "NOW WE ATTACK."

Fadius felt tears running down his cheeks. "Yes, Lord," he agreed, then started picking the potions up again. A sense of hopelessness was building inside him. Eternity. He would be Jenny's for eternity. He didn't even know if there was an eternity. He didn't know he could live for eternity. What had he done?

"FADIUS," came the voice. "ARE YOU READY FOR YOUR REWARD?"

"Yes," said Fadius, miserably. Would anything make him feel better?

Heat, strength and power blasted through his body. His muscles screamed with strength, his head buzzed with blinding glory. He stood up, his arms outstretched as ecstasy took over his body. Nothing could stop him. Nothing. Jenny's eternity was irrelevant. He was strong.

He was powerful. He could kill the witches with his bare hands. Nothing would get in his way. His Lord loved him.

"PICK UP THE POTIONS, FADIUS," the voice commanded. "IT IS TIME TO DO YOUR DUTY."

Fadius gathered up the bottles then hesitated. "Lord," he said, noticing something for the first time. "There are only six. I have potions for each witch, but none for the genie."

There was laughter in his head. "THE WITCHES WILL DISPOSE OF THE GENIE THEMSELVES," Fadius boomed. "YOU WILL BREAK THEM DOWN TO THE POINT OF DESPERATION. THEY WILL WISH FOR YOUR DEATH. THEN THE GENIE WILL BE GONE."

"Yes, Lord," said Fadius. My death, he thought with an irreverent smile. Irrelevant. Nothing can kill me. Nothing. I am invincible. I am power. I am strength.

ð

"This is Anya, Sebastian and Nico," said Monroe, gesturing to three small but fierce looking Fae that stood in Emerald's mother's kitchen.

"We are ready to battle in Hannah's honour," said Nico, his voice shockingly deep considering his height.

"They are the heads of my sect," said Monroe. "We have seventeen below them ready to fight."

"Okay," said Emerald. "Erm, hello there."

Monroe nodded proudly.

"I have a question," said Carla, standing up. She towered over the Fae but they didn't look intimidated. "I know what we can do. But I don't know what you can do."

"We can fight," said Anya.

"Yeah, that's great," said Carla. "But how? I mean, do you have powers? You're fairies right?"

"Fae," said Georgette.

"Fae," repeated Carla. "Sure. But here's the thing, I'm our muscle. I'm the one who takes these guys down normally. But we work together, we work as a team. If I'm supposed to rely on you to be the muscle next to me, I'm going to need to know what I'm working with exactly. I need to know if I can count on you to have my back. And I need these guys to know they can feel safe. That's how we work."

Monroe pointed at the three Fae. They stepped forward, feet apart, then beautiful pearlescent wings suddenly burst forth from their backs with a rippling sound.

"Oh my God you're really fairies!" gasped Lila, her hands clasped to her chest in delight.

"Fae," Georgette repeated.

"So you're like The Wasp?" asked Ben.

"Wasps?" asked Nico, stepping forward with a furious look on his face. "You're calling us insects?"

"No!" said Ben, holding his hands up. "No, no, no. The Wasp. From the comics."

"Human stuff," said Georgette.

"It's a compliment! She's cool!" insisted Ben, looking at Emerald apologetically.

"You witches," snorted Nico. "You're so unfocused. So easily distracted. You're split in your magic, split in your interests and motivations, you're so...."

"Nico," Monroe snapped. "Enough. Emerald is leading us. You answer to her now."

The three Fae looked startled but folded in their wings and nodded respectfully to Monroe, then turned their faces to Emerald, expectantly waiting for orders.

"What else?" asked Emerald. "Do you have magic?"

"We do," said Monroe. "But it's different to yours. We can move things, change things. But we're affected both positively and negatively by the world around us. Our magic is old, tied into nature."

"Like what?" asked Celeste. "Are you telekinetic like me?"

"Yes, and no," said Monroe. "Fae magic, stemming from pure fairy magic, is so much more complex than simply being born of power. It's closer to celtic or Virilicae magic. But more complex still."

"What's that?" Ben whispered to Abi who shrugged.

"We can fight. Our strength and skills will aid whatever magic you use," said Georgette. "We will come in from above, throw Fae magic at him, wrong foot him."

"We need to take out the man quickly," said Monroe. "Once the man's body is dead the demon will be revealed. He is weakened when exposed. He will move to take over a new human body quickly, so unless we want to sacrifice another human life that is our time to move, before he obtains a new vessel."

"Do we have to kill him?" asked Lila.

"Yes," said Emerald, her heart hurting. "We do. He killed Tig, he killed Hannah, he's killed so many other women I can't even... If he gets a new body he will kill again. Us, other women, who knows how many. So yes, unfortunately, we have to kill him."

Lila nodded sadly. "Okay."

They fell silent for a moment when Abi stood up. "He's coming!"

Chapter Twenty-Eight

Monroe clicked her fingers at the Fae and they followed her obediently out of the back door. Emerald's mother retreated upstairs where she had been instructed to wait and not come down unless Emerald herself told her to. Guinevere climbed onto the windowsill and took up sentry duty.

Emerald stood in front of her coven and looked at them. They were frightened. Last time they'd faced him he'd been unprepared and he'd still murdered one of them, maimed the rest. Now he knew their powers and was coming armed and prepared with magic so dark it was unknown to the authorities. They were right to be frightened.

"We can do this," Emerald said.

"How?" asked Celeste.

"Because we can," said Emerald. "Because we're strong and we're smart and we're capable. Because we're going to make it right for Tig. Because we have each other. Because The Commission may be total bastards but they're pretty damn powerful and they're confident we can do it."

"But..." said Celeste, looking anxiously at Maram. "But how many of us will die?"

"None of us!" said Emerald, glaring across at them. "None of us will die. Do you hear me?"

"Come on Em," said Maram.

"No!" shouted Emerald. "Now listen to me. All of you. Maram is not going to die. None of you are going to die." Her heart began to race. She felt herself begin to swirl, spiral. She let it go. "Now, take my hands. We're together. We're always together."

The coven formed a circle, taking one another's hands and holding on tightly. Emerald felt it. The unity, the strength. She knew they could do it. The magic flowed between them.

"I see him," said Guinevere from the window.

Everyone stared at Guinevere, eyes wide, then back to Emerald. She was growing. She felt strong. Powerful. She felt huge. There was a collective gasp.

"Let's go!" Emerald commanded, then burst out of the kitchen door and onto the driveway where all those years ago she had first let her power grip her, first unleashed fury on a male who had dared to harm Maram. And now she would unleash it on the man who planned to do it again. He would never, ever, hurt her. Not whilst Emerald was standing.

The coven flooded out behind her into the dark grey of the descending evening.

ð

Fadius saw before him an enormous woman, taller than himself by several feet, her muscles huge and her face contorted. Behind her stood the witches. At her side stood the genie.

"DESTROY THEM ALL!" commanded the voice. "KILL THE GENIE!"

ð

Emerald stood tall. She felt, for the first time ever, in control. She wasn't going to fight this, it was her power and with it she could save them. She could save Maram.

Looking down on the man as he stormed down the long dark driveway towards her she saw that he didn't look afraid. But he would be. She would make him. The rain fell down hard as he stared up at her, a look of triumph on his face. Emerald flexed her fingers.

"Abi!" she called down. "What can you see?"

Abi looked frantic, her hands to her head, and her eyes screwed up in concentration. "Nothing!" she shouted, shaking her head and smacking at herself. "I can't see anything!"

"Nothing?" asked Carla, putting a hand to her.

Abi took her hands down and looked at Carla who let out a scream of shock. When Abi looked up at Emerald she understood why. Abi's eyes were completely black. "I can't see!" she howled. "I can't see anything!"

As Carla pulled Abi to her, looking at her face and trying to offer comfort, Emerald turned to Ben.

"Throw the biggest you can," she commanded him. "Let's see how much defence he's got to work with!"

Ben stepped past Emerald, moving a fireball in his hands. His arms outstretched he held it out, ready to throw. Watching them, the man smiled and took a bottle of black liquid from his pocket and swigged it down.

Ben looked up at Emerald, a questioning look on his face. Emerald didn't know what to suggest so gave him a nod and he sent it soaring through the air towards the man.

As it reached him, the fireball dissolved with a loud fizzing sound and a turned into a thick, black smoke that spread out forming a shield around him, moving and swirling and growing.

"Where is he?" cried Celeste, looking frantically around.

"Carla!" Emerald commanded. "He's in there!"

With one last look at Abi, Carla stepped forwards with her hands towards where the man had been standing. She gritted her teeth and sent magic into the smoke, a determined look of fury on her face, but then screamed and fell to the groud, clutching down at her leg.

"What happened?" asked Maram, crouching down to her.

"My leg!" Carla cried out and Emerald saw the bone in her thigh had splintered and torn through the skin. Carla held out her hands again. Through tears and pain she threw more magic towards the smoke cloud then screamed an agonised scream as her arm suddenly bent back, the bone breaking with an ear splitting snap.

"Stop!" Emerald shouted. "He's turning it on you!"

Abi fell to her knees at Carla's side, feeling around to find her beloved. "We've got to get her out of here!" she wept. "Someone help me! Help!"

The wind was picking up now as the rain lashed against them, hammering against the house and the ground in a cacophony of drumming. Overhead the clouds thickened in a dark mass that mirrored the growing smoke on the ground below that dominated the long driveway before her.

Behind her, Emerald saw her mother step out from the kitchen and rush over. "Here, I'll help," she said, and carefully lifted Carla in her arms.

"Mum! Get back in the house!" Emerald shouted. "You're not safe out here!"

"I'm never going to abandon you, Emerald!" her mother shouted. "Now let me help!"

Carefully, Emerald's mum moved the bleeding and agonised Carla into the house, Abi keeping a hand on her arm to follow her lead.

Emerald turned back to the cloud of smoke. Where was he?

She had to figure out what to do. She had to get in there and find him. He could be anywhere, masked by smoke and ready to attack.

But what should she do?

He burst through the smoke with a roar of fury. He seemed to glow and pulsate, a power crazed look on his face like Emerald had never seen. Ben tried again, throwing another fireball but again it changed into smoke, masking the man from view. From behind the smoke they heard a terrifying laugh of victory. Celeste threw her arms out to clear it but the more she tried the thicker the smoke became.

"I can't move it!" she shouted. "I'm just making it worse!"

"We're useless!" Ben shouted in frustration.

Overhead, Emerald heard shouting. She looked up and saw Monroe and Georgette, wings outstretched and buzzing with vibrations, leading the army of Fae. They shot downwards and into the smoke which moved about them in a swirling tornado as overhead a flash of lightning forked across the sky, followed moments later by the crash of thunder.

There were screams and roars from the smoke and suddenly Nico skidded across the gravel driveway and landed in a bloodied heap at Emerald's feet. Celeste crouched to his side, then Emerald's mother appeared again, gathered the wounded soldier into her arms, and carried him into the house.

"I can't see anything!" Maram cried. "What's happening?"

Another Fae, wings torn from her body, was thrown from the smoke cloud, screaming and landing with a crunch. Then another. Their bodies twisted and blooded. The cacophony of shouting and crashing and raging was almost deafening. The smoke that surrounded them bloomed and moved, thick and black and growing.

"You've got to get in there Emerald!" shouted Ben. "He's killing them!"

Emerald felt her heart racing. She looked down on her coven below her. They were watching her, depending on her. Now was the time. She had to do it. She had to take a life once more. She felt her heart racing, her muscles throbbing. She had to do it. She had to do it.

"I can't see where he is!" she shouted as another fork of lightning tore the sky in two.

"Just go!" screamed Celeste, as another Fae was thrown through the smoke, a wing torn in two, her face mottled with bruising and blood.

The smoke was thick, there were Fae embroiled in battle. Emerald couldn't hurt one of them, she couldn't do that to Monroe or to herself. She had to be clear, to know where she was going in case she lost control.

"I don't want to go in until I know where everyone is!" shouted Emerald. "I can't see! We need to get over the smoke!"

At her side Lila stepped forward. "I can help!" she looked up at Emerald and she looked alive. She looked confident in a way Emerald couldn't remember seeing before. "I know what to do!"

Lila ran forwards towards the smoke then in a heartbeat she transformed and became a sparrow. The tiny brown bird swooped into the sky, high above the swirling smoke and soared in a circle. For a moment Emerald watched her, enchanted by the realised freedom, then saw the tiny bird dive bomb down to the left of the smoke cloud.

Emerald roared and raced forwards, her heart pounding, and tore into the smoke. She could do it!

She burst through the smoke and found herself in the centre of the swirling mass, face to face with the man as Fae, armed with spears and glowing spells that moved from their hands and blasted against him, swarmed over him. He flung them to the ground with roars of fury, his fists colliding with skulls with a sickening crunch. He was wounded and weakened, and he was raging, but he seemed to be winning.

Lightning carved open the sky overhead, shooting down and stabbing into the old oak tree behind them. A branch was torn from the tree, and fell to the ground with flames leaping from the wood, giving the smoke a violent orange glow.

As Monroe was flung from the man's body and landed with a crunch at Emerald's ankles she let out a howl of fury and ran at the man, her fist out ready. She would end this now.

ð

Lila swooped with joy overhead, the rain and the thunder not bothering her, so happy to finally be in flight.

She looked down through the rain and saw Emerald below her shrinking and crying out in agony, the man looming above her. Why wasn't she stopping him?

Behind the smoke screen Maram was staring, desperately trying to see anything, but the smoke was too thick. Lila flew down, transforming as she went, and landed in front of her.

"Emerald's hurt," she said. "He's done something to her."

Without pausing for a second, Maram ran into the smoke, disappearing from sight.

Lila watched her, hesitated, then transformed into a wolf. Her teeth were bared, her hackles raised, and she followed Maram into the smoke, ready to do what her grandmother had trained her to do. Ready to finally be who her grandmother had needed her to be. Ben and Celeste flanked her, racing into battle at her side.

ð

Emerald felt her muscles screaming in agony. Everything hurt. She couldn't move, couldn't walk. She staggered backwards and landed heavily, crying out in pain. She tried to force herself to grow, to fight, but every attempt induced such a pain through her limbs that it felt like muscles were being ripped from her bones.

"That hurts, doesn't it," said the man with a cruel laugh as he flung a fist into the face of a Fae warrior.

Emerald tried to speak but she just cried. She couldn't stop him. She couldn't kill him. She tried to move but the pain was so bad she feared she'd pass out.

"Emerald!" Maram cried out, bursting through the smoke at her side.

Emerald looked up. "No!" she cried out. "Go! Run! Quickly!"

"No!" cried Maram, falling to her knees at Emerald's side. "I'm not leaving you!"

"Neither are we!" cried Celeste as she, Ben, and Lila in wolf form landed behind them.

They looked at the man who stood over them. He did not look afraid. Instead he smiled.

"He's done something to me," Emerald wept, trying to stand but collapsing to the ground again.

The man laughed. "You're all alone now," he said, looking at Maram. "Nobody can save you."

Lila snarled a blood thirsty, guttural growl, then launched herself at the man, her claws out and her teeth exposed.

As she landed on him, her mouth aimed straight at his jugular, the wolf form changed and she landed against him as a girl, clinging to his clothes with a desperate fear. She screamed and flung herself away from him but he caught her by the throat.

"Lila!" shouted Celeste as Lila frantically scrambled to free herself, her eyes bulging with horror as he began to crush her windpipe.

"No!" screamed Emerald.

Ben and Celeste ran at him, grabbed his arms and pulled, kicking and fighting. The man laughed again.

"You have no magic," he laughed as his hands crushed at Lila's neck and she started to lose her fight.

"I have to stop him!" wept Maram. "I can't let this happen again!"

"No!" Emerald choked out. "He'll kill you!"

"But he's going to kill Lila!"

Ben and Celeste fought him, bit at him, smacked at him, but he seemed to barely notice as his face, illuminated by the glowing orange of the fire that roared behind them, grinned with a demonic smile.

"No he isn't," said Emerald.

She forced herself, pushed herself to her feet, made herself feel the flood of strength and rage through her body and, screaming in agony, raced towards the man.

He looked up in surprise as Emerald ripped his arms away from Lila, who dropped limply to the ground below, and swung her fist into his face with a thud against his chin.

As Ben and Celeste grabbed Lila, pulling her away, the man landed with a thud on the stones below, and Emerald collapsed on the ground screaming in pain, weeping in despair, as she felt her flesh tearing from her bones with a burning agony.

ð

The smoke around them started to clear as together they got Lila away from the fight.

Monroe hurried to their sides. Her face was bruised and bloodied. "I can help," she said, and crouched down next to Lila. Carefully, she opened Lila's mouth and put her own mouth to it, breathing into her until Lila started to choke and cough.

Monroe quickly moved Lila onto her side and she began to vomit what looked like sparkling water across the stones.

"Let's get her into the house," said Ben.

"Who's that?" asked Celeste in confusion.

Ben and Monroe looked in the same direction, past where the man was starting to get to his feet, to where an old woman had started walking down the long driveway towards them.

ð

Maram rushed to Emerald's side, crying desperately, but Emerald could barely see her. The pain was so intense she felt like her face was going to explode.

"He's coming!" Maram cried. "Emerald he's coming again! We have to kill him!"

"I... can't," Emerald choked out.

She forced her eyes open and looked up to see him standing over them. He reached down and grabbed Emerald by the shoulders, lifting her up with a smile. She tried to fight, the panic in her brain swirling but the more she panicked and the more she fought, the more her body screamed in searing agony that took her breath away.

"Emerald!" Maram screamed, standing up and pulling at his arm, putting all her strength against him to no avail. "Wish! Wish him dead! Emerald wish it now! Wish! Wish it!"

"No!" sobbed Emerald. "I won't do it!"

She wouldn't do it. She would never do it. She gritted her teeth and stared into the man's eyes. She would do the job herself. Even if she died in the process.

Forcing herself to feel the rage, feel the fury, Emerald pushed her body to release its strength. She felt herself grow as agony ripped through her flesh. She howled in anguish but pushed through, her body ripped itself to shreds but she was able to break free of his grip.

She fell to the ground with a crunch, her head smacking hard on the gravel below.

"Emerald!" Maram cried and landed next to her on her knees. "Emerald please! Wish it! Oh god please wish it!"

Shaking her head, tears pouring from Emerald's eyes, she whispered, "Never."

ð

Fadius watched the women on the ground below him. The witch could easily have saved herself by sacrificing the genie, but was choosing her own pain over doing it. The genie was desperately offering her own life to save the witch's.

"END THEM BOTH," the voice commanded.

Fadius looked down at them. He could. He could do it now. He blinked.

"NOW FADIUS! NOW!"

Why would they do that? Neither woman posed a threat to him. The witch was too weak, the genie without strength. None of the watching witches or Fae could stop him. He was the strongest. He could walk away.

"FADIUS!"

He looked up. The sun was setting. Through the clouds and the storm, the last strains of light were creeping in from the west.

He could walk away now and the prophecy wouldn't come to fruition. If he walked away from the genie she would not kill him, she would not kill his God. They had won. This was no longer about saving a God. It was about vengeance. It was about power. It was about murder.

"KILL THEM!"

Fadius looked down towards the women again but something caught his eye. He looked up and saw Jenny watching them. He felt a stinging sensation and held up his hand and saw the blue on his thumb glowing.

"NOW FADIUS! NOW!"

He turned to look down at the two women.

Emerald stood up, her face betraying the pain she was in to the point he had no idea how she was managing to do it, and faced him. "I won't wish you dead," she shouted over the rain and the wind, her voice cracking from the pain in her body. "But I will die before I let you hurt her."

Her body was ripping itself to pieces, and he knew she was taking it for one reason only. For love.

"NOW!" the voice roared. "OR I WILL MAKE YOU SUFFER!"

Fadius stepped towards them. They squared up to him, side by side, standing him down even though they knew they couldn't stop him. Still willing to die for each other.

He looked into their eyes. He saw the faces of all the women he had killed suddenly flash in front of him. All the lives he had ended for this voice he thought was God. It wasn't God. He had been lied to. He had lied to himself. He had done it all for a lie, for the addiction. It was bullshit. He had become the monster he had feared as a child, but worse.

Pain ripped through his body and he stumbled, crying out in pain. "I WILL HURT YOU AGAIN, FADIUS!" boomed the voice, splintering through his head. "KILL THEM OR FACE THE CONSEQUENCES!"

"Please," Fadius wept.

"DO IT FADIUS," instructed the voice. "DO IT."

"If you don't kill him," the genie said to the witch, her face full of desperation and fear, "The demon will never be exposed. We can't kill the demon if we don't kill the man! Please, Emerald, wish it. Wish it."

Demon. The monsters of his childhood, the monster he had become, none compared to the monster in his head.

He looked over at Jenny who was waiting patiently. Eternity.

"THROW HER INTO THE FIRE," the demon roared into his head. "THROW THEM BOTH INTO THE FIRE! LET THEM BURN!"

Fadius roared and ran forwards. The witch and the genie braced themselves to fight with every ounce of strength they had, but Fadius flung himself past them and onto the burning log, screaming in agony as the fire carved into his aching flesh.

ð

Celeste, Lila and Ben ran to Emerald and Maram's side.

Emerald turned to them. "He... he did that!" she gasped.

"We saw," said Celeste, then threw her arms around Emerald, pulling Maram in by the neck and kissing her cheek.

"It's not over," whispered Maram.

Monroe marched over. "Now we fight," she said, her face concentrating hard as every Fae that was still able to stand circled around them.

Emerald turned back to the fire, her heart pounding in her chest. The rain began to slow and they watched in silence.

With a sudden roar, a huge black shape loomed up from the fire, spreading and growing, until enormous arms clawed at the sky and the shadowy shape of Ubel blotted out the moon.

"YOU!" he roared, pointing down at Emerald, his eyes red and glinting evily in the firelight.

"We shall not go down without a fight!" shouted Monroe, and behind her the Fae raised their fists to the sky and cheered a ferocious battle cry. "FOR HANNAH!"

"FOR HANNAH!" they shouted, then launched themselves into the air, ready to fight.

Chapter Twenty-Nine

The fire raged wildly behind them, catching the trees around them as the wind whipped the flames, and from the fire Ubel loomed high.

The Fae, lead by Monroe, flew straight towards the monstrous form of the demon, tiny shapes against the towering darkness. Ubel laughed and swatted them from the air as though they were gnats. Their bodies spiralled to the ground and crunched on the stones.

"PATHETIC!" he roared, then using an enormous clawed hand he ripped a burning branch from the tree behind Fadius' body and held it high, staring down on the watching coven below. His eyes glowed red and his enormous teeth glinted in the firelight. "YOU'LL BURN!"

ð

Emerald felt panic in her chest. They were going to die. Would she see Tig again? Would she be able to apologise?

Tig.

She frowned for a moment then felt in her pocket.

As Ubel hurled the flaming branch towards them, Emerald pulled out three pouches of Tig's enchanted sand.

She flung it as hard as she could straight towards the burning branch.

The fire immediately went out with a hiss and the branch was thrown backwards by the force for the magic sand hitting it. The demon roared in outrage. "I DESTROYED YOUR MAGIC!" he raged.

"Not all of it!" shouted Emerald. "You might have killed Tig but you didn't kill her power!"

To her surprise, Ubel laughed then looked down at them. He smiled, shining silvery teeth spreading across his jaw, his eyes landing on Ben. The beast stared intensely at Ben, then let out a roar like thunder.

"He's chosen his human!" shouted Monroe. "We do it now!"

Ubel roared again, then began to dissolve into smoke, swirling and twisting into a point, moving like a giant snake about to pounce on its prey below.

Ben stumbled backwards, horror on his face. "Emerald," he said, turning to her. "You have to kill me. If he gets into me, you have to kill me. You promise me? Kill me. I won't do those things! I won't murder women for him! You kill me, Emerald, you kill me!"

The smoke monster swirled higher and higher into the sky, then shot forwards towards Ben who screamed and covered his face as he fell to his knees in fear.

"I WISH UBEL DEAD!" Emerald screamed.

The smoke monster vanished with a pop.

And so did Maram.

Emerald stared at Ben.

"Emerald, I... I..." Ben stuttered.

"Maram?" said Emerald, looking around her, panic rising in her chest. "Where is she?!"

Behind them they heard a cough and Emerald spun around. The fire had gone out and a blackened body lay on the log. The body was coughing. An old woman was approaching it with a smile on her face.

"Hello, Fadius dear," she said, smiling down at the body. "I'm here to collect my payment."

"Where's Maram?" asked Emerald, turning away from the bizarre scene. It didn't matter. She stared around frantically. "Maram! Maram!"

"She disappeared," said Ben, his voice a strange hollow noise. "When you wished."

"You killed the demon," said Monroe, walking towards her. "You did your duty. My daughter has been avenged. Thank you."

"MARAM!" Emerald screamed. The Fae, the woman and the body, Ben, none of it mattered. She had used her wish. Maram had gone.

The lamp. She had to find the lamp. She ran from them and headed into the house. Carla was now propped against a cushion, leaning on the wall, two of the wounded Fae were tending to her, moving their hands across her broken bones.

Emerald ignored them.

"Emerald, are you okay?" asked her mum as she ran past but Emerald didn't stop.

She ran past them and into the living room then up the stairs to her bedroom. She flung open the wardrobe, rummaged through the sweaters that were in the bottom, and pulled out the shoe box. Pausing a second, she pulled off the top and found the box empty.

"NO!" she howled, throwing the box to the floor and sobbing.

"Hey," she heard a voice behind her, but she didn't turn around. She couldn't. She couldn't look at them.

She felt a hand on her back and looked up. Her mother was knelt at her side, stroking her gently, behind her Celeste, Abi, Ben and Lila were watching her, worry on their faces.

"I killed Maram!" Emerald sobbed, then fell into her mother's arms. "She's gone! The lamp is gone! She's gone!"

"Oh my darling," whispered her mother, stroking her hair and kissing her head.

Downstairs there was a knock at the door.

"I promised her," Emerald whispered. "I promised her. I promised I'd never use that last wish! From the day I met her I've promised!"

The knock from downstairs came louder.

"Someone's here," whispered Celeste, looking around nervously.

"I don't care," said Emerald, sitting up from her mother's lap.

"What if... is it..."

"I don't think demons knock..." said Carla.

The door banged again.

"I'll go," said Ben and hurried away.

"Mummy," Emerald said, picking up the empty shoe box, tears falling from her chin and landing on the bottom of it. "I killed her."

Quiet settled over the room as Emerald wept, her friends cuddled one another, and her mother softly stroked her back.

A moment later they heard footsteps.

"Erm," Ben said as he came back into the room. "There's a man here. He says he's Emerald's grandfather. His name's Stuart Wren."

Emerald's mother tensed. Emerald looked up. "He's here?"

"Erm, yeah," said Ben, shuffling on the spot awkwardly. "He's... intense."

Emerald's heart raced. Her grandfather had brought Maram to her.

She stood up and, sniffing heavily, headed downstairs with her mother and friends following behind. Her face felt sore from the tears, and her hands were shaking. What did he want? Why was he here? Did he know she'd used her last wish? Was she in trouble or was he proud?

He sat in the living room with Guinevere at his side. He looked exactly the same as she remembered. Smart suit, neat grey hair, sharp blue eyes.

"Emerald," he said. "It's good to see you."

"Hello grandad," she said.

"And Olivia, my dear," he stood and approached her mother with his arms out. "It's been a long time."

"Years," agreed Emerald's mother stiffly. "Since before Eric left."

Emerald twitched, she hadn't heard her mother use her father's name in years.

"Yes," he said, stepping back and nodding. "I realise I perhaps should have been in touch."

"With the wife and child your son abandoned?" said Olivia, cocking her head to the side. "That implies we matter. Of course you didn't bother. You and your son are cut from the same cloth. What are you doing here?"

"I am here to see Emerald," he said, no sign of any emotional response to her criticisms.

"Why?" asked Emerald. "What do you want?"

"Can we sit?" he asked. "Perhaps your friends would like to wait in the kitchen whilst we speak?"

"No," said Emerald. "They wouldn't. They're fine here."

Her grandfather sighed and nodded. "As I expected. Very well."

"Emerald," said Guinevere from the sofa. "Please listen to Mr Wren."

"Mr Wren?" asked Emerald, glaring at her. "Whose side are you on?"

Guinevere looked down at her paws but didn't answer.

Emerald sat on one of the chairs and her grandfather sat back down next to Guinevere.

The door opened and a hobbling, but healed, Carla walked into the room. "I didn't want to miss anything," she said. "Monroe says to tell that old goat that he's an ass but she'll see him tomorrow."

"Carla!" chastised Guinevere.

Carla shrugged and went to Abi's side.

"You work with Monroe?" asked Emerald.

"Yes, I do," said Stuart Wren. "Well, not directly. She works with my colleagues but I am anticipating an extensive debriefing at which we will both be present."

"You're Commission," said Emerald.

"Yes," he said. "I am."

"That's why you brought me the lamp?" she asked.

"It is," he said. "You were destined to face Ubel."

"But I was just a little girl," she said. "I was a child. How could you do that to me?"

"I didn't do anything to you," he said, leaning forwards. "You didn't have to rub the lamp, nor save the last wish for this time. You did it because it's who you are and what you're destined for. I simply made sure the genie got to her rightful place."

"She had a name," Emerald snarled.

"Of course," he said. "Maram. Now. To business."

"Business?" asked Emerald. "What do you want from me now?"

"I would like to discuss the next step," he said, resting his chin on the ball of his hand and fixing her with a stare that made her feel like he was looking straight into her brain. "I'm extending an offer of employment to you."

Emerald sat upright, scrunching up her nose in disgust. "What? At the Commission? With you?"

"With us," said Guinevere, gently.

"You too?" asked Emerald, her face crumpling. "You've gone back to them? Even after everything?"

"Emerald, we aren't the evil you think we are," said Stuart Wren.

"Did you know Tig would die?" Emerald asked.

"Everything is destined to be what it will be," he answered.

"What kind of answer is that?" demanded Carla.

"What about Maram?" Emerald asked, terrified of the answer. "You brought her here. Did you know she'd die? Did you know I'd kill her?"

"Kill her?" Stuart Wren repeated, leaning forwards. "Emerald, Maram isn't dead."

Emerald blinked. "She isn't?"

"No," he said. "She fulfilled her duty as your genie. She has gone back in the lamp to be found by her next master."

"Her next *master*?" said Emerald, curling her lip in disgust. "You have no idea what you're talking about, do you? Her next *master* is also her next *rapist*, her next *owner*."

"You could find her," said Stuart Wren, sitting back and folding his arms. "Find her lamp. Bring her back."

Behind her Emerald heard gasps. "How?" she asked, her heart racing.

"With our help," said Stuart Wren. "Join the Commission and you'll have access to the best resources that the world has to offer."

"That's why you're here," said Emerald quietly. "You want me to join you. Was this your end game all along? Pitch me against a demon and if I survive then I've got what it takes?"

"We've observed you for a long time," said her grandfather. "You've impressed us, and now you're ready."

"You've observed me, have you?" asked Emerald, glaring at Guinevere who dropped her eyes and flicked her tail. "Well then you should have observed that it wasn't me. Not just me. It was us. All of us. We've done good because we've been together! Maram included... Tig included."

"Perhaps," said Stuart Wren. "But the offer for you is there."

"No," she said, feeling tears welling up and forcing them down again. "Never."

"Emerald..." interjected Guinevere, but Stuart held up his hand.

"If you're certain?" he asked.

"I am," said Emerald.

"Very well," said Stuart Wren, standing up. "Well, it was good to see you again Emerald. Congratulations on your success with the demon. Olivia," he said turning to

Emerald's mother. "My son is an embarrassment, and an utter ass."

Emerald's mother looked a bit startled then laughed. "Yes, he is."

"Goodnight all," he said, then vanished.

"Woah," said Ben. "That was cool."

Emerald turned away from him. She couldn't bear to look at him. She had sacrificed Maram to save his life. He hadn't asked for it, and she knew that, but she hated him for it.

"I'm going to bed," she said. "Guinevere, I don't want to see you here when I come down."

Without waiting for a response Emerald left the room, climbed the stairs, went to her bedroom. She picked up the empty box from the floor and stared at it for a moment, then let out a scream of despair and threw it against the wall.

ð

For three days Emerald stayed in her bedroom. Her mother brought her food and drinks which she barely touched, tried to speak to her but Emerald couldn't talk.

"Come downstairs, sweetheart," her mother tried to coax her. But Emerald couldn't move. Couldn't think. Her head was drained of tears, drained of the ability to speak.

On the third day there was a knock at her bedroom door. "Emerald, Celeste's here," said her mother. "I'm going to let her come in, okay?"

Emerald didn't move. She felt someone sit on the bed at her side then heard the door close.

"Hey," came Celeste's gentle voice. "How you doing?"

Emerald blinked.

"We've missed you," she said. "We've been worried about you."

Emerald turned to look at her.

"The shelter's being rebuilt," she said. "This amazing charity took us up and they've done so much already. I've been working non stop with the women in their temporary housing. They're frightened but we're getting there."

Emerald looked away again. She didn't care.

"Tig's body should be released to us soon," she went on. "We're making arrangements. Carla's insisting we play Five Finger Death Punch as her coffin's carried through the crem."

Emerald felt a small laugh come out. "Tig would love that," she whispered.

"True," said Celeste with a smile.

Emerald felt fresh tears start to slide down her cheeks. They were planning Tig's funeral.

"It's Lila's grandmother's funeral this weekend," Celeste went on, one hand slowly rubbing Emerald's shoulder. "I think the music might be a bit more appropriate. I'm guessing some Hall and Oates followed by Nelly Furtado. We're all going. Ben says he'll pick you up after me."

Emerald turned sharply towards her. "No."

"No?"

"No! I'm not getting in a car with him. No."

"Hey," said Celeste, putting a hand on Emerald's. "He's absolutely breaking his heart. And it's not his fault. You know that."

"She's gone because of him!"

"You did the right thing," said Celeste gently. "You have to cut yourself some slack, Emerald."

"I saved him not her!"

"You saved him and how many other women?" asked Celeste. She slipped off the bed and knelt in front of Emerald, resting her head on the mattress so she was face to face with her. "We were broken, Em. The Fae were literally ripped apart. None of our magic was doing what was needed. If he'd taken Ben he could have used Ben to not only kill all of us but how many other women too?"

"But..."

"But nothing," said Celeste. "It is fine to be sad. Feel everything you need to feel. But do not blame that boy. He didn't ask Ubel to target him and he didn't ask you to save him. He did nothing wrong. We know bad men, we know them far too well, but Ben is not one of them. Feel what you need to feel but be honest about it."

"I'm sorry," Emerald whispered, then began to cry. "I'm so sorry."

Celeste gently stroked her hair and kissed her cheek. "I know, my darling, I know," she whispered.

After a few minutes Emerald sat up. "Let's go downstairs," she said.

"Erm no," said Celeste. "First you're going to go and have a shower," she said. "Then we're going to go downstairs."

Emerald looked down at herself and put a hand to her hair. "Yeah," she said. "Okay."

She showered and dressed then headed downstairs. Her mother silently greeted her with a hug, then pushed a cup of coffee towards her. "Here."

Emerald gratefully accepted it and sat down. "Where's Guinevere?" she asked after a moment.

"Gone," said her mum. "She disappeared after you told her to go and I've not seen her since."

"Oh," said Emerald. "Good. I mean... I wonder where she is though..."

Celeste sipped a cup of coffee and looked nervously out of the window.

"You know where she is," said Emerald, peering at her friend.

Celeste sipped her coffee again and mumbled something incoherent.

"Where is she?" asked Emerald.

"At your flat," said Celeste, looking at her hands.

"How do you know?"

"We've been... meeting there," said Celeste. "Like before. Only... different."

"Oh," said Emerald.

"Abi's still getting visions only much clearer now," said Celeste. "We aren't as strong as we were without you there with only the five of us, but Guinevere's been helping. We've already done some good."

"Oh," said Emerald again.

"She's trying to get a vision about Maram," said Celeste.

Emerald looked up at her, tears in her eyes. "Has she managed?"

"Not yet," said Celeste. "But honestly she's getting so much stronger than she ever was before. She's going to keep trying. If we can find out where her lamp has gone then maybe..."

"I'll go wherever I have to go," said Emerald. "I'll do anything I have to do. If I can get her back."

"Us too," said Celeste. "We're in, okay? I promise. All of us."

"Thank you," said Emerald.

"Moira's funeral is on Saturday at eleven," said Celeste, standing up and kissing Emerald on the cheek. "We'll come pick you up at half past ten."

"Okay," said Emerald.

"You did the right thing," she said quietly. "Try to forgive yourself."

"I can't."

"I know."

Chapter Thirty

"Door!" Emerald shouted from the bathroom where she was carefully applying concealer to hide the dark grey blotches below her eyes that exposed her lack of sleep.

She heard her mother cross the kitchen and open the door, then let out a cry.

Dropping the concealer wand she opened the bathroom door and hurried into the kitchen. Her mother stepped aside, a look of shock on her face.

"Dad?"

"Hey there, baby girl," said the man in the doorway.

He was shorter than she remembered, with salt and pepper hair where it was once black, but he was definitely her father.

"What are you doing here?" Emerald asked, walking towards him and standing between her mother and him.

"I came to see you," he said.

"Now isn't a good time," said Emerald. "I'm going to a funeral."

"I only need a few minutes," he said, stepping forward. Emerald stepped backwards and looked at her mother who still looked shell shocked then back to her father. "Alone."

"Excuse me?" asked Emerald. "Alone? You don't get to dictate terms here, *Dad*, as I recall you gave up that right when you fucked off and left us."

"I understand that, Emerald," he said. "But this doesn't concern your mother. It can't. It's not her world."

"My mother is part of my world," said Emerald. "Both of us or neither."

"It's okay, Emerald," said her mother, putting a hand on her shoulder. "You go into the living room. I'll be here."

"Mum..." Emerald protested.

"Honestly," said her mum, putting a hand to Emerald's cheek. "I trust you. And you know I'll never be far."

"Okay," said Emerald. She kissed her mother's cheek then led her father through the kitchen and into the living room. She sat in the chair her grandfather had occupied just days before. "What do you want?" she asked him.

He sat down and leaned back in the arm chair, his left foot resting on his knee. Emerald got a flashback. It was how he had always sat.

"You are a powerful young woman," he said, smiling at her. "Impressive. Strong."

Emerald screwed up her nose. "That doesn't answer my question."

"I made a mistake when I left you, Emerald," he said. "I know that now. I walked away when I should have stayed and been there for you."

"Right..."

"It recently came to my attention just how much you needed me," he said. "How much you would have benefited from having me around. If you're this strong now, imagine how much power you'd have been wielding if you had been raised by me instead of Olivia."

"I think mum did an alright job, actually," said Emerald. "And Guinevere taught me well."

He put his feet on the floor and his head in his hands. "My daughter reduced to the ward of a Guardian," he said.

"Come with me now, Emerald. Come with me. I can take you somewhere where you can learn to be so much more."

"I don't want to be more," said Emerald. "I'm happy with who I am."

"You want to find your friend?" he asked her. "Your genie?"

Emerald hesitated. "Yes."

"Come with me," he said, leaning forwards.

"Why?"

"I can help you," he said. "You and I, side by side, Emerald. Just how it was supposed to be. We can find her together. There are so many powers at Adamantine, so many witches. So many Beings. If there is anywhere in the world could help you find her, it's there."

Emerald stared at him. He looked so eager. So many witches... so many powers...

She couldn't betray her mother by going with him, it'd be so wrong. But to find Maram? If he really could help find her then wasn't this the opportunity she needed? Since rejecting her grandfather she'd not been able to think of any way to find the lamp and now her own father was here offering her exactly what she needed.

Could she afford to reject the offer? Could she afford to take him up on it?

She chewed her lip. She didn't know what to do.

"I..." she said. "I don't know... I just..."

"Emerald," he said. "Imagine how much we could achieve together. Imagine what we could do with the power of a genie's wishes..."

"Get out."

He sat upright. "What?"

"Now."

He stood up, perplexed. "Why?"

"Are you kidding me?" she shouted. "You're not interested in helping me save Maram! You don't give a shit about her! Or me! You just want what we can do for you! Are you crazy? Get out! Get out now!"

"Emerald..." he said, approaching her.

"GET OUT!" she screamed, feeling herself start to grow. "You're a fucking psychopath! The best thing you ever did was to walk out of this house! We didn't need you! We never needed you! Mum's amazing. Amazing! And I didn't need you when I had her." She was huge now. Her father staring up at her in horror and fear. "And you tell me she's not part of my world? Who was here when we fought Ubel? Who? It wasn't you! It was her! She had a chance to be safe and she didn't take it! She stuck by me and saved people when she had no chance to defend herself!" Her father backed away towards the door, trembling, his mouth hanging open. "Get out! NOW!"

Her father howled in horror, threw open the living room door and staggered away through the kitchen, the front door slamming behind him.

Emerald felt her breathing start to slow as her mother poked her head around the door and looked at her.

"So your dad just left," she said.

Emerald felt herself shrinking, her heart rate slowing, her brain clearing. "Funny that," she said.

"You ripped your dress a bit," said her mum.

"Yeah," said Emerald. "I did."

"And the state of your face. It'll take more than concealer to fix that."

Emerald laughed and allowed her mother to envelope her in a hug. "I love you Mummy."

"I love you too, baby."

ð

The funeral service for Moira was remarkably moving, thought Emerald. The room was filled with a fascinatingly eclectic mix of primarily women. Women who told stories of her bravery and support, women who had lived with her during times of crisis, women alongside whom she had stood in protests. The old woman had had quite a life, even aside from her secret life as the man-killing werewolf.

"It was a beautiful service," said Celeste, hugging Lila as they walked out of the crematorium.

"Your grandmother had a fascinating life," said Emerald.

"You're not kidding," said Lila with a sad smile.

"See you in a bit, yeah?" said Carla, kissing Lila's cheek.

"I'll need a drink after this," said Lila.

The five of them walked away and left Lila to embrace the rest of the mourners. Small groups gathered in the cold sunlight, talking and hugging, and they walked through them to a cluster of trees further back so they could talk in private.

"So, my dad came to visit me this morning," said Emerald, wrapping her arms around her waist.

"He what?" demanded Carla, rage on her face. "What the hell did he want?"

"Me," she said, shrugging. "And Maram."

"What?" asked Ben.

"To go find her, to use her," said Emerald. "To become her new master."

"Sick bastard," sat Carla in disgust.

"Are you okay?" asked Celeste.

"No," said Emerald. "I mean, yeah. I just... I don't know how I'm going to find her. I feel like I'm walking away from the only chance I have, you know?"

"I'm trying," Abi promised her. "It's like there's a block in my brain. I can't even get a feeling."

"It's okay," said Emerald. "It's not your responsibility."

"Are you going to call your grandfather?" asked Ben.

"What? No! No. Of course not," she said. "There has to be another way. There has to be."

"Excuse me?" came a voice behind Emerald.

She turned and saw a woman she recognised, but couldn't place, with a little girl clinging onto her leg. "Hello," she said.

"You're Emerald, right?" she asked.

"Yes."

"And... Ben?" she asked, looking at Ben.

"Sophie?" said Ben, staring at her.

"Yes," she said, smiling warmly.

"Oh my god," whispered Emerald, her mouth dropping open. Sophie. Sophie the first girl they had ever saved. Sophie who had looked so weak, so afraid was now tall and plump with lustrous dark hair and a confident smile.

A man came up behind her and slid an arm around her waist. "Hello," he said. "So you're the famous Emerald? I'm Leo." He stuck a hand out and Emerald shook it. Then he did the same to Ben. "I've heard so much about you."

"Sweetie," said Sophie, bending down to the little girl who was clinging to her leg. "Baby, come here." She lifted the girl into her arms. "Darling, mummy and daddy want you to meet somebody very important. This is Emerald Wren."

"Wren?" said the little girl. "That's like my name!"

"It is!" said Sophie, kissing her cheek. "Emerald, this is my daughter, Wren."

"Oh my god," whispered Emerald, tears starting to pour down her face.

"Oh please, don't cry," pleaded Sophie, handing the child to her husband and then taking Emerald's hands. "She's alive because of you. I'm alive because of you. You and your friends. You saved my life that day and I've never seen you to say thank you. I'm so grateful to see you now. I've always wanted to tell you what a difference you made to my life. I couldn't name her anything else. Thank you, Emerald Wren, thank you."

Emerald felt hands on her back as her friends rubbed her shoulders. She took Sophie in a hug and held on tight, crying on her soft black cashmere cardigan. "I'm sorry," she said, pulling away and trying to wipe it.

"Oh, no," said Sophie, smiling. "Forget it. It doesn't matter. So, is Maram anywhere? I'd love to see her too."

Emerald opened and closed her mouth. "No," she said eventually. "She's... gone... away..."

"Oh, that's a shame," said Sophie. "Well, when you see her would you please send my regards? Please? I've thought of you all so often. I'd love for her to know how grateful I am."

"Of course," said Emerald.

Sophie rummaged in her handbag and pulled out a card "This is my number," she said. "I run a charity that funds refuges, that's how I knew Moira. She was one of our biggest supporters, always doing things for us."

"You're Sophie Hunter?" asked Celeste.

"Yes," said Sophie. "I'm sorry, have we met?"

"Your company has come in to fix the refuge on Waterside Street," said Celeste. "I work there."

"Oh wonderful!" she said. "Yes, that's us. After Emerald, Maram and Ben saved me that day it gave me a new focus. There are hundreds of women in every town in situations like I was in, trapped and needing help. And you guys can't be there for all of them. So I want to be. I can't bear for any more women to feel they've been abandoned or forgotten, as if they don't matter."

"That's amazing," said Emerald.

"Thank you," said Sophie. "For giving me the chance to do it."

"Mummy?" said Wren. "I'm thirsty."

"Come on baby," said Sophie, taking the girl in her arms. "Say bye bye."

"Bye bye," said the little girl, smiling a toothy grin.

Emerald watched them go then felt herself start to cry again.

Celeste wrapped her arms around her, "You did a good thing. Don't cry."

"Maram is abandoned," wept Emerald. "She'll feel abandoned and forgotten. Maram saved Sophie and I can't save Maram!"

"Oh honey," said Celeste, holding her close.

"I need to go and see Guinevere," she said.

"Come on then," said Ben. "I'll take you. We'll meet you all at the wake, okay?"

Celeste, Abi and Carla all kissed her cheek, then Emerald and Ben walked to the car.

They rode in silence, Emerald staring out of the window and Ben not intruding into her thoughts, until they got to Emerald's flat.

"I've not been back here," she said quietly as she got out of the car. "Not since I was here with Maram."

"I know," he said. "We've been looking after it for you."

"Thank you," she said, smiling at him then looking up at the building she knew so well. A strange empty feeling filled her. This wasn't her home anymore. This wasn't her sanctuary.

They headed up the stairs then went to her front door. It felt weird to be there. Like it was a stranger's door. She pulled out a key and pushed it open, stepping into the flat.

"Oh!" she gasped.

"Hello Emerald," greeted her grandfather from the chair by the window.

"Don't worry," said Guinevere from the table. "Please, stay."

"What are you doing here?" Emerald demanded.

"I'd like to speak with you," said her grandfather. "In private please, young man."

"Emerald?" asked Ben, peering round her.

"It's okay," said Emerald, turning to him. "He's my grandad."

"I'll erm... be outside," said Ben. "Yell if you need anything, yeah?"

Emerald nodded vaguely and he closed the door behind her. "What are you doing here?"

"I'm here to see you," he said.

"Why? How did you know I was coming?" she asked.

He smiled at her. "You are going to learn so much with us, Emerald," he said. "I want to introduce you to Nahla Hussain. She's your new boss."

"My what?" asked Emerald, then stepped around the corner and saw a woman standing by the fireplace. "Who are you?"

"My name's Nahla," she said, holding out a hand which Emerald took, not because she wanted to particularly but because it was just what you did. "I am head of the Beings department at the Commission. Monroe is one of my staff members, as well as working with the Underworld Initiative of course."

"The what?" asked Emerald, blinking and looking back and forth between the two.

"It was my team that helped acquire Maram's lamp," she went on. "We are ready to work with you on finding it again."

"I... I..." Emerald stuttered.

"We have a team ready," Nahla went on. "And we are tracking her. With your help we can bring her in. We can protect her. Imagine the good you and she could do with the resources of the Commission behind you. Imagine the lives you could save."

Emerald hesitated. "But how could I trust you?" she asked. "You lied to me. Guinevere lied to me."

"I'm sorry, Emerald," said her grandfather. "Unfortunately there are aspects of my work that I do not always agree with. However, I respect that sacrifices must be made."

"Sacrifices?" asked Emerald, the word smarting. She stared at him with furious tears in her eyes.

"It's a big world, Emerald," he went on. "Far more complicated, far more filled with danger and potential disaster than you could ever imagine. I am terribly sorry for what has happened to your friends, truly."

"Emerald," said Guinevere, her voice calm and reassuring. "My time with you is over. I'll be taking on a new charge soon. A new witch who needs me. You're destined for greater things and joining the Commission is how you can achieve them."

"You're leaving me?" she asked, her lip starting to wobble, tears forming in her eyes yet again.

The cat jumped from the table and came to her, leaning against her legs. Emerald crouched down and stroked her head. "You're grown, Emerald," said Guinevere. "And now you can move on."

"But I don't know how to do this without you," she whispered. "I've never done this without you."

"You took down Ubel without me," said the cat, looking at her intently. "Remember?"

"But I lost Maram," she cried. "Please, Guinevere, I can't lose you too. I don't know how to do this without you!"

"I taught you well," Guinevere purred. "You've not needed me for a very long time."

"But..." said Emerald, tears running down her cheeks. "I do need you."

"No, you don't," said the cat. "And I was selfish staying with you when someone else really does need me. I only stayed because I love you."

"I love you, too," she whispered.

"I know," said the cat, and nuzzled against her. "And I'll always be your friend. But now I need to be somebody else's Guardian."

Emerald nodded, tears falling down her face. "Okay. I understand."

"I'm ready to take you to your new home," said her grandfather.

"I haven't agreed to anything yet!" Emerald protested, wiping tears from her eyes.

"Then why did you come?" asked her grandfather.

"Because I... I..."

"You came because you wanted me to help you get in touch with Mr Wren," said Guinevere. "Didn't you?"

"Yes," admitted Emerald. "I suppose I did."

"We're ready to go," said Nahla, smiling. "As soon as you are, Ms Wren."

"Then let's get on with business, shall we?" said her grandfather.

"Can't I say goodbye?" she asked, looking towards the door where Ben was waiting on the other side.

"Yes," he said. "Of course you can. You're not my prisoner, you're my employee."

"She is *my* employee actually, Mr Wren," interrupted Nahla.

"Quite right, Ms Hussain," said Stuart Wren, flashing a grin at Emerald that seemed to both be apologetic and full of mischief at the same time. "Emerald, say goodbye to your friend then we can go. This won't be the last time you see them, don't worry."

Emerald staggered to the door and opened it. On the other side was Ben, loyally waiting for her, playing on his phone.

"You okay?" he asked her, concern on his face.

"I'm going," she said.

"Where?"

"To find Maram."

"How?"

"With them."

"The Commission?"

"Yes," she said, nodding and crying. "They can find her. They can protect her. I have to do it, Ben, I have to do it. You understand, don't you? It's Maram. I can actually save her."

"Hey, no judgment," he said, putting a hand on her shoulder. "Whatever it takes is what you said, whatever it takes is what you meant. I think we all knew this was coming."

"Ben... I..."

"Yeah?"

"Thank you," she said. "I'll see you again. I promise."

"I know," he said.

"Will you tell the others?"

"Of course," he said.

"Bye," she said.

"Goodbye, Emerald," he said.

She hesitated for a moment, then threw her arms around his neck and held on tightly. He was still for a moment, then slowly wrapped his arms around her waist, his hands gently against her back.

She pulled back and kissed his cheek. "I'll miss you," she said to him.

"I'll miss you too," he said.

Emerald nodded then straightened her jacket and stepped back into the flat, closing the door behind her.

"Right," said her grandfather. "I have informed your mother of your new address and packed your bags. Shall we go?"

"Erm, okay," she said, overwhelmed and anxious about the new life she was about to start.

"Are you ready to change the world?" her grandfather asked, smiling at her proudly.

"I am," said Emerald. "It needs to be changed."

"I'll see you bright and early for work on Monday," said Nahla.

"I... right... yes," said Emerald, nodding formally and standing straight.

Emerald's grandfather took her hand and before she could say anything, before she could even consider acting on the impulse that suddenly surged through her to change her mind and run as far and fast as she could, a sudden rush of air hit her and the living room vanished.

ð

"Good work, Guinevere," said Nahla, once Stuart and his granddaughter had disappeared from sight. "You are an excellent Guardian. I'm glad to have you back on the team."

Guinevere smiled wanly, looking around the flat. "It'll be strange to leave this place. And these people. They're good people."

"Are you ready?"

"I suppose," said Guinevere.

"I've got your new charge ready," she said. "She's in a women's refuge near here. A young healer named Lotta."

"A healer?" asked Guinevere, a smile spreading across her face. "I know a coven that need a healer."

The End

Read More

Siren Stories: The Ultimate Bibliography

Lilly Prospero And The Magic Rabbit (The Lilly Prospero Series Book 1)
By J.J. Barnes

Lilly Prospero And The Magic Rabbit is a young adult urban fantasy exploring the corrupting effects of absolute power on a teenage girl. When the unpopular and lonely Lilly Prospero is given a talking pet rabbit, her life begins to change. She is thrust into a world of magic, mystery, and danger, and has to get control of a power she doesn't understand fast to make the difference between life and death. The first in a new series by J.J. Barnes, Lilly Prospero And The Magic Rabbit is a tale full of excitement, sorrow and mystery, as Lilly Prospero shows just how strong a girl can be.

Available in Paperback and for Kindle.

Alana: A Ghost Story
By Jonathan McKinney

Alana is a ghost, trapped in the New York Film Academy dorms, where she died. She has friends, fellow ghosts, with whom she haunts the students living there, passing her time watching whatever TV shows and movies the students watch.

But she is restless. She wants to move on. And when a medium moves into the dorms, Alana gets a nasty shock, which turns her mundane afterlife upside down.

Alana is a light yet moving short story about a miraculous love that travels many years and many miles to save a lost, trapped and hopeless soul.

Available in Paperback and for Kindle.

Emily the Master Enchantress: The First Schildmaids Novel (The Schildmaids Saga Book 1)
By Jonathan McKinney

Hidden, veiled behind the compressed wealth of New York City, is a dank underbelly of exploitation and slavery, which most people never see, or sense, or suffer. A cruel, expanding world.

And when Emily Hayes-Brennan, a proficient enchantress with a good heart and a tendency to overshare, is recruited to the world renowned crime fighters, the Schildmaids, she will find that that cruel world threatens to expand around her, and everyone she cares about.

She will be confronted by conflicts of fate and choice, as she seeks to find her place in the world.

Available in Paperback and for Kindle.

After the Mad Dog in the Fog: An Erotic Schildmaids Novelette
By Jonathan McKinney and J.J. Barnes

Emily Hayes-Brennan wants to get through a simple night out in her home city of New York, introducing her new boyfriend Teo to her friends, so she can get him home and have sex with him for the very first time. But when an obnoxious admirer and old flame shows up, she begins to fear that her plans are going awry.

After the Mad Dog in the Fog is a wild and energetic novelette about love and desire, and about the free joy that comes from prioritising the one you love before all others.

Available in Paperback and for Kindle.

Lilly Prospero And The Mermaid's Curse (The Lilly Prospero Series Book 2)
By J.J. Barnes

Lilly Prospero And The Mermaid's Curse is a young adult, urban fantasy following Lilly Prospero and her friend Saffron Jones on a magical adventure to Whitstable.

Whilst on a family holiday, Lilly and Saffron meet mermaids under attack from a mysterious and violent stranger, work with a powerful coven of witches, and fight to save not only the lives of the mermaids, but their own lives as well.

Available in Paperback and for Kindle.

The Inadequacy of Alice Anders: A Schildmaids Short Story
By Jonathan McKinney

Alice Anders can summon vision of the future, which guide her heroic friends through heroic acts. Sometimes she'll see vulnerable people in danger; sometimes she'll see her superhero friends in places where they can help those who can't help themselves.

But, for the last three and a half weeks, she's not been able to summon a single vision—and given that she started working for the superhero team of her dreams, the Schildmaids, exactly three and a half weeks ago, she's becoming anxious about her worth. And to figure out why her power has gone away, she'll have to push herself, and face some hard truths.

The Inadequacy of Alice Anders is a light and bittersweet short story about the pain of loss, and about facing that pain when it threatens to hold you down and hold you back.

Available in Paperback and for Kindle.

The Fundamental Miri Mnene: The Second Schildmaids Novel (The Schildmaids Saga Book 2)
By Jonathan McKinney

Miri Mnene is the Syncerus, a warrior, and the strongest of the Schildmaids, the New York team of legendary crime fighters. But she was not always the Syncerus. Once, she was the Xuétú Nánrén Shashou, the final student of the man-hating, man-killing Guan-yin Cheh.

And when she is sent to South Dakota to investigate a mystical brothel, which has been kidnapping women, kidnapping girls, and forcing them to work, she is confronted by the darkness that lives within her when her past and present collide.

The Fundamental Miri Mnene is a powerful novel about the lengths to which you should go, the lengths to which you must go, in order to see justice in the world.

Available in Paperback and for Kindle.

The Relief of Aurelia Kite: A Schildmaids Novella
By Jonathan McKinney

Aurelia Kite is a young New Yorker at Christmas, trapped in an abusive relationship, dreaming of escape. And when her controlling boyfriend Trafford takes on a new job, her path crosses with two highly serious female crime fighters, causing her to make a big decision about what she will and will not tolerate.

The Relief of Aurelia Kite is a harsh novella with a soft centre, about hope in the face of toxic romance, and about the salvation that can be found just by talking to a sympathetic stranger.

Available in Paperback and for Kindle.

Not Even Stars: The Third Schildmaids Novel
By Jonathan McKinney

Teo Roqué is journeying through Europe with Emily Hayes-Brennan, the woman he loves, when ancient hostilities give way to a war between powerful, clandestine organisations. A war which puts the young couple's lives in danger, as well as all those they care about.

And as a new threat emerges, fanning the conflict's flames, Teo and Emily must work together to end the war before it leads to a disaster much, much worse than they'd imagined.

Not Even Stars is an incredibly intense novel about all-consuming love, about awe-inspiring heroism, and about the cost of making the right choice when the fate of the world hangs in the balance.

Available in Paperback and for Kindle.

The Mystery of Ms. Riley: a Schildmaids Novella
By Jonathan McKinney

Alice Anders and Rakesha McKenzie are members of the Schildmaids, the legendary New York crime fighters. And when Alice sees visions of Nina Riley, a young New Yorker carrying a deep, hidden pain, the two heroes fight to determine what has caused that pain, and how to save Ms. Riley from a prison she cannot even see.

The Mystery of Ms. Riley is a harsh yet hopeful story about self-doubt, about ordinary, everyday oppression, and about the kind of love that defies the testimonies of everyone around you.

Available in Paperback and for Kindle.

Unholy Water: A Halloween Novel
By Jonathan McKinney

In the misty Lancashire town of Ecclesburn, kids go missing. But no one talks about it. Everyone knows why, but they don't talk about it. The grown ups smear garlic and holy water over their necks and wrists while walking the dog after dark, but they never say the V word.

And when one of the local pubs is taken over by a group of undead monsters, and a trio of vampire hunters is called to clear them out, a terrible series of events begins to play out, which will change the way Ecclesburnians live forever.

Unholy Water is a dark and bloodthirsty novel about desire in wild excess, about whether you should defy your circumstances or adapt to them, and about the kind of inflexible determination that can save or destroy those that matter most.

Available in Paperback and for Kindle.

Emerald Wren and the Coven of Seven
By J.J. Barnes

As a child, Emerald's grandfather gives her a magic lamp with the promise that she can change the world. As an adult Emerald is working hard as a waitress by day, and as part of a crime fighting coven by night.

And when they get news of a man working his way across the country, burning women to death in his wake, Emerald's coven of seven must take on the biggest challenge of their lives, and risk everything to save the people they love.

Available in Paperback and for Kindle.

Printed in Poland
by Amazon Fulfillment
Poland Sp. z o.o., Wrocław